Nightmare on the Northern Dream

A Southeast Alaska Mystery • Book 2

GRETA MCKENNAN

Kenmore, WA

Epicenter Press Inc.
Alaska Book Adventures™

published by Epicenter Press

Epicenter Press
6524 NE 181st St. Suite 2
Kenmore, WA 98028.
www.Epicenterpress.com
www.Coffeetownpress.com
www.Camelpress.com

For more information go to: www.Epicenterpress.com
Author's website: www.gretamckennan.com

Nightmare on the Northern Dream

ISBN: 9781684922772 (trade paper)
ISBN: 9781684922789 (ebook)

LOC: 2025942366

For Mike, with all my love

Southeast Alaska Mysteries

Death at the Shipshape Bookshop
Nightmare on the Northern Dream

Acknowledgments

Thanks to Jennifer McCord and the folks at Epicenter Press for turning my words into a book.

Thanks to Jessica Faust and the folks at BookEnds Literary Agency for all their support.

Thanks to Bob McKee, who has a boat.

Thanks to my family: Mike, Jamie, Laura, and Johnny, for believing in me always.

Chapter One

"I can't believe you're planning an Alaska cruise with your ex-fiancé!" My best friend, Marcy George, rolled her eyes at me with a grin. Her voice changed to a singsong as she gently bounced her baby daughter, Lisa, in her arms. "I know, sweetie pie, you can't believe it either. What is Auntie Junetta thinking?"

Lisa just gurgled. What did she care about cruises or fiancés?

I let out a mock groan. "It's not a cruise, and I'm not planning it. I'm just the host, and … and I've lost my mind, haven't I?" I plumped down at one of Marcy's café tables and rested my chin in my hands. "When we were engaged, I kept telling Liam how beautiful Southeast Alaska is. He couldn't even imagine our rocky beaches. He thought all beaches were covered with white sand like in Florida. I guess it's my fault that he wants to bring his entire bridal party here for a pre-wedding vacation. But it'll be fine. What could go wrong?"

Marcy shifted Lisa to her shoulder for some gentle patting. The three-week-old couldn't hold up her head yet, but she had already taken her rightful place at the center of Marcy's world. "Do you want an honest answer to that ridiculous question, or should I just let it slide?"

I couldn't help laughing. "Yes, please, just let it slide. We'll be out on the water for five hours, tops. It's high summer, the days are long, and the temperature is supposed to get up into the sixties. As long as no one gets seasick, it'll be fine. I'm not the slightest bit interested in Liam anymore, and it will be fun to show off our little bit of paradise." I tickled Lisa's tiny toes. Although I wasn't related by blood, I relished my role as 'Auntie Junetta' and loved every minute I got to spend with the new baby. Her presence also gave me an excuse to avoid Marcy's scrutiny. It was just an outing on the water, after all. What could go wrong?

I had been surprised when Liam Blackwood contacted me out of the blue, a full year after I handed him back his ring and abandoned sunny Florida for my rainforest hometown of Ptarmigan Port, Alaska. I was happy for him when he told me he was engaged to Lacey Carver, a writer for a Florida cuisine magazine. I managed to refrain from asking if she was a hockey fan. Liam's obsession with hockey is what finally drove me away from him. He was a die-hard Tampa Bay Lightning fan who lived and breathed hockey from the start of the season to the awarding of the Stanley Cup. When he proudly presented me with an engagement ring in the shape of the Stanley Cup, I knew that I would have to either embrace the ice or leave. I chose Alaska ice instead.

Liam had never visited Ptarmigan Port when we were together, so I was a bit surprised that he would choose to bring his whole wedding party here. But who could blame him? I gazed out the window of the café, savoring the mist that rose from the water in a thick swirl of fog. As the day warmed up, I knew the fog would dissipate and the surrounding mountains would become visible. Ptarmigan Port was nestled along a long stretch of beach at the base of 4000-foot peaks. From rocky beaches to tree-lined slopes to alpine meadows overlooking the Tongass Glacier and the Juneau Icefield, our small fishing town offered something for everyone. Marcy and I were in the midst of it all, me at the Shipshape Bookshop and her at the adjoining Last Chance Café.

Marcy shifted Lisa to her other shoulder. With her long, dark hair and her apron printed with formline images of whales and salmon, Marcy embodied the Tlingit culture of her family. She filled my coffee cup and handed me a mug of warm milk to mix in. "I can't wait to meet Liam and his gang. When are you expecting them?"

"They should come in on the ferry this morning." I sipped the hot brew. Just a few more minutes before I needed to knuckle down and sell some books before my excursion on the water this afternoon. First things first—a good cup of coffee was meant to be savored.

I was almost finished when Annalisa Martin slipped through the front door of the café. A respected Tlingit elder and Marcy's grandmother, Annalisa was one of my favorite people in town. I knew I could always count on her sunny disposition and her fount of traditional wisdom. Marcy knew she could count on Annalisa's devotion to her newest great-grandchild, Lisa.

Annalisa gave Marcy a hug and caressed Lisa's tiny head. "It's a beautiful morning, little one. Come to Grandma." She held out her arms and Marcy settled Lisa into her grandmother's loving care. "We'll be back every two hours for nursing," Annalisa said. "You could say that Lisa is the most faithful of your regulars." She stroked Lisa's soft cheek. "I'll take over the café in the meantime." She winked at me. "I can make coffee with the best of them."

Marcy laughed. "You taught me everything I know." She gave her baby a kiss on the top of her head. "Thanks, Grandma."

Annalisa slipped back out the door, cradling her precious charge. She nodded to Rachelle Simonson, who burst into the café with her usual flair. Throwing her arms wide, Rachelle proclaimed, "We've made the national news!"

Marcy and I both froze. In my experience, the national news was not a good thing. Last time we had that honor, it was because a landslide had taken out the road leading from the ferry terminal to town. Two cabins had tumbled into the channel. Luckily no one was home at the time, so we didn't lose any of our friends and neighbors. A reporter from the Associated Press had contacted Rachelle asking for details, and the resulting story made front page news for two days, until something more exciting pushed it out of the news cycle. I hoped that the current situation was not a similar disaster.

Marcy closed the door firmly behind Rachelle. "What happened?"

Rachelle laughed, an almost maniacal sound in the quiet café. She tucked her wiry gray hair behind her ears and peered at Marcy through thick glasses. She rubbed her hands together in the perfect cliché of glee. As editor and publisher of the *Ptarmigan Times*, she was clearly elated by this event. Whether the news was fabulous or tragic, she would have reacted in the exact same way.

I joined the chorus, "Rachelle, what happened? Why did we make the national news?"

She pulled out her phone and punched in her password. "Here we are. *New York Times*!" She waved the device in my face.

I eased it out of her hands and held it still so Marcy and I could both read the story. 'Where are they now?' the headline ran. Clearly not a disaster, thank goodness. I skimmed the story, then looked up at Rachelle in some exasperation. "There's nothing new here. This is just a story about a couple of Russian Orthodox icons that were stolen from St. Michael's church ten years ago. They haven't found them. I don't know why the *New York Times* would bother."

Rachelle snatched her phone back and scrolled down to the bottom of the article. Pointing a stubby finger at the screen, she read, "An anonymous source indicates that the icons might be hitting the art market in the next few months." She held her breath for a dramatic pause. "The art world was roiled by the theft ten years ago. Those icons are irreplaceable. The five-thousand-dollar reward that the church is offering doesn't scratch the surface in terms of their worth. If they're about to show up on the market now, in 2015, that's a big story."

Marcy handed her a cup of coffee. "Sounds like a slow news day to me."

I tried to hide a smile.

Rachelle slurped down the coffee and banged the cup on the table. "I need to get to work. It's not every day that the *New York Times* prints the words, 'Ptarmigan Port.' You girls might not care, but I know there are plenty of people in town who do." She bustled out the door, waving her phone triumphantly behind her.

Marcy watched her go. "There goes the original drama queen. I'm just glad it wasn't bad news that got her so excited."

"I guess she comes by it naturally." In addition to running the newspaper, Rachelle was the director of the Ptarmigan Port Players. "I'm glad it wasn't anything to worry about."

Marcy gathered up the dirty cup and wiped down the table. "Three big ships are due in today, Junetta. Are you going to be able to get away to tour Liam and company for the whole afternoon?"

I gave my café au lait a swirl. "Uncle Vance can hold down the fort. As long as the weather clears up, it'll all be good."

"So you say now. The weather's supposed to turn ugly later this afternoon. They're calling for sideways rain and twenty-foot swells by suppertime."

"Liam and his party will be cozying up with a beer at the Grizzly Bar by suppertime." I finished my coffee and hopped up from the table. "Time to sell some books before I hit the water."

I rustled through the beaded curtain that separated the Last Chance Café from the Shipshape Bookshop. I couldn't hold back a smile as I walked through the low bookshelves to the front door and turned the hanging sign to 'Open.' I loved everything about my bookshop. I loved the clean, bright shelves of new books, carefully organized by subject, that attracted the cruise ship tourists. I loved the crowded shelves of used books, running heavily to paperbacks, that provided a cheap read when needed. I loved the library-bound books organized by the Dewey Decimal system, that kept the locals entertained through the long winter nights. And I loved the *Northern Dream*, my floating bookmobile that sailed out to the Native villages in the summertime to bring books to the children.

My young employee, Patrick Wickham, came in as I was opening the blinds. "Sorry I'm late," he gasped, in full agitation mode even though he was only three minutes late, if that. "When I went out to my car this morning, I found that a bear had gotten into it overnight. What a mess!" He whipped out his phone and scrolled through a series of pictures to show me the front seat of his dark SUV scored by claw marks and covered with mangled candy wrappers and smears of chocolate.

I bit back a smile. "Did you leave a bag of candy in your car overnight?"

"Yeah, I forgot about it. I loaded up on peanut butter cups at the store yesterday." He gripped his bright purple hair with both hands. "They're my favorite. I was really looking forward to a sweet and savory treat. All I've got now is a chocolatey mess." He shot me an anxious glance. "You don't think I'll get in trouble for creating a nuisance bear, do you?"

"Contributing to the delinquency of a beast?" I patted him on the arm. "As long as you cleaned it up and don't leave out any more bear snacks, you should be fine." I winked at him. "I'll never tell."

He gave me a tentative smile, as if he couldn't tell if I was serious or not. But he didn't have a chance to puzzle it out. The front doorbell jangled, and the crowd was upon us.

• • •

There was a steady stream of customers throughout the morning. Tourists browsed, sipped coffee in the café, and bought book after book. I loved chatting with each one, trying to guess their hometown by their accent and answering question after question. "What is the elevation of Ptarmigan Port?" "Where can I find the best salmon in town?" "Do you take American money here?"

"Where can I go to see these rocky beaches that I've heard so much about?"

I looked up from the book I was gift wrapping, to see a handsome man beaming at me. "Liam!" I hustled around the counter to greet him with a big hug. He was every bit as attractive as when he was my fiancé. "The ferry doesn't come in until 11:00. How did you get here?"

"We flew into Juneau and chartered a float plane to bring us here. I didn't want to be out on the water until we go out with you and your boat." He smoothed back his thick brown hair and grinned at me. "It's great to see you after all this time, Junie, and in your natural habitat too."

I laughed. "I feel like I should let out a roar or something. Where's everyone else?"

"Hither and yon. There's plenty to see in town before we set out on the high seas." He reached out to take the hand of a slim woman who was browsing through the cookbooks. "This is Lacey Carver. Darling, meet Junetta Beale, our host here in Alaska."

Lacey favored me with a wide smile. She was a petite woman, fashionably dressed in tailored slacks and a bright magenta rain jacket. Wispy curls hung down to her shoulders, giving her the look of a Dickensian waif despite her expensive looking clothing. "Hello, Junetta. Liam has told me all about you." She drew Liam close to her side, twining her arm through his and keeping a tight hold on his hand. The protective gesture was unmistakable. "It's so nice of you to offer to take us out on your boat."

"I'm looking forward to it." I scooted back behind the counter to finish wrapping up the book for the gentleman from Minnesota.

Over the next half hour, the party assembled in the Last Chance Café for a bite to eat before setting out. Aside from the bride and groom, there was the best man, Flint Sands, and the maid of honor, Teena Styles, who had yet to arrive at the café.

"You know, Flint, right Junetta?" Liam's deep brown eyes regarded me. "He's from Ptarmigan Port, just like you."

I looked at the tall man at Liam's side, surprised by this connection. When I was with him in Florida, Liam never mentioned that he had a friend originally from Alaska.

Truly, Flint could have passed for an Alaskan. He was tall and tanned, with dark brown hair and a well-trimmed goatee. He could fit in either on the fishing boats of Southeast Alaska or the courtrooms of Florida where he worked as a lawyer alongside Liam. He wore a sturdy waterproof jacket that looked like it could withstand even the sideways rain if it came to that. His hiking boots had seen some miles on them, in contrast to the squeaky-clean ones that Liam wore. He appeared to be a couple years older than me. I couldn't for the life of me say if I had ever seen him before.

I smiled at Flint, happy to be set straight. "I don't know if we've ever crossed paths before. Did you grow up here?"

He shook his head, a smile pasted on his face. I probably offended him by not remembering him. "I only moved here my junior year of high school. I graduated in the class of 2002 from Ptarmigan Port High. The principal made a big deal about the year being a palindrome."

"That was my sophomore year." I turned to Liam and Lacey. "Our principal was legitimately a numerologist. Every day at 12:34 pm he came on the intercom to make the daily announcements at the proper auspicious time." I stole another glance at Flint. He probably didn't have a goatee in high school—maybe that was why I didn't recognize him.

Lacey looked from me to Flint and back again. "You really don't remember Flint, Junetta? In such a small town, I would have thought everyone knew everyone else." She poked Flint in the ribs. "You must have been completely unremarkable in high school."

I saw Flint's jaw clench. I wasn't sure what Lacey's opinion meant to him, but I, personally, felt uncomfortable with this conversation. Hard to tell who was coming out the worst, me, for not remembering him, or Flint, for being unmemorable.

"Well, to be fair," I said, "I was a lowly sophomore when Flint was a senior. I'm sorry, but my mind is blank."

Marcy bustled up to our table, a pot of coffee in one hand and a basket of muffins in the other. I could have kissed her. "Welcome to Ptarmigan Port." She deposited the muffins on the table and began filling coffee cups. "Banana and cinnamon muffins on the house, to welcome the bride and groom-to-be." She whipped out an order pad. "I'm Marcy George, and I do remember Flint from high school. You hung around with Timmy Everson, who I had a huge crush on. Don't mind Junetta, she was fully occupied with Kirk Dunbar at the time."

Suddenly, Flint laughed, breaking the tension. "Goofy old Kirk. You didn't end up with him in the end, did you?"

"Kirk and I dated in high school, but that was a long time ago. He's still here in town, you know. He's the bartender at the Grizzly Bar. I'll take you all over this afternoon when we get back from the cruise." I refrained from mentioning that while I had moved on from Kirk, he still nurtured a fantasy of some happily-ever-after for the two of us. He hadn't been fazed by my short engagement to Liam, and he wasn't worried about my budding relationship with Angus Montgomery, the charming New York historian who had recently brought his treasure map to town and disrupted Ptarmigan Port's equilibrium. Angus had returned to Columbia University to finish his dissertation with the hopes of moving to Alaska permanently to take charge of the Ptarmigan Port Historical Society. We texted and called on a regular basis, but it wasn't the same thing as being there. As far as Kirk was concerned, Angus was down south, while Kirk was here where I was. Simple as that.

Marcy broke into my thoughts. "I thought there were four bridal party members coming. Did you lose one?"

"Oh, Teena. She said she was going to do a bit of beachcombing before we take off." Lacey laid a soft hand on my arm. Her nails were beautifully manicured and polished with a delicate peach hue. "She's an artist. She makes treasures out of the most mundane items. She's probably arranging driftwood on the beach right now." She turned back to Marcy. "We'll just grab a sandwich for her." She took a dainty bite of muffin. "This is delicious—spicy and mellow at the same time. Beautiful!" She picked up an untouched muffin, placed it deliberately on the table, and pulled out her phone to take a close-up photo. We all watched in silence as she proceeded to bend down and pivot the camera in different directions, finally settling on an angle that framed the muffin with Marcy's carved wooden plaque depicting the Tlingit story of Raven stealing the sun in the background. She snapped a few photos, before suddenly noticing that we were all staring at her.

"I write for the magazine, *Fave Flavors of Florida*. I might want to do a piece on the cuisine of Southeast Alaska. It's never too early to make a start."

Marcy and I were admiring the photos when the café door banged open and a woman breezed in. She tossed her head, jangling her long feather earrings adorned with tiny jingle bells. She wore ripped jeans and an oversized tunic sweater woven with thick, multicolored yarn. A silver Celtic knot on a black leather cord dangled around her neck. She dropped a handful of mussel shells on the table, heedless of the mess they brought. "Coffee?"

Liam smiled sheepishly. "This is Teena Styles, Lacey's maid of honor."

Teena wiped a hand on her sweater and stretched it out to me. "Happy to meet you. I can't wait to get out in the Alaska wilderness."

Lacey pocketed her phone and stood up. "How about we get started?"

"Let's get a group photo before you go." Marcy handed me a bag of plastic wrapped sandwiches and held out her hand for my phone. "You're going encounter the wedding paparazzi on the day, so you might as well get used to it." She posed the wedding party for a series of shots and then motioned for me to join them as, 'your Alaska connection.' We all smiled for the camera, looking forward to an amazing sea voyage. What could go wrong?

Chapter Two

I led the group down the dock to the *Northern Dream*. Captain Evan had moored it at the cruise ship dock to make things easier on my guests. A taciturn man who knew everything about boats and navigation and next to nothing about polite conversation, he stood on the deck of the boat as if it were his private domain. In truth, it was.

I flung out my arm like a prize-giver on a game show. "Ta da! The *Northern Dream*!"

The women oohed and aahed over the sleek white boat with its gleaming wooden accents that reflected the loving ministrations of Captain Evan, while the men talked about seaworthiness and speed. I could vouch for the seaworthiness of the aged craft, but I knew the guys would be disappointed by its serene cruising speed.

I chattered away as the party came on board, leaning into my new role as a tour guide. "The *Northern Dream* was originally built as part of the 'Presbyterian Navy,' a fleet of evangelical mission boats that sailed through the Inside Passage to the Native villages. My great-great-grandfather, Rev. Raymond Denton, sailed on the *Northern Dream* on her maiden voyage in 1932. He would visit each outlying village to preach at the church there at least once a month. Now, I use the *Northern Dream* as a floating bookmobile, to serve those very same Native villages with a cabin full of children's books." I led the group into the cabin, which was indeed lined floor to ceiling with bookcases crammed full of kids' books. With the limited space, I couldn't afford to use low, child-friendly bookshelves, so I had the books organized from board books on the bottom shelves to picture books on the lower shelves all the way to young adult books on the very top rows.

Liam and Flint moved on pretty quickly to quiz Captain Evan in the wheelhouse, but Lacey and Teena browsed through the bookshelves, exclaiming over their childhood favorites mixed in with the newest releases.

"What have you got going on here?" Lacey asked, pointing to the door frame leading into the cabin. The painted wood was scored with numerous horizontal lines accompanied by names, dates, ages, and various feet and inches.

I drew a gentle finger along the highest line. "I measure the kids from time to time. They're all looking forward to growing taller so they can reach the big-kid books on the top shelves."

Lacey murmured, "How quaint," and turned away to scan the entire space. "No books for adults, then?"

I slipped a Roald Dahl book back into its proper place. "No, this collection is just for the kids. But I do have a lending library at the Shipshape Bookshop, and I'm happy to deliver any books that adults want to check out."

Captain Evan forestalled any further explanation of my business model. "Ready to go? I want to get out and back before the weather sours."

"Let's do it!" I led the way out on deck, so we could all watch Captain Evan casting off from the dock and getting the boat underway. Flint made a move to give Captain Evan a hand, but Evan ignored him as if he'd never existed. I saw Flint's face go red. I was able to get to him before he said something we would all regret.

"Captain Evan never lets anyone help with the *Northern Dream*, Flint. Don't take it personally."

"I know a thing or two about boats," he huffed. "I crewed on a fishing trawler after I graduated from high school. But if he wants to do it the hard way, more power to him."

I shrugged with a smile. "That's just his way. He's the captain, he's in charge." I pointed to a stand of trees along the beach, hoping to change the subject. "I see three eagles in that tall tree there. Look, there's a nest in the tree just behind where they're sitting."

Lacey and Liam crowded close, peering through binoculars at the eagles perched in the treetops. I pointed at the thick mass of sticks that made up the eagle's nest. It was obvious to me, but neither Lacey nor Liam could see it. "See the eagle on the right. Go two fingers down from there and then pivot slowly to the right. See it?"

Lacey gave out a squeal, but Liam shook his head in defeat. "I don't see anything that looks even remotely like a nest."

I reached around his shoulders and positioned the binoculars to the correct spot for him. "Now, quickly. We're cruising away from it."

Liam relaxed back into me, his hand coming up over mine on the binoculars. The caress was so unexpected that I jumped, knocking the binoculars out of both our hands. They skittered across the deck with me in close pursuit. The chase gave me a minute for my whirling brain to slow down. Liam's touch was so intimately familiar, and so completely inappropriate. He was practically a married man, for crying out loud. I scooped up the binoculars and held them out to Liam. "Sorry about that. You've missed the nest now. Next time..."

Liam just shrugged and threw an arm around Lacey's thin shoulders. "I'm glad you saw it, sweetheart."

Lacey gave a pale smile. Yeah, she'd seen it, all right.

I turned away and leaned on the boat railing. Why hadn't I listened to Marcy? Me with my, 'what could go wrong?'

• • •

Teena wandered over to the rail, a rapt expression on her sunburnt face. "Will we see any whales on this trip?" She snapped a picture of the rapidly receding eagles.

"You never know about whales," I said brightly, hoping to cover up any awkwardness. "They're always a treat, just like the Northern Lights."

The *Northern Dream* slipped quietly along the shoreline of Havoc Strait, approaching the site of our famous shipwreck. I pointed at the murky depths. "Not far below us lies the wreckage of the SS *Fortunate*, a passenger ship that went down in 1915 with a load of Yukon gold. There's a glass-bottomed boat tour in town if you want to see the shipwreck. It's a constant reminder to us in Ptarmigan Port that the sea is a dangerous place, to be treated with respect." My family and I knew the dangers of the sea all too well. That was a story I didn't care to share at the moment. No need to dampen the cheery mood.

Liam peered over the side, but there was nothing to see without the strong lights of the Saltwater Tours glass bottomed boat. I felt bad for Liam—he couldn't see anything I was showing him.

A light rain began to fall, and the forested slopes breathed in the mist as we slipped past them. The mountains come right down to the sea in my part of Southeast Alaska, with rocky, barnacle-covered beaches that ebb and flow with the tide. I loved the feel of the soft rain on my face, but the bridal party drifted into the cabin to stay dry. There wasn't really any place for them to sit, aside from the child-sized benches attached to either side of the wall.

I stood in the doorway with rain dripping off my waterproof windbreaker. "It's really nicer to stand on the deck and watch the scenery." I flung out my arms and lifted my face to the pattering raindrops.

Teena was the only one who took me up on my invitation. She pulled out a battered green umbrella and followed me on deck. "Are we going to be stopping on any of these little islands, Junetta? I'm always on the lookout for bits of nature to collect for my artwork."

"We might be able to make one stop, depending on the rain. There's a deposit of garnets along the cliffside twenty-five knots from here. It belongs to the Boy Scouts, but if you go and collect there, you can pay them back later."

Teena laughed out loud. "Seriously? The Boy Scouts?" She shifted her body to try to keep dry under her umbrella.

I chuckled along with her. "Seriously. Don't mess with the Boy Scouts. My brother Nels was a Boy Scout back in the day. He gave me a handmade garnet necklace one Christmas."

"Then, he grew up to be an Alaska State Trooper, huh?" Liam crowded under Teena's umbrella, throwing an arm around her shoulders to take advantage of the limited space. She seemed quite comfortable with the physical closeness. Maybe I was reading too much into his touch earlier. Maybe Marcy was wrong, after all, and nothing untoward was going to happen.

I tore my eyes off the pair of them before things got awkward again. "That's right. Trooper Nels is the law in Ptarmigan Port. Don't mess with him either. There's nothing worse than butting up against the law in the person of one's little brother."

Liam and Teena both laughed.

Lacey poked her head out of the cabin. "What's so funny out there?" She ducked back in when a fat raindrop smacked her on the forehead.

Liam slipped out from under the umbrella to go to her. "We're just picturing Junetta breaking the law and having to answer to her little brother, the trooper." He clasped her hands in his and flung a wide smile over his shoulder at me. "We'll just have to keep you out of trouble, Junie."

Nobody else called me Junie. His use of this pet nickname combined with his endearing smile to set a flock of butterflies dancing in my belly. I wondered what his pet name for Lacey was.

Captain Evan stepped out of the wheelhouse to break into this tricky train of thought. "The weather forecast is calling for increasing rain and heavy swells. We'll need to turn back in half an hour at the latest."

Flint popped out of the cabin. "Can we swing past the lighthouse on Forgotten Rock? It shouldn't be much more than forty-five minutes at this speed." He gazed around the group of us, all staring at him as if he'd just held aloft a gold nugget. "I told you, I crewed on a fishing trawler in these waters after high school. The Forgotten Lighthouse is very picturesque, even in the rain."

Captain Evan nodded grudgingly and retired to his sanctum. He turned the boat slightly to the west. We broke out the bag of sandwiches in the cabin as we continued through the darkening water.

By the time the Forgotten Lighthouse was in sight through a strong set of binoculars, the light rain had morphed into a proper Southeast Alaska downpour. Teena's umbrella was no match for the sideways rain, and even my waterproof windbreaker was tested to its limits. We all gathered in the cabin, taking care not to touch the books with wet hands or dripping sleeves.

"What do they say about happy is the bride who gets rained on?" Liam sat on the deck with his back to the board books and Lacey snuggled up on his lap. He stroked her damp hair absentmindedly.

She pinched his other arm which encircled her waist. "Don't be silly. It's not my wedding day today. I'm hoping for blazing Florida sunshine on the day."

"Well, that's gotta be bad luck." Liam twined a lock of Lacey's hair around his finger. "Can we go up into this lighthouse, or is it just to gaze at from afar?"

I turned to look out the doorway. We were coming up fast to the lighthouse. "Normally we could get out and explore. There used to be a live-in caretaker at the lighthouse, but the light is automated now, so there's no need. I think the door is unlocked and you can go in. We'll have to save it for another time, though, with this weather coming on." I trained my binoculars on the lighthouse. "We'll be in photo range in another minute. It really is lovely."

The bridal party crowded behind me in the cabin, straining to see while still staying dry. The sturdy white two-story building with a red slate roof stood on Forgotten Rock like it had for the past century. A flock of seagulls perched on the rocky shore, calling out to each other with their raucous cries. It wasn't quite dark enough for the light to be circulating. The heavy rain obscured the mountains along the shoreline, so their photos wouldn't be as dramatic as they might have been, but that was the reality of visiting Southeast Alaska for just one day—you take what you get in terms of weather.

All of a sudden, I realized that we were cruising far too close to the rock. I pushed my way out of the cabin and booked it to the wheelhouse. "Probably time to turn back, Captain," I called out. I flung open the door to the wheelhouse—and froze.

Captain Evan was slumped over in his chair, his right hand dragging the wheel over. As soon as I saw the wheel, I recognized the difference in the motion of the boat. She was starting to veer to the north, toward the shoals surrounding the rock. We were perilously close to grounding.

I hollered out the door, "Help me!" I pried Evan's fingers from the wheel and eased it over to straighten out our course, hoping that it wasn't too late. The *Northern Dream* was an historic boat in my care—I couldn't allow her to be dashed to pieces on the rocks of a lighthouse.

Teena and Liam came running, followed by Lacey. "Take care of Evan," I hollered, struggling to keep the boat on a safe course.

Teena took charge of the captain, laying him down on the deck and searching for a pulse. "He's breathing erratically, and his pulse is fluttery. Maybe a heart attack? Find me a blanket."

Liam whipped out his phone. I thought he was about to take a picture of the stricken captain, but he appeared to be trying to call 911. Out on the water like this, there was, of course, no signal. I shoved the boat's radio into his hands. "Call for help." Lacey shivered next to him, both hands clapped over her mouth, her face pale. She looked like she was going to be the next one down.

Flint appeared in the doorway of the wheelhouse. He took in the sight of the fallen captain and the boat's proximity to the rocks in one glance. He shouldered me aside and grabbed the wheel with both hands. "Fishing trawler," he barked, as he spun the wheel around to set the boat on a whole different course.

I let him do it. He was one of those guys who needs to be in control—a lot like Captain Evan, in fact. His touch on the wheel was sure, and I knew instinctively that he wouldn't let us crash onto the rocks. I ran out of the wheelhouse and clattered down the ladder below to grab a wool blanket off Captain Evan's bunk. I hustled back on deck and pushed past Lacey and Liam to kneel down next to Evan and tuck the blanket around him. "How's he doing?"

Teena kept one hand on Evan's wrist. "He doesn't need CPR, at least not yet. Do you know if he has any health conditions, or takes any medications? How old is he?"

"I have no idea how old he is. He's been a fixture in Ptarmigan Port my whole life. I'd guess seventies? I can look around his cabin for medications." I locked eyes with this ditzy artist who seemed so capable in this emergency. "Lacey said you're an artist. Are you a nurse in another life?"

She smiled. "I'm an elementary school art teacher. Working with young kids involves blood, puking, and all kinds of crises on a daily basis. I'm trained in first aid and CPR, but the biggest thing is to stay calm, so the kids don't freak out."

I blew out a sigh. "That's exactly what we need right now. Between your first aid training and Flint's skills on his fishing trawler, we should be okay."

I turned to Liam, who was slapping the boat's radio in his palm. "Did you raise anyone?"

"I don't think this thing is working." He handed it over to me. "I pushed every button I could find, but there's no sound."

I took the transmitter and pressed the button I knew was the right one. As he said, nothing happened. I checked the cord to make sure it was plugged in properly and tried again. Nothing. I felt like slapping it like Liam did, but I knew that wouldn't make the radio work any better. "Okay, we're not reaching anyone on the radio, and there's no cell service this far out. Liam and Lacey, could you go back to the cabin to stay dry, but keep an eye out for any passing watercraft. If you see any, let me know so I can signal them for help."

Liam put an arm around Lacey and led her back to the cabin. She huddled up to him like he was an anchor in a storm. I watched the two of them make their way back to the comfort of the cabin. Clearly, they were going to be no use in a crisis. Thank goodness for Teena and Flint!

I headed below again to see if Captain Evan took any medications. I hesitated in the doorway to his cabin. He was a very private man who didn't talk about himself at all, ever. It felt like a huge violation of his privacy to root through his things looking for pill bottles or something. But his privacy wasn't worth anything if he was dead, right? I started with the cupboard next to his bunk and worked my way through his things.

In the end, the only thing I found was a bottle of sleeping pills, which I had forgotten that I actually knew about. When we made our biweekly trips to the villages with the floating bookmobile, both Captain Evan and I would sleep on board. He had once remarked, in a rare moment of sharing, that he suffered from restless leg syndrome and sometimes took sleeping pills so he wouldn't be aware of the unwanted movement. I wasn't sure if that was a treatment or just covering up the problem, but I knew better than to question a man like Captain Evan about his personal health habits. As long as he woke up in time to pilot the boat, he could take any sleeping concoctions he wanted to.

I went back on deck with the bottle in my hand. "This is all I found," I said to Teena, and told her about Captain Evan's restless leg syndrome. She didn't think there was a connection.

I left Captain Evan to Teena and turned to Flint at the wheel. "Thanks for getting us out of peril, Flint." I checked the GPS against the chart of the Inside Passage hanging on the wall. "You're taking us straight back to Ptarmigan Port, right? No more sightseeing for today, I'm afraid."

He just grunted, peering through the streaming front windows of the wheelhouse. I stood at his shoulder, peering along with him. I couldn't exactly tell where we were through the haze of rain. I always trusted Captain Evan to find our way through the maze of little islands as we picked off the villages one by one.

"Do you need a pilot, Flint? I can help you with navigating if you'd like." I threw him my hundred-watt lightbulb smile, hoping to influence him.

Didn't work.

"I know my way," he barked, fully focused on the sight before him. Again, I left him to it.

I turned my attention to the radio, trying to figure out what was wrong with it. I knew Captain Evan kept everything on board in pristine working order, all the time. How the radio came to be inoperable at a time of crisis was a mystery to me.

Suddenly I heard a shout from the cabin. Had Liam and Lacey sighted a passing vessel? I zipped out of the wheelhouse. I didn't make it to the cabin.

A strong, noxious smell was emanating from below decks. A thin cloud of smoke swirled up the ladder leading to the engine room.

The *Northern Dream* was on fire!

I pulled my jacket neckline up over my mouth and rushed down the ladder. The haze of smoke thickened around me as I hit the lower deck. A wall of smoke poured out of the engine room. It was completely impassable. I couldn't even reach the doorway where a fire extinguisher hung on the door jamb for just such an emergency.

I heard Liam's voice calling me from above, "Junetta, get out of there!"

I ran to the bottom of the ladder. "Grab the fire extinguisher in the wheelhouse and throw it down to me. Now!"

Liam's face disappeared, and an instant later he tossed down the fire extinguisher. It almost beaned me.

I scrabbled in the smoke to snatch up the fire extinguisher. Coughing and choking, I ran back to the engine room and started shooting foam everywhere. The smoke intensified, billowing out the door in toxic waves, beating me away. I wasn't going to be able to save the *Northern Dream*! I slammed the engine room door shut and stumbled back to the ladder. "We have to abandon ship," I hollered, pulling myself up the rungs.

I burst into the wheelhouse, coughing until I thought I was going to throw up. "We have to abandon ship," I repeated. "Flint, is there an island we can get to in the dinghy?"

He looked over his shoulder in astonishment. Seriously, did I have to spell it out for him?

"The engine room is on fire. We need to get away in the dinghy. Everyone, put on the warmest clothes you have and grab any food you can carry. Life jackets are in the bench by the picture books. Don't go below. Liam, help me drop the anchor." I doubled over, coughing.

No one moved.

"Now!" I yelled.

The next few minutes passed in a blur of panicked activity. Liam and I managed to drop the anchor, so the boat wouldn't drift off with no one tending to her. If she didn't blow up or burn to a crisp, at least she wouldn't ground herself on the rocks. Small mercies.

With the boat on anchor, Flint was freed up to help me with the dinghy. This was a small inflatable boat that Captain Evan kept ready for use on a line allowing it to trail behind the *Northern Dream* in the water. It had a small outboard motor, but no shelter from the rain. We pulled the dinghy close to the side, so Teena and Lacey could clamber aboard. I held it steady while the two women positioned themselves on either side of the dinghy, midships. Then, Flint and Liam lowered the still unconscious Captain Evan wrapped in the wool blanket into their waiting arms. Lacey squealed when the dinghy rocked, but she didn't lose her head or cause the boat to capsize, thank goodness.

I pressed the line into Flint's hands. "Be right back. Liam, come with me." I ran into the galley, hoping he would follow without questioning. I rooted through some bench lockers, tossing coils of rope and a couple blue tarps into Liam's arms. Blue tarps are an Alaskan's best friend, second only to duct tape. I tossed him a few rolls of duct tape for good measure.

The smell of smoke was getting more toxic. I grabbed a boat tote and shoveled in as many bottles of water as I could carry, along with a supersized box of granola bars that sat on the counter. The last thing I grabbed was the first aid kit, complete with a sturdy utility knife, flares, and matches in a waterproof container. "Time to go, Liam!" Together, we ran back to the dinghy.

Flint held the line tightly while Liam and I tossed in the supplies and then crowded on board. I felt like maybe I should have been the last one to leave the *Northern Dream*, since it was my boat, after all. But such honorable notions of heroism meant nothing to me in the face of the practical need to ensure the safety of Captain Evan and Liam's bridal party.

I braced the dinghy against the side of the boat while Flint clambered on board and tossed off the line. We were adrift.

Chapter Three

I picked my way to the stern to fire up the outboard motor. We were in ten-foot swells, which threatened to swamp the dinghy if it sat dead in the water. But if we could get under way, we had every chance of staying afloat. Beyond that, I wasn't sure what our prospects were. I pushed that thought out of my mind and concentrated on the engine.

"I feel sick," Lacey moaned, clinging to Liam as the dinghy pitched in the waves. The two of them sat on the one seat, with Flint crowded in beside Liam. Teena sat on the bottom in the bow cradling Captain Evan, who she'd curled up into a fetal position to try to conserve space. I crouched in the stern to tend the engine. The dinghy was only intended to hold four passengers. The rain pelted down. I fired up the engine and eased the dinghy into motion.

I closed my eyes for just a second, visualizing the boat's position on the GPS when we cut her engine and bailed. Calling up the chart of the Inside Passage in my mind, I tried to remember if there was a logical island nearby where we could land and take shelter. I had no illusions about our chances of making it safely back to Ptarmigan Port with an overloaded dinghy and ill passengers in this rough weather. It was up to me to find safe harbor in the storm. I took a deep, cleansing breath.

"We're going to make for Price Island. It's not far away. Everything's going to be all right." I spoke in my most calming tone, picturing a classroom full of panicked children reacting to their classmate's vomit. If Teena could do it, so could I. "I'll bet you've been there before, Flint. It's got a nice beach where people like to pull off and have a picnic. There's even a rope swing that sails you out over the water. We'll hole up there and figure out a way to be rescued."

Liam gave me a weak thumbs up. He clutched Lacey close to his chest, his arms encircling her. I could see her shivering from where I crouched in the stern. That's when I noticed that I was shaking as well. I hoped we could find some dry wood on Price Island. We could all use a roaring fire right about now.

Flint spared me a glance over his shoulder. "I do know Price Island. Good thinking, Junetta." That was high praise, coming from him.

Teena drooped over Captain Evan's prostrate form. "How far do you think, Junetta? Captain's in a pretty bad way."

"Soon." That was the best I could do.

The rain hissed down, the waves tossed the dinghy about, and the engine putt-putted through the storm. Lacey was sick over the side, her face ashen. All I could see was the sea in all directions. "It's going to be okay," I repeated, as much to reassure myself as anyone else. "We're almost there."

I was so intent on what was in front of the dinghy that I never looked behind to see the fate of the *Northern Dream*. We'd been tossing about in the waves for hours and hours, or at least half an hour, before it dawned on me that I hadn't heard any explosions from the rear. Maybe I'd been able to contain the fire after all. Maybe I would have a boat to sail in another day. If only I could bring this tiny craft to shore so I could reasonably expect to have another day in my life...

"Are you sure you're going in the right direction, Junetta? Shouldn't we be there by now?" I could hear the fear in Liam's voice. He was shivering as much as Lacey by this time.

Lacey stirred in his arms. She let out a keening wail. "We're all going to die out here! We never should have left the boat. We're going to die!"

"Shush, honey, shush." Liam threw me a panicked glance.

I sucked in another deep breath, beating down my own fear. "We'll be fine, guys. We're almost there, truly."

"If you say that one more time, I'm going overboard," Lacey screeched. She struggled in Liam's arms, bending over the side for another bout of retching. He murmured into her shoulder.

I bit my lip to keep from snapping at her. I was doing the best I could—what more could she expect? I focused on the engine, shutting out all thoughts of the cold, unforgiving depths below us.

Suddenly, Flint sang out, "Land ho!" Those two words could not have come at a better time.

• • •

It took another half hour or more to reach the island and navigate to the sheltered bay that I remembered from my younger days. Finally, the dinghy stopped rocking as we entered the calmer water of the bay. Through the unrelenting sheets of rain, we could just make out the long rope with a sturdy board on the end that had entertained so many kids from Ptarmigan Port over the years.

"Just like you said," Teena murmured. She wiped some rain off Captain Evan's face. "I was starting to think you were making this whole thing up, just to give us some hope."

I stared at her, stunned. "I guess I'm not that subtle. It's the real deal." I piloted the dinghy close to the rocky beach before cutting the engine. I vaulted over the side, gasping as the icy water washed over the tops of my boots and numbed my feet in seconds. Grabbing the line, I pulled the dinghy the rest of the way to shore, steadying it so nobody tipped over the side at the last minute.

Flint climbed out when we reached the shore, and together we dragged the dinghy along the beach and out of the surf. Liam stepped over the side, supporting a shuddering Lacey. She was going to need some immediate care to ward off hypothermia.

I reached a hand to pull Teena to her feet. "We can leave Captain Evan in the boat while we pull it up to higher ground. The tide is coming in."

Flint and I pulled the boat up the beach, groaning under the weight of Captain Evan, who never stirred as we bumped him over rocks. The rest of the wedding party stumbled alongside us. I hoped the exertion might warm us all up a bit. It was high summer, and the temperature when we left on our doomed cruise was a balmy 62 degrees. But the temperature had dropped with the storm, and the soaking rain, inaction, and stress could easily bring on hypothermia. The best thing we could do was get a fire going and dry everyone out.

I stamped my icy feet and flailed my arms against my chest. "I remember a little clearing in a stand of tall pine trees. It might be a good place to take shelter."

Flint glanced at me. "It's pretty amazing that you know this island so well."

I gave him a genuine smile. "Flint, thank you for your efforts. We wouldn't be here safe without you."

He ducked his head with an inscrutable expression on his face. Evidently, he wasn't one to accept a compliment gracefully. I didn't have the energy to care.

We got the dinghy safely to the high-water line. I leaned in and touched Captain Evan's cheek. It was cold as ice. I quickly felt for a pulse in his neck and was rewarded by a faint beat. The wool blanket enveloping him was soaking wet. Hypothermia was a very real danger for him as well. The sooner we could get a fire going, the better.

I looked around at our bedraggled group. Lacey and Liam sat on the wet rocks, huddled under their raincoat hoods, clinging to each other as if their very survival depended on it. If left to themselves, they would likely sit there together in the rain until they turned to stone. Teena also sat on a rock, seemingly exhausted from her care of Captain Evan. Flint alone was on his feet, bent over with hands on his thighs, panting as if he'd just finished a sprint race.

Lucky for them all, they had good old Junetta to save them.

I pulled the boat tote out of the dinghy and handed out water bottles to each person. "Have a drink, but not too much. There's a limited amount of clean water. Hang onto your own bottle."

Lacey started laughing, a note of hysteria in her voice. "There's plenty of water. There's water pouring out of the sky.

We're surrounded by water. We're soaked in water. Water, water, everywhere…"

Liam tightened his arm around her shoulder. "Shh, darling. It's okay…"

I knelt down and gripped Lacey by both shoulders, getting right in her face. "Hang in there, Lacey. We're safe on land. We're not going to drown. People at home know where we went, and they will notice when we don't come back. They'll come looking for us tomorrow, because that's what we do in Alaska. They will search by air and by water, and they will find us. I promise." She stopped laughing, her eyes locked on mine as if she trusted me to fix everything. I smiled warmly. "All we have to do is make it through an uncomfortable night in the rain. We can do that. Let's get a fire going and set up some tarps for shelter, and we'll all feel a lot better."

I stood up and reached down a hand. "It'll warm you up to walk around. Let's go look for that clearing and find some firewood. Come on, Liam will help you."

She let me pull her up and turned to take Liam's hand. Teena struggled to her feet as well. "I'll stay with the captain. Don't forget about us."

The rest of the group straggled behind me away from the beach and toward a wall of trees. I hoped I was leading them to the right place.

"I haven't been to Price Island in years, but I remember there's an outer ring of trees and then an inner clearing parallel to the beach where you can camp, build a fire, or play an amazing game of hide and seek." I chattered on, while anxiously searching for this elusive clearing. "Have you been here before, Flint?"

He just shook his head, whether yes or no, I couldn't tell. It looked like it was up to me.

I pushed through the wet underbrush, calling, "Watch out for that devil's club." The wide, umbrella-like leaves on their tall stalks reached to my shoulders. Every bit of this plant was spiny, from the hidden barbs on the undersides of the leaves to the thorns festooning the stalks. Even soaking wet, devil's club was a formidable foe.

Liam swore lustily as he pushed his way through, dragging Lacey behind him. "Where's this clearing, Junetta? Lacey hasn't got much left."

I chose to ignore him, so I wouldn't say something I might regret. I simply kept on bushwhacking my way through the undergrowth, intent on nothing except putting one foot in front of the other in my quest for the clearing. I was sure it was around here somewhere. It was due to this single-minded focus that I missed the smell.

"Do you smell smoke?" Flint pushed past me and shouldered his way through the bushes. I stopped in my tracks, stunned. He was right, there was a smell of campfire smoke, mingled in with the unmistakable savory scent of food cooking over a fire. Someone was camping in the very clearing I was making for.

We weren't alone on this island!

Chapter Four

I shook myself and struggled to follow Flint through the devil's club and blueberry bushes. He was going so fast that I couldn't even see him anymore. I could hear him calling, "Hello, anybody there?" as he ran. Liam and Lacey tripped and stumbled their way behind me, with Liam swearing all the while.

I left Flint to pave the way for us and turned back to encourage Liam and Lacey. "Someone has a campfire going. It couldn't be better. We'll be dry in no time."

Liam perked up at the news and redoubled his efforts at getting Lacey to walk. "Just a few more steps, darling. I can smell supper cooking already."

Again, I bit my tongue. No need to dash their hopes too soon. The camper might not want to share dinner with a party of six, but they wouldn't be likely to deny us some room at their fire. The Alaska ethos of caring for one another, especially in the wilderness, was very strong. I pushed my way past the last tangle of devil's club into the clearing.

The first thing I saw was a crackling fire surrounded by a welcoming circle of logs to sit on. The cheery flames drew me into their warmth. The second thing I saw was a hunting rifle pointing straight at me, held by a big man shrouded in waterproof camouflage. "Get out of my campsite," he hollered.

So much for that Alaska ethos of care for one another! I stood stock still, holding out a hand behind me to stop Liam and Lacey from bursting out of the underbrush into this standoff. I didn't see Flint anywhere. "Sorry, we didn't mean to intrude. It's just that we had to abandon ship and there's quite a storm blowing right now."

I pulled my coat close around me to indicate that I was freezing. "Can we warm up at your fire?"

The rifle barrel lowered slightly. "Are you from the government?"

I forced a laugh. "No, not at all. I'm a shopkeeper in Ptarmigan Port. We were just out on a sightseeing cruise when my boat caught on fire."

The man growled, "When you say, 'we,' what exactly are you talking about?"

I took a deep breath and assumed my most calm, noncommittal voice, hoping to neutralize the paranoid vibes he was giving off. "There are six of us. We left the captain on the beach in the dinghy with one person—he's unconscious. Liam and Lacey are right behind me—Lacey is close to hypothermia, I think. Flint was ahead of me, but I'm not sure where he is." Oh dear, I hoped he wasn't laid out by the hunting rifle. I'm sure I would have noticed the sound of a shot. "My name is Junetta. What's your name?"

Surprisingly, the man threw down his hunting rifle and waved his hand in a welcoming gesture. "I'm Chuck. Come on and get warm."

Never taking my eyes off Chuck, I reached behind me and took Liam's hand, pulling him and Lacey into the clearing. "Meet Chuck," I said to them, and drew them into the warmth of the fire.

Lacey crowded close to the flames, fat tears rolling down her face. I wasn't sure if they were from the smoke coming up from the damp logs, or if they were tears of relief or hysteria. I didn't really care. I'd managed to bring her safely to warmth out of the storm. Mission accomplished.

Well, not completely. "Did you see where Flint went?" I asked Chuck. "He was ahead of me in the woods, so he must have come to your fireside before me."

"Tall guy, black hair? He ran off when he saw my gun. I was sure he was a government dude. Why else would he take off like that? I was about to go find him when you showed up." Chuck chuckled a little, an eerie sound that set my teeth on edge.

"I'll just go look for him. I need him to help me bring Captain Evan to the fire." I waved Liam off when he made a move to come with me. "You stay here and take care of Lacey. I'll be back with Flint in no time."

I pivoted around the clearing, taking in the battered tent set up in a nice, dry spot, and the scatter of dishes, clothing, and trash that indicated that our host may have been living here for a while. Off to my left, not fifty yards away, was the unmistakable sight of a well-worn path pointing back to the beach. How could I have missed it? We could have avoided all that pesky devil's club if I had only walked for one more minute along the beach.

I scoped down the path, but I didn't see Flint on it. Turning back to Chuck, I said, "Which way did Flint go when he ran off? Was he on a trail or bushwhacking?"

Chuck turned without a word and pointed to a spot opposite the trail I had just noticed. I could see that someone had recently trampled through the bushes. I entered the underbrush once again, calling out, "Flint, come on back. It's all good!" I shoved my way through the dense blueberry bushes, ignoring the ripe berries that I longed to pluck and eat. "Flint! We need you!" Oh, how could he have gotten lost at the last minute, when it seemed as though our troubles were over? "Flint!"

Finally, I was rewarded with a "Yo!" Flint appeared seconds later, his arms full of sticks. "Don't get all in a panic, Junetta. I just gathered up some wood for the fire."

His sardonic tone stayed my mad rush to him. I simply shook the rain off my shoulders and said, "I need your help to get Captain Evan from the beach to the fire. There's actually a path that I missed, so it won't be nearly so hard. Come on."

Together, we walked back to the campsite.

It took another half hour for Flint, Teena, and I to drag Captain Evan in the dinghy down the lovely, easy path to the fireside. Once there, we lifted him out of the boat, unwrapped the wet blanket from around him, and basically laid him out on the ground to dry. He still hadn't regained consciousness, but his breathing and pulse were steady. He would need help to make it through the night.

I rooted through the first aid kit and pulled out a survival blanket. One of those silver mylar blankets that looked amazingly like tin foil, it was compact enough to fit into a gallon-size plastic bag, along with a camp towel. "Teena, help me undress Captain Evan and dry him off so we can wrap him in this blanket." I gritted my teeth at the task. I had known Captain Evan since I was a little girl and had always looked up to him as a venerable adult, to be respected, not stripped naked in the rain in the wilderness. But I knew we had no choice. Evan would not thank us if we left him to die of hypothermia because we were squeamish about removing his clothes. Once he was as dry as we could get him, we wrapped him in the space blanket. We laid him down by the fire with his head pillowed on a life jacket. Then, we heaved the dinghy over to let the water drain out before propping it up next to his prostrate form. It could serve as a windbreaker, shielding him from the worst of the weather. "It's the best we can do for him," I said to Teena.

She nodded, tucking in the blanket with a gentle hand.

Chuck watched this activity without comment. I hoped he didn't interpret it as somehow threatening. The guy sent off some seriously weird vibes.

He had plunked himself down on a log and was staring into a pot perched on the edge of the fire. It smelled like baked beans or some other canned food. Normally, I'm not big on baked beans, but this pot smelled like the most delicious meal in the whole world. I gestured at the pot. "Is there enough to share?"

In a flash, Chuck snatched up his rifle and pointed it at me. "You think you're going to steal the food from my lips? Think again, Missy!"

I backed off with my hands in the air. "I would never steal your food, Chuck. Just asking." I pointed at the tote bag I'd brought. "No worries, we've got granola bars for dinner." I checked my watch—it really was dinner time. Marcy's excellent sandwiches seemed like a long time ago, and she seemed very far away at this moment. I wondered how long it would be before I saw her or anyone else from Ptarmigan Port again.

Chuck dropped the rifle on the ground by his feet, and I moved to retrieve the box of granola bars. I wanted to set up a tarp to protect us from the rain, but I was afraid that Chuck would run us off from his campfire. At this moment, it seemed like the fire was more important than keeping the rain off. I handed out the granola bars, one to each of us.

Chuck held out a hand. "I'll take one of those." He nudged the rifle at his feet.

I handed over a granola bar.

Liam made a sharp movement with one hand, but I shook my head at him. There was no need to antagonize someone as punchy as Chuck, especially while he had a gun. Charm was what was called for.

I sat down on a log on the other side of the fire and unwrapped my granola bar. "It's really great to run into you here, Chuck. We had to abandon ship when the engine room caught on fire. Poor Captain Evan was passed out at the wheel—we're not sure exactly what's going on with him. Your fire is a lifesaver." I threw him an encouraging smile.

He wasn't much for cheery conversation, that Chuck. He simply pulled the pot toward him and started shoveling beans into his mouth.

When I finished my meager supper consisting of one soggy granola bar, I stood up and held Captain Evan's wet blanket from the boat out to the fire. Instantly, clouds of steam billowed up from its soaked surface. It was as good as sending out a smoke signal, except for the sheets of rain that continued to fall. The clearing was somewhat protected from the ravages of the storm, but rain penetrated through the canopy of treetops, dripping down on us in a continuous patter. I positioned the heavy blanket on a log next to the fire and turned to check on Evan.

He lay unmoving, breathing shallowly. I touched his pale face, saying a silent prayer for his health. I had always counted on Captain Evan to keep me and the *Northern Dream* safe on our voyages through the Inside Passage. The sight of his capable hands lying limp at his side filled me with fear. Would I have what it takes to see us all safely through this night, until we had a chance for rescue in the morning?

As if reading my thoughts, Liam spoke up. "So, when will the cavalry come out and save us, Junetta?"

I smoothed Captain Evan's wet hair as if he were a sleeping child, and turned to Liam with what I hoped was a reassuring smile. "Here's how it'll go down. My best friend, Marcy, who gave us sandwiches, is very interested in this sightseeing cruise of ours. She knows when to expect us back, and she will have already noticed that we didn't make it on time. When she looks out the door, she'll see the storm raging and know that we're in trouble. She won't waste any time before calling my brother, Trooper Nels, and telling him to mount a search. Nels will grumble about his sister's foolishness at getting caught out in the weather, but he will start to organize a search. Problem is, the searchers won't be able to go out until the weather clears up. If they go out too soon, then they might need rescuing too. Nobody wants that. So, all we have to do is hunker down here for the night, and the Civil Air Patrol will be out as soon as the weather breaks. They'll see the *Northern Dream* at anchor and start searching this area. I'd give them no more than a few hours to find us after the weather clears up."

This cheerful account glossed over the stark flash of fear that Nels would experience at taking Marcy's call. He was only ten when our dad's commercial fishing boat went down, but I knew he remembered that dreadful night when the two of us clung to each other in the depths of my closet, trying to block out the sounds of Mom's frantic phone calls as we all waited and prayed for good news. When it finally came, the news was bad.

I pulled out my phone with trembling hands, hoping against hope for any kind of signal, just so I could let Nels know that he didn't need to worry. Nothing.

"So, what are we supposed to do, sit up in the rain all night long?" Lacey sounded exactly like an elementary school kid who wasn't getting her own way. I tried to remind myself that she was from a city in a tropical climate and wasn't used to fending for herself in the wilderness of Alaska.

"Well, we could… or we could put up some shelters for the night." I pulled out a blue tarp, a survivalist's best friend. "I was at camp as a teenager where we were turned loose in the afternoon to build ourselves shelters for the night with nothing but what we carried in our pockets. Nobody had pockets big enough to hold a tarp, but we did make sure to have a pocketknife, some waterproof matches, and as much rope as we could stuff in without the camp counselors accusing us of cheating. I learned how to build a shelter out of branches and a soft bed out of moss. I was so tired from all the work that I slept like a baby."

Flint took the other side of the tarp and helped me stretch it between two trees. "I did something similar in Boy Scouts. I didn't sleep well that night, though. I kept hearing things in the woods and imagining bears and wolves galore."

Chuck snorted into his baked beans. "Yeah, there's bears here on this island. Better watch out, Boy Scout!" His cackle sent shivers up and down my spine.

Flint's face flushed. He turned away from Chuck, furiously tying a piece of rope to one corner of the tarp.

Liam jumped up from the log he was sitting on. Dashing rainwater out of his face, he advanced on Chuck. "Who do you think you are, making fun of us all like this? We never did anything to you."

Chuck plunked down his pot of beans and scooped up his rifle in one smooth motion. He leveled it at Liam's chest. "I think I'm the boss."

Chapter Five

Lacey screamed, "No!"

Flint grabbed Liam's upraised arm, hissing, "Leave it." He struggled to hold Liam back.

I jumped in front of Liam, facing Chuck and the barrel of the rifle. In as calm a voice as I could muster, I said, "What kind of bear did you see, Chuck? Brown or black?"

Chuck poked the fire with the barrel of his rifle, sending sparks flying. "There's a sow with two cubs," he confided to me, as if we were best of friends. "Black bears. Your hothead boyfriend better keep an eye out."

"Yeah, he's not my boyfriend," I said, still keeping up that light, conversational tone. "My boyfriend has only ever seen a bear once. My brother, on the other hand, is a trooper in Ptarmigan Port. He's dealt with many a bear, and a slew of criminals too. Just saying."

Behind me, Flint persuaded Liam to sit back down on the log. Lacey pulled him into a crushing embrace.

Chuck glowered at me. "Are you threatening me with your brother, the trooper?" He spat the word out as if the taste of it was gagging him.

I shrugged. "I just wanted to let you know the lay of the land. You're the boss here, fine, but you can't go shooting us, or my brother, the trooper, will come find you. He gets grumpy when somebody messes with his sister." I smiled sweetly. "So why don't you lay down the gun and we can all enjoy your lovely fire. Then, when my brother shows up tomorrow morning to take us off the island, there won't be anything bad for me to tell him."

Chuck stared at me for a long, long beat. I didn't know if he was going to burst out laughing or launch an attack on me. In the end, he did neither. He simply set down the rifle and went back to his beans without a word.

I took a deep breath, blowing it out slowly like the puff of a whale. It was always helpful to have a trooper in the family, for intimidation if nothing else. I turned back to Flint to resume hanging up the blue tarp for shelter.

"Nice job taming the beast," he muttered to me.

I heaved another cleansing breath. "All we have to do is make it through the night, and the cavalry will come over the hill in the morning. I don't care if Chuck's the boss until then, as long as nobody gets shot." I threw a glance over my shoulder, to see that the man in question was fully intent on his meal. "I wish we had a bottle of Captain Evan's sleeping pills, so we could all go to sleep and wake up in the morning to sunshine and a Coast Guard cutter in the bay."

Flint chuckled. "I'm not planning on sleeping at all. That maniac could slit our throats in our sleep for no reason. Seriously, someone should keep watch at all times."

I tied off the rope on the high side of the tarp before stretching it out like one side of a tent. "I'm sure that's a good idea."

• • •

Between the two of us, Flint and I managed to construct two passable shelters with the two blue tarps I'd grabbed on the boat. We positioned the tarps to block the wind and rain. There was room for three of us to lie down under the larger tarp, if we didn't mind touching one another. The smaller tarp would provide shelter for two more of us in a pinch, leaving one person to sit by the fire and keep watch.

Teena stumbled up from her seat on a log to check on Captain Evan again. "Let's settle him under the small tarp, and I'll hunker down next to him for the night," she said. "If anything happens, I'll know about it."

Flint and Liam lifted Captain Evan and laid him down in the shelter of the tarp under Teena's supervision.

I gave her an impulsive hug. "You're amazing, Teena! Your elementary school kids are lucky to have you."

She grinned, tucking the blanket close around the captain. "I'll have a new set of stories to tell them when this is all over."

Liam surveyed the enclosed space under the tarp. "This looks cozy. Do you have another one of those survival blankets lying around? Lacey can't stop shivering, even right next to the fire."

"Nuts! I only have the one." I followed Liam back to the campfire. Indeed, Lacey looked terrible. Her whole body shuddered with every breath. She sat glued to a log, clutching the heavy, wet wool blanket around her shoulders. The wool still breathed off steam, making her look like some kind of ethereal being surrounded by a wispy aura. There was a mystical beauty about her, but I would have preferred to see sturdy flesh and blood, myself.

"Lacey, you need to get moving, get your blood pumping." I took her hand and hauled her to her feet. "Jump up and down for a minute, it'll warm you up."

She gazed at me vaguely.

I grabbed her other hand, and vigorously pumped both hands in a piston motion. I could feel the movement warming me up already. "What's your song for your wedding, Lacey? Are you and Liam going to do a first dance kind of thing?" I flung our hands back and forth, back and forth, hoping to get her blood moving.

"We're going with salsa music," Liam said, taking Lacey's icy hands from me. "We've been practicing some moves." He started humming a catchy tune, and twirled Lacey out and back with an experienced hand.

I remembered what a good dancer he was. He used to take me out to the Corner Club, a little nightclub on the beach in Florida with an open-air dance floor lit by hundreds of string lights in all colors. He had proposed to me there, pulling out a ring and dropping to one knee in the middle of the dance, with people swirling all around us. It was very romantic.

I squashed these dangerous thoughts and focused on the task

at hand. We needed to keep Liam's fiancée warm, so they could have that first dance at their wedding later in the summer.

It looked like some color was coming back to Lacey's cheeks. She tottered through the dance steps, but she didn't collapse. I gave Liam a thumbs up.

Across the fire, Chuck watched silently. He had finished eating by now. I watched in disbelief as he tipped the rest of his baked beans into the fire and stood up. "I'm turning in." He reached behind him for a bucket. Before I could stop him, he flung the water over the campfire, drowning the flames.

I gasped out loud, both hands over my mouth.

"Nighty, night," Chuck chanted.

"What the heck!" Liam pushed Lacey away and rounded on Chuck. "We're trying to keep warm here, buddy."

I caught Lacey before she fell over. Liam barely noticed. He scowled at Chuck; his hands balled into fists.

Chuck waved an arm at the smoking mess of the fire. "Always put out your fire completely before bed. Or maybe you weren't a Boy Scout, eh lover boy? Where's your other guy gone now?"

I looked around quickly. Where was Flint? Hopefully he was gathering up more wood. We were going to need it.

I took Liam's arm, trying to gently pull him back from the brink of another confrontation. "Goodnight, Chuck," I said. "We'll take care of your fire from here. It will be fully extinguished before the last of us goes to bed. No worries." I pushed Liam back to Lacey.

Chuck cackled, and ambled off to his tent, toting his rifle. He waved it over his head, saying, "If any bears come around in the night, just call me. I've got protection."

Liam glowered after him. He stirred the charred mess with a stick. "What a jerk! He could have left us the fire, at least."

I closed my eyes, just for a second. I was so tired. "The coals are really hot. We can find some more wood and get it going again. Where's Flint, do you know?"

"My ears are burning," Flint called out. He entered the clearing, his arms full of sticks. He took in the soggy firepit in a glance. "Guess we'll be needing these."

We should have scooped out the wet coals and started over, but none of us had the energy for that. We simply piled on the fresh sticks and fanned the smoldering coals back to a flame. Thick smoke rose from the fire, but nobody cared, as long as the flames lasted.

By this time, it was getting dark in the clearing. Flint disappeared into the woods again to continue searching for sticks for the fire. Between the continuing rain and the advance of twilight, we didn't have much time left to gather firewood. I scanned the makeshift campsite, wondering if, by chance, Chuck had laid in a stock of wood that we could raid instead of scouring the forest for windfalls.

It's amazing what you can find if you're looking for it. On the edge of the clearing, nestled underneath a blue tarp, was the finest woodpile you would ever see. The wood was uniformly cut, like it had gone through a splitter. Chuck never gathered or cut all this wood on the island. He must have brought it with him somehow. I thought back to our landing on the beach. Was there another boat in the bay, either pulled up onto the beach or moored in the water? I had been so intent on a safe landing that I hadn't noticed anything of the sort. I shrugged off the faint uneasy feeling that crept up my spine. Who cared where the wood came from? It was going on the fire, to keep us warm. I vowed to replace whatever we used in the fullness of time and loaded my arms with the lovely dry logs.

We soon had a crackling fire going. I sat down on a log and let the blessed warmth flow over me. Between the shock of the fire on the *Northern Dream*, the exertion of piloting the dinghy safely to the island and then setting up a campsite, and the stress of keeping our bedraggled party from being shot by the maniacal Chuck, I was completely exhausted. I looked longingly at the cozy spot under the larger tarp. I could lie down and let my worries drift away until morning. But I knew I wouldn't be able to sleep. I would be snuggled up with Liam and Lacey. Even if I positioned Lacey between myself and Liam, I didn't think it was a good idea to spend the night in such close quarters. Who knew what Liam might do?

"I'm going to set up a shelter with branches for myself," I announced, as if anyone cared. "That will leave you more room under the tarp." I heaved myself to my feet and set about gathering long branches to prop up for a shelter.

I found an inviting stand of saplings to make the framework for my shelter. I pulled their trunks closer together and lashed them up with rope. I laid the long branches along one side to make a lean-to. I secured them with rope as well. A pile of ferns formed a covering for the roof, and a bed of moss invited me to lie down and rest. Sheltered from the wind, I could curl up and stay relatively dry throughout the night. I stepped back to survey my handiwork, going so far as to take a picture on my phone. My camp counselor would have been proud.

Liam got up from his seat by the fire to stand beside me. "Are you sure you want to hunker down under this mess rather than the tarp?" He put an arm around my shoulder.

I threw him an exasperated smile. "This is a state-of-the-art wilderness shelter." I shrugged out from under his arm. "I'll be the most comfortable one of all of us."

I fussed over the fire, piling on more wood. Liam disappeared into the surrounding brush. Lacey just sat, her arms hugging her chest, her eyes vacant.

I sat down next to her on the log. "Are you getting warmed up at all, Lacey?"

She turned to look at me. "A little." She leaned close to me, holding me pinned with her gaze. "Liam sure seems happy to see you, Junetta. Really happy."

I conjured up a cheery smile. "It's nice to see him too, but just as a friend, Lacey. I'm seeing someone—a sweet guy from New York." I pulled out my phone and clicked on a picture of Angus sitting on a rock in the sunshine with the Tongass Glacier spread out in the background. His curly brown hair peeked out from beneath his cap, and he caressed the wriggling body of Uncle Vance's little white dog, Cosmo. Somehow, the photo captured Angus's eager joy as I showed him the wonders of my little corner of Alaska. I looked at the photo for a long beat before holding the phone out to Lacey. Angus was so very far away!

"This is Angus. He's a grad student in history at Columbia University. He's hoping to take over the Ptarmigan Port Historical Society when he finishes his dissertation." I ran a light finger over the photo.

She gave me a weak smile. "He looks nice. He's in New York right now?"

I nodded. "Yup. It's a long ways away."

"And we're all here in Alaska," she mumbled, turning away from me.

• • •

Liam reappeared at the fireside and wrapped his arms around Lacey, nuzzling the side of her head. "Come on darling, let's get you settled for the night." He pulled her up and led her to the shelter of the big blue tarp.

I pocketed my phone and bit my tongue. Lacey probably could have benefited from the heat of the fire more than the shelter of the tarp. Maybe Liam intended to lie down with her and lend her some body warmth. I grabbed a long stick to poke the fire. No use going down that train of thought. Lacey and Liam together under the blue tarp was something I didn't want to see or even imagine. I got up to throw a few more logs on the fire and looked around for my water bottle. I thought I had left it by the overturned dinghy, but it was nowhere to be seen.

In a flash, I went from merely wanting a swallow of water to being consumed by thirst, feeling like I would pass out if I didn't get a drink in the next second. I started searching around for my water bottle. I had dutifully marked it with my name so as not to use up our meagre stash. My frantic search didn't turn up anything. Finally, I gave in and reached into the boat tote for a fresh bottle. The marker was in the tote so I could label this new one. I pulled out a bottle that was only half full. I rotated it in my hand until I found the writing on the side: 'Junetta.'

It was my missing water bottle. I was sure I hadn't stashed it in the tote filled with unopened bottles. Who was messing with my water?

I held the half-filled bottle in my hand for at least a minute, trying to figure out if there was something to be concerned about here. Was someone trying to keep me from staying hydrated? Chuck, perhaps? I peered over at his tent. The flap was closed and zipped up for the night. I imagined that I would hear snoring if I wandered over to stand next to the tent. I didn't have the energy. I screwed off the top of the bottle and gulped down the cool water. Maybe someone simply saw my bottle on the ground and picked it up and put it in the bag. What was sinister about that? I tipped up the bottle a second time, draining it completely. There was more water for tomorrow.

"Hey, don't drink up all the water, Junie. Save some for the rest of us." Liam plopped down on the log next to me, swatting at a pesky mosquito.

I took a deep breath, beating back the panic that had flooded me at the thought of not having water. The stress must have been getting the best of me. I threw Liam a small smile. "Is Lacey settled, then?"

He looked over at the tarp. "She's completely exhausted. As soon as we lay down, she dropped right off to sleep."

I frowned. "Is she warm enough?"

Before he could answer, Flint appeared on my other side. He flung a load of sticks onto the fire, sending up a shower of sparks. "It's going to take us all night just to gather enough wood to keep this fire going."

I pointed to the woodpile sheltered under Chuck's tarp. "Good old Chuck has laid in a supply for us. We can pay him back later."

Flint stared from me to the woodpile and back again. He opened his mouth and then snapped it shut again.

Liam started to laugh. "She's pretty amazing, our Junie. You can sit and warm up, Flint, or you can go get some rest. You've been working nonstop since we set foot on land."

Flint rubbed his hands down his pants. "Somebody's gotta do it."

Liam's face flushed, but he didn't engage. "Go lie down next to Lacey. You can keep her warm while you get some rest. I'll take the first watch, from midnight till 2:00 a.m. You can take the second watch, and Junetta the third."

Flint snagged a few logs from the dry woodpile and threw them on the fire. "Okay, sounds like a plan. Poke me at two if I don't come out. I'll keep Lacey warm for you."

I huddled under my wet jacket, soaking in the warmth of the crackling fire. I was too tired to try to sort out the undercurrents swirling between Liam and Flint. One was the groom, and the other was the best man. It seemed to me that the wrong one was going to keep the bride warm, but I didn't have the energy or the inclination to interfere.

Flint rustled off to lie down under the tarp beside the sleeping Lacey. He laid a hand on her cheek and then gathered her in close to his body. I was sure that's what she needed to make it through the night.

Liam leaned forward, holding out his hands to the blaze. "I'll bet this isn't what you had in mind when you said you'd tool us around on your boat."

I smiled at him, sitting close beside me. "Absolutely not. I hope you won't hold it against me for landing us in such a mess."

"Of course not." He leaned closer and took my hand. "This isn't your fault. Things happen. You've been a hero ever since we had to abandon ship." He stroked my fingertips, a very sensuous touch. "Flint thinks he's taking care of us all, but we'd be at the bottom of the ocean if not for you. Really." He slid even closer and drew me into his arms. "We owe our lives to you." He stroked my hair and ran a wet hand down my cheek, whispering, "Oh, Junie, I've missed you."

For maybe a nanosecond, I missed him too. But that ship had sailed a whole year ago. I pushed him away from me so forcefully that he toppled right off the log. "Liam, get a grip! You're getting married in a few weeks, and not to me." I staggered to my feet. My limbs felt so heavy, like I was struggling to tread water offshore. "I'm going to lie down and get some rest. Alone!"

Liam gaped up at me from the ground. "I'm so sorry, Junie. I don't know what I was thinking. Please forgive me."

I closed my eyes, just for an instant. "Of course. We're all under a huge amount of stress. Keep the fire going until Flint spells you at two." I stumbled off to my wilderness shelter.

I crawled in under the canopy of branches, my mind whirling. I could use a stiff drink right now. I thought longingly of the small cabinet over the tiny sink in the galley of the *Northern Dream*. Captain Evan kept a bottle of whiskey there for himself, and I stocked it with wine for me. I could go for the whiskey right now. What was Liam's problem? Lacey was a beautiful woman, if a bit whiney and inadequate in a crisis. He had no business snuggling up with me on his pre-wedding trip.

I groaned out loud. I could just as well ask, 'What is my problem?' I was the one who broke things off with Liam in the first place. I was done with him. I had moved on, and met a sweet man from New York who made my heart beat faster when I thought about him. I pulled out my phone and opened up my photos. There was Angus, posing on the ferry, his curly hair blowing in the wind. In the water behind him a whale's puff was just visible. I couldn't help chuckling. I'd taken my time framing the picture before letting him know that there was a whale swimming behind him. I could almost hear his laughing voice accusing me of holding out on him.

I wanted to hear his voice. I flipped to my voice mailbox. I only had two recordings of Angus, one of which had to do with a murder investigation. I chose the other one.

I pressed the phone to my ear, listening. 'Hey, Junetta, just called to say goodnight. Okay. Goodnight, then.' Short and sweet. I played it again and then again, before I realized that I should preserve the phone battery. Who knew what tomorrow would bring? I turned off the phone and snuggled down into my bed of moss to try to get some rest.

I never thought I would fall asleep, but exhaustion overcame me. It wasn't a restful sleep, however. I dozed in and out, feeling an extreme heaviness in my body while my mind skittered from one alarming thought to the next. *What are Liam's intentions? What would Lacey think if she saw us? Will Chuck leave us alone through the night and on into the morning? He has a gun. How long will it take Nels to find us? Chuck said a sow and two cubs. Is Captain Evan going to be okay? Do we have enough water? When is this blasted rain ever going to stop? What's that noise?*

I strained in the darkness, trying to make out what I'd heard through the steady din of the rain. Was it a cry? Sometimes ravens fooled people with their multitude of calls. But why would a raven be calling out in the middle of the night in the rain? No, not a raven. It sounded like voices, one male, one female, talking with animation. I caught the words, "…see you again…," and "…what are you up to…," and then, "…what are you saying?" I couldn't tell who was saying what, or why.

I groaned and struggled to sit up. It was probably time for me to stand watch. My head whirled and I sank back down to a prone position. I didn't have it in me to get up. I drifted back to my uneasy sleep. On the edge of consciousness, I heard a rustling in the bushes, and what sounded like a heavy tread. I hoped it wasn't the bears. I tried to open my eyes to check, but nothing happened. They felt like they were glued shut. I gave up the fight, and slept.

● ● ●

I was awakened by an earsplitting scream. I sat bolt upright, dashing my head against the branches that sheltered me. The pain knocked the cobwebs out of my brain. I crawled on all fours out of my shelter, calling out, "What's going on?"

Lacey stood with her back to the tarp, pointing off into the bushes.

It was full daylight, although my watch said it wasn't any later than 5:00 am. I was just in time to see a small, dark, furry form scampering away into the bushes, sending a shower of spray behind it.

Whenever I see a bear cub, I'm always on the lookout for the mama. One thing you don't want to tangle with in the Alaska wilderness is a mother bear protecting her young. I couldn't see any evidence of the sow, though. Thank goodness.

I staggered to my feet and lurched my way over to Lacey. I took her shaking hand in mine. "It was a bear cub, Lacey. It's run off. No worries, now."

She turned to me as if she'd only just noticed that I was there. "It touched me," she whispered, "in the night. I could smell it, but I couldn't move." She shuddered. "It was horrible."

"I had a bear sit on me once, in the night," I said lightly. "I was in a tent, camping. It sat down on the outside of the tent, squashing me underneath. Scared the heck out of me."

Suddenly, Lacey started to laugh, with no hint of hysteria. "You've got an answer for everything, don't you, Junetta?"

I just shrugged. I would have bowed like a diva, but I was afraid I would fall over. "I aim to please."

Despite her fright, Lacey looked a lot better than she had last night. Her cheeks were pink, and she seemed far more aware of her surroundings. When Liam reached her side, she linked arms with him. "It was a bear cub. We saw it run off, so it's all good. At least, that's what Junetta tells me."

Liam threw me a grateful smile.

I narrowed my eyes at him. He had materialized at Lacey's side from the opposite direction of the big blue tarp. Evidently, he had not been lying beside Lacey when she was startled by the bear cub.

I glanced at the fire. The logs had burned down to nothing but coals. Hardly any heat emanated from the sodden mess. It looked like no one had been keeping watch through the night.

Oh, right, that was supposed to be me.

I limped over to the woodpile and gathered up an armful of logs. Luckily, there was enough of a spark left that I was able to rekindle the fire. Once the flames were crackling, I was able to look around and notice that the rain had finally stopped.

While the trees all around us dripped steadily, I could see the tiniest bit of blue sky through their tops. With any luck, the day would stay fair, and our rescuers would find us in a matter of hours.

Lacey and Liam sat together on a log, stretching their hands out to my blaze. I looked over to their tarp, but I didn't see Flint there. The other blue tarp had slipped down in the night, almost covering its inhabitants. I tottered over to check on them, surprised to see Flint snuggled up to Teena, with Captain Evan on her other side. All three slept soundly, despite Lacey's screaming.

I glanced at Chuck's tent, wondering if he had been disturbed. I definitely didn't want him charging out of his tent brandishing his gun. But Chuck's tent was unzipped and empty.

I tiptoed over to peer inside. Chuck's sleeping bag lay in a jumble in the center of the tent, with a scatter of clothes in the corner. A few puddles around the edges of the tent revealed that his rain fly wasn't sufficient to keep out the heavy overnight rain. His gun was nowhere to be seen.

For some reason, his absence gave me the willies. The thought of Chuck traipsing around in the forest toting his rifle filled me with a nameless dread. There was no telling what he might do next. Unpredictable—that was his middle name.

Lacey's soft voice broke into my thoughts. "What's our program for the morning, Junetta?"

I sat down across the fire from her and Liam. "Looks like the rain has stopped. All we have to do is sit tight and wait to be rescued." I soaked in the blessed warmth of the fire, trying to shake off the heaviness that persisted in my limbs. I felt like I was emerging from a drugged sleep. I didn't know that being shipwrecked would exhaust me like that. "We can go back to sleep until a decent hour, or we can just hang out by the fire." I gave another anxious glance at Chuck's tent. "Any idea where Chuck went?"

"I heard him rustling around in the night," Lacey said. "I think he was peeking in on us."

"What a creep!" Liam scowled in the direction of Chuck's empty tent. "I hope he's gone for good."

"No, he'll be back for his tent and stuff." That feeling of unease was creeping over me again. Where was Chuck sneaking off to with his gun in the middle of the night?

I popped up from the log to check on Flint, Teena, and Captain Evan again. All three breathed slowly and deeply, sound asleep. It would be a disservice to wake them.

I pushed my way through the underbrush, searching for a private spot to answer the call of nature. There appeared to be a fresh path headed away from the little campsite, marked by trampled moss and broken branches on the bushes. Hoping that I wasn't following in the footsteps of a sow and two cubs, I took the path of least resistance. It took me to another clearing in the trees, smaller than the one Chuck had selected for his campsite. A quick glance showed me that there wasn't enough cover to afford me any privacy. As I turned away to retrace my steps, I saw them.

On the edge of the clearing, a rugged pair of boots lay on the ground, their muddy soles facing me, their toes pointed to the ground. I approached them slowly, my heartbeat quickening. Boots were a survival tool in the Alaska wilderness. People didn't just leave them around on the ground for other people to find. Nor did they in this instance, either.

The worn boots were connected to a pair of legs encased in waterproof camouflage pants. I parted the thick underbrush to reveal a dirty camo slicker with its hood pulled all the way up. One arm was flung out at an angle. Stubby fingers dug into the mossy ground. I held my breath and pulled back the waterproof hood, revealing the close-cropped head of that maniac, Chuck. A patch of blood spread across the back of his scalp.

I let out a scream to rival Lacey's.

Chapter Six

I stumbled backward away from the body. I barely noticed Liam charging into the small clearing, calling out my name.

"Junie! Are you all right?" He caught me by the shoulders, spinning me around to face him. "What's the matter?"

I pointed to the boots. "It's Chuck," I croaked. "I think he's dead."

I hugged my arms around my chest, while Liam bent over the body. He pulled back the hood like I had and checked the back of Chuck's head. Then, he bent down to touch the hollow of his throat, feeling for a pulse, no doubt.

"He's dead, all right. Looks like he got hit on the back of the head." He straightened up, dusting his hands together as if to shake off the feel of death. "You and Lacey saw a bear cub. There must have been a mama bear nearby, as well."

I slowly approached the body, buoyed by the close presence of Liam. I was grateful to not be alone in the horror of this moment. I peered at the bloody wound on the back of Chuck's head. "It doesn't look like a bear did this. There would be some slash marks from her claws, or bite marks." I raised my eyes to Liam's. "It looks like he was hit with something heavy." I scanned the area, looking for low-hanging branches that he could have run into. The clearing was surrounded by a circle of spruce and hemlock trees, their sharp needles threatening to scratch anyone who pushed their way through. The branches were thin and spindly, hardly likely to knock someone out. I stared at Chuck's head again. If the wound was on his forehead, it would make more sense. I supposed he could have pushed his way through a thicket, only to have a branch snap back and hit him on the back of the head. Somehow, I doubted it, though.

I looked around again, to see that Liam and I weren't alone in the clearing any longer. Lacey and Flint had wandered in, with Teena just emerging from the makeshift path.

"What's going on?" Flint said.

Liam turned his back on the body. "It's pretty horrible." He waved a hand behind him. "Chuck is dead. Looks like he was hit on the back of the head. Lacey saw a bear cub this morning—it could have been an angry mama bear who attacked him."

Lacey yelped, "Dead?" She averted her eyes, scanning the edges of the clearing. "Where are the bears now?"

Teena froze on the edge of our little group. She held both hands to her mouth, her eyes round with fear.

Flint, on the other hand, pushed past me to bend over the body. He pulled out his phone to take a picture of the back of Chuck's head and took hold of his arm to roll the body over.

"Wait," I called. "We shouldn't touch anything until the troopers can secure the scene." I could just hear Nels scolding me, "Why didn't you wait for me?"

Flint ignored me. He rolled Chuck's body over, bending down to stare at his face.

I looked away, averting my eyes like Lacey.

"I don't think a bear did this," Flint said, echoing my own thoughts. "Looks more like a blow from something hard, like the butt of a gun." He scrabbled around in the moss and dead leaves under Chuck's body. "Where's his rifle?"

We all stood in the small clearing, staring around at each other in mystification. Flint's words rattled around in my head, gaining volume as if he had shouted from the top of a mountain. Where was Chuck's rifle? A quick search throughout the clearing didn't turn up anything. The gun was missing.

All this time, neither Lacey nor Teena had moved or said a word. Now, Teena stirred. She slid her hands down to clasp her elbows, hugging her chest as if to ward off a blow. She crept over to peer at the body. I watched her lean down and reach out to lightly touch Chuck's cheek with her fingertips. She snatched her hand away and staggered to her feet. She locked eyes with Flint. "You think somebody killed him?"

• • •

My head started to whirl. After an uncomfortable night of weird sleep and very little to eat or drink, I felt like the slightest puff of wind, or shocking suggestion, could topple me over. Clearly, I wasn't the only one who was shocked.

"Murder?" Lacey's voice rose to a shriek. "Who would have murdered him?"

"Don't be ridiculous," Liam shouted. "Watch what you say, Flint. There's nobody on this island except us. Are you suggesting that one of us bashed him over the head with his rifle and then took it away and hid it? You think one of us is a murderer?"

"What else could he be saying?" Teena cried. "You don't think a bear did it, and you think he was clobbered by his rifle, which is gone. It's obviously not a case of suicide. Bears don't hit people over the head with rifles. Only a person would do that."

Lacey looked wildly around. "Is there someone else here that we don't know about? Maybe someone landed a boat in the night."

"I'll go look," Teena said. She took off at a run in the direction of the beach. Flint sprinted close behind her.

"Maybe he threw his gun when he got hit from behind," Liam said. He started rooting frantically through the underbrush until he was out of sight.

"What about Captain Evan?" Lacey said. She turned to run back to the campsite, stumbling on the rooty ground.

"Wait," I shouted, but nobody listened to me. In an instant, I was alone in the small clearing, standing next to the dead body of Chuck. I didn't even know his last name.

I slowly approached the body again. I really didn't want to look, but I felt like I needed to know. Was it a bear or a person who killed him? I gritted my teeth and unzipped his coat, looking for any evidence of a bear attack. It was too late to leave the scene undisturbed for the troopers. I lifted his shirt, to see unmarked skin beneath. He clearly hadn't been mauled by a bear. Before my brain fully registered what I was doing, I had slipped a hand into his coat pockets. I pulled out a billfold, a small penknife, and a folded-up piece of paper. I unfolded it to see a phone number scrawled across it, with no other writing. I stashed the items in my own pocket. When Nels arrived, I could turn them over to him as evidence. In the meantime, I could keep them safe from a murderer.

I straightened up slowly, my breath coming fast. Flint was right, Chuck had not been attacked by a bear. He had been murdered, struck down from behind in the middle of the night. Unless we could find evidence of another human being on the island, we had to assume that one of Liam's bridal party members was a murderer.

Was it Liam? He hadn't been next to Lacey in the night, nor was he keeping watch by the fire. What was he doing all night? Was it Teena? She had touched Chuck's cheek in such a way as to look like a caress. I shuddered at the thought of his cold, wet skin. Why would she want to touch him like that? Was it Lacey? I couldn't picture her having the strength to bash someone over the head with a rifle. But what did I know about her, really? What about Flint? He was an extremely capable person—I wouldn't put anything past him. If he was a murderer, then Teena might be in danger while the two of them dashed off to the beach.

I shook myself before I lost my head and went running off willy-nilly like the rest of them. If one of them was a murderer, the most important thing was to find out who, while making sure that no one else got hurt. I knew that I wasn't a murderer. It was up to me to find out who was.

Chapter Seven

I turned to return to the campsite. My first thought was for Captain Evan. Of our whole party, he was the only one who didn't respond to my scream and the discovery of Chuck's body. That would indicate that he was still unconscious from yesterday. He would be very vulnerable to a killer. I picked up my pace, so that by the time I reached the campsite I was running as fast as the others who had scattered to the four winds.

Captain Evan lay under the blue tarp where I had last seen him. He breathed slowly, shallowly, like a sick man. No one had disturbed him.

With my mind set at ease about Captain Evan's safety, I threw a few more logs on the fire and sat down on a log to plan out my next steps.

It was still quite early in the morning, too early for Nels to have mobilized his searchers yet. I scanned the sky anxiously. The rain had stopped, and I could see a fair amount of blue sky through the tree canopy. It looked like the perfect weather for an air search, as long as the fog didn't come up. Southeast Alaska was notorious for fog, which usually appeared in the morning under clear skies. I remembered one summer day when the forecast called for three days of uninterrupted sunshine. We got three days of heavy fog instead. I stopped listening to meteorologists from that day forward.

My stomach grumbled loud enough to startle a Stellar's jay perched on a branch on the edge of the clearing. It flew off with a sharp cry. I heaved myself up off the log and went in search of my tote bag from the *Northern Dream*. It was under the big tarp, still soggy from yesterday. There were four damp granola bars left. I counted in my head—there were six of us, counting Captain Evan, who may or may not be able to eat something. I hoped he would recover enough to be hungry like the rest of us.

Dividing four granola bars between six people was too much math for me to attempt at the moment. I could make it easy on myself and just eat one straight up, while no one was looking. Then, there would be three bars to split in half and portion out among six people. My stomach growled again. No one would ever know.

I unwrapped a bar and took a bite before my conscience kicked in. I had read *Lord of the Flies* in high school. I could easily imagine the breakdown of social mores in the service of survival. Our current situation had evolved from a life-and-death sea voyage to an uncomfortable night in the rain to the grisly discovery of a dead body in our midst. Polite society it was not. But I didn't want to be the one to start us down the slippery slope of self-preservation at the cost of others, especially not over a whole rather than half of a granola bar.

I carefully broke the bar in two, wrapped up the unbitten half, and stashed it back in the tote bag. I finished the rest of my half and washed it down with a frugal swallow of water. When we got back to Ptarmigan Port, I was going to order every single thing on the menu at the Last Chance Café and ask Marcy to bring me cup after cup of hot tea until I floated away in bliss.

Teena and Flint straggled into the clearing and made for the fire. "We couldn't see any evidence of other people along the beach," Teena said. "Looks like it's just us."

"How about a boat in the bay?" I said. "Chuck got to the island somehow."

She looked up, startled. "I didn't see any boats. We couldn't see too far out to sea—there was a lot of mist on the water."

I held out a granola bar. "There are only a few left. You can each have half, to take the edge off."

Teena took the bar, broke it in half, and held out one half to Flint. "I guess we'll need to start harvesting berries and figuring out how to catch some fish."

I gave her a warm smile. "Hopefully we'll be rescued before we have time to cook a fish over the fire."

Flint chewed his bit of granola bar. "We might be here for a while. That early morning mist on the water is starting to look like some serious fog."

I stood up and walked across the clearing to peer down the path to the beach. As soon as I got away from the smoke from the fire, I could see that Flint was right, again. The woods on the edge of the clearing were starting to fill up with fog. I jogged down the path until I broke out of the trees and stood on the edge of the beach. Sea grasses tickled my ankles, and the salty smell of the sea was strong. But I could barely see where the rocky beach ended and the water began. A solid wall of fog was rising up from the water. No morning mist now, it swirled up to obscure the tops of the trees. I could still see my way along the path back to the clearing, at least for the moment. I hurried back to the fireside, hoping that Lacey and Liam had returned.

Liam stood by the fire, bending over to hold his hands out to the blaze. He spoke over his shoulder, "I didn't find any sign of Chuck's gun. I can only assume that someone hit him over the head with it and then took it away somewhere."

"Someone?" Teena laid a hand on his arm. "Someone... like who?"

Liam straightened up slowly and turned to Teena. It felt like it took him half an hour to make eye contact with her. "Someone who killed that menace, Chuck. That someone." He shook off her hand.

"Someone who came to this island aboard the *Northern Dream*," Teena persisted. "Someone who is standing around the fire even as we speak. One of us killed Chuck."

I scanned the faces around the fire. One of them was a killer. Could it be Liam or Flint, Teena or Lacey? Wait a minute... "Where's Lacey?"

The four of us swiveled around in all directions, searching for Lacey. I called her name. I could feel a sense of panic rising in my throat. I could barely get a sound out.

"She's the one," Flint said, wild-eyed. "She hit him over the head and now she's hiding out from the rest of us."

"Don't be ridiculous," Liam shouted. He shoved Flint on the chest, hard. "Lacey wouldn't hurt a fly. You're saying that because you're the one who did it."

Flint shoved him back. "Are you accusing me of being a murderer?"

I sprang in front of Flint before he could haul off and sock Liam in the face. I held out both hands in opposite directions, hoping that the visual barrier would keep the two of them apart. "Come on, guys! Lacey must have gotten lost in the fog. She needs us to find her, not accuse her of murder or fight over her." I found that my left hand was resting on Liam's chest. I could feel his heart beating a mile a minute. I pushed a little bit with my hand, so he would realize that I was holding him off, not trying to caress him. That was my hope, anyway. "Did anyone see where she went when she ran off from Chuck's body?"

"She said she was going to check on Captain Evan." Teena hugged her arms to her chest again. "He's over there, under the tarp. He was still asleep but doing fine when I peeked in on him a minute ago. I didn't see Lacey, though."

Flint backed off from his altercation with Liam. "We need to find her. But we need to keep ourselves safe. Nobody should go off alone."

Liam glowered at him. "If you suggest one more time that Lacey is a killer, I will…" He balled his hands at his sides.

"You'll what?" Flint glared at him. "What will you do? Kill me?"

"Stop it!" Teena cried. "Just stop it. Nobody's killing anybody." She cracked a smile. "I'm going to put you both in timeout if you can't stop acting like children. We need to find Lacey. She's probably scared."

Liam turned his back on Flint. "Yes, we need to find her. Shall we split up, two and two?"

"That's no good," Flint said. "You might pair up with a killer, and never come back."

I heaved an exasperated sigh. He was right, dang it. "Come on, we'll all go together. Liam, you go first, and Flint, you can bring up the rear. Which direction do you think she went?"

There followed a long, excruciating time of beating around in the brush, stumbling through the fog, calling out Lacey's name. Teena and I followed close behind Liam, close enough to be swatted in the face by the branches he blundered through. I could hear Flint behind me, tromping through the underbrush and swearing at the mosquitos that we scared up. The fog curled around our bodies, blotting out everything farther away than three feet in front of our faces. I kept a hand on Teena's shoulder so I wouldn't lose her in the fog. It made it harder to navigate the underbrush and avoid the spikes of devil's club, but I didn't want to get separated from the group.

I considered in my mind if Lacey could be a killer. I couldn't imagine it. She had been nearly comatose yesterday, shivering with the wet and cold and counting on others to save her. Unless she was a fantastic actor, she didn't possess the physical or moral strength to get up in the middle of the night and whack someone over the head, for any reason. But I could totally see her getting lost in the fog and needing to be rescued. Unless… I stopped in my tracks. Could someone have struck her down too? Would we stumble upon her lifeless body as we cast about in the merciless fog?

Flint crashed into me from behind. "What the heck, Junetta! Keep up."

I reached out in front of me, but I'd lost contact with Teena. I ran forward a few steps, my arms stretched out in front of me. "Slow down, Liam. Teena, are you there?" My cries were muffled by the billowing fog.

I turned around and clutched at Flint. "I've lost Teena and Liam." I shivered in the clammy fog.

Flint called a few times, peering ahead of us through the mist. "Blast Liam! He should have made sure everyone was keeping up." He bent over, his hands on his knees, breathing hard. "Can't be helped. We should retrace our steps back to the campsite. Maybe Liam and Teena will find Lacey, or maybe she's all cozy by the fire while we stumble around in the woods looking for her. The best we can do is get ourselves back safely at this point." He reached out a hand. "I'm not a murderer. Are you?"

I accepted his hand. "Absolutely not."

"All right, then. Let's get back to that clearing."

Together, we walked through the woods. I hoped we were going in the right direction. Nothing like fog to confuse one's senses. I pulled Flint to a stop. "There. Do you smell the fire? We're almost there."

"You're a regular bloodhound," he said.

I wished he had chosen a different breed of dog for that remark.

Finally, we pushed through the bushes to regain the clearing. The campfire still flickered feebly. No one sat on the logs surrounding the fire pit.

I gathered up an armful of logs and built up the fire. No need to worry about replenishing Chuck's wood in the fullness of time. The dry logs flared up, crackling cheerfully.

Flint plumped down on a log. He started to unzip his jacket and then changed his mind and pulled the zipper up to his throat. "Lacey probably just got turned around and headed straight back here when she realized she was lost. She's causing us a lot of unnecessary trouble, if you ask me."

I dusted the dirt from the wood off my hands. "I'm going to check on the captain." I could just see the blue of the tarp through the fog. I approached the makeshift lean-to. Things looked different underneath. I caught my breath at the sight of Lacey, curled up next to Captain Evan, both of them under a fluffy green sleeping bag. They both breathed deep and slow, sound asleep.

I returned to the fire and sat down across from Flint. "Lacey is sleeping next to Captain Evan—safe and sound just like you said. It looks like she borrowed Chuck's sleeping bag for warmth."

Flint started to laugh. "You wouldn't catch me touching that jerk's bedding, dead or alive. He's likely got fleas, if nothing worse."

I couldn't help laughing with him, laughing until tears ran down my cheeks. It was hard to tell if they were from mirth or the aftermath of fear. Probably a bit of both.

Finally, I calmed down enough to speak. "I hope Liam and Teena can find their way back."

He nodded. "Got any more of those granola bars?"

I shook my head sorrowfully. "I wonder what supplies Chuck laid in. He won't be needing them anymore."

Flint hauled himself to his feet, and the two of us began to search systematically through Chuck's campsite, looking for a cache of food that we could partake of. I guessed that he knew enough about camping in bear country to avoid storing food in his tent, but I crawled inside just the same. In the back of my mind was the latent thought that I needed to figure out who had killed Chuck, and why. Maybe I would learn something by going through his things.

Lacey had taken Chuck's sleeping bag, but his sleeping pad was untouched. A pile of clothes was jumbled on one side of the tent, away from the puddles that collected on the outer edge where the rain fly failed to keep out the wet. I gritted my teeth and systematically went through the pockets of Chuck's clothes, coming up with nothing.

The only surprising thing I found in the tent was a thin paperback book titled, *Iconic Icons of the East and West*. I flipped it open, to see that it was actually more of a graphic non-fiction book, illustrated with comic book style pictures of Orthodox priests, classic artists, and holy icons. I sat back on my heels and regarded this remarkable volume. I couldn't imagine why Chuck might take an interest in the religious art of the Russian Orthodox church.

I crawled out of the tent, to see that Liam and Teena were just returning to the campsite.

"What the heck is going on here?" Liam demanded, glaring at me coming out of Chuck's tent.

Teena sidled up to the fire and held out her hands.

I chose to ignore his aggressive tone. "Sorry, I stopped for a second but you two kept on going, and then you were gone." Before he could take breath to argue with me, I said, "Lacey's here. She's sleeping next to Captain Evan. I didn't want to disturb her."

He swung away to peek at Evan and Lacey under the blue tarp. "Is that the dead man's sleeping bag?"

"It is. Lacey must have brought it out. You've got a resourceful woman there, Liam." I scooped up my soggy tote bag and pulled out the half granola bar and handed it to Liam. "Here's your rations."

He took the morsel from me and popped it in his mouth, dropping the wrapper on the fire. A coil of noxious smoke rose up. Plastic fouling up a nice wood fire was one of my pet peeves, but I decided to let it go, just this once. I fanned the offending smoke away from my face and sat down on a log and looked around for Flint. "Any luck finding something to eat, Flint?" I called.

Flint came around from the far side of Chuck's woodpile. "I found his food stash. Looks like he didn't plan on camping out here for much longer. There are a few cans of pork and beans and a pile of individual sized chip bags, but that's all. Luckily the cans have pop tops." He popped the tops off of three cans of beans and set them on the edge of the fire. "Your flames will burn this food before it's properly cooked, but the edges aren't so hot."

I sucked in a big breath to keep from snapping at him for criticizing my efforts to keep us warm. There was no pleasing some people!

"So, where's the cavalry, Junie?" Liam said, sitting down next to me on the log. "It's mid-morning already. They'll show up any minute now, right?"

"Alas, no. Nels can't send out any airplanes in this fog. We have to wait until it burns off."

"You're kidding me, right?" Liam's voice rose. "Are you telling me that planes can't fly in the fog, so everything just stops until the sun comes out again? That's ridiculous!"

I conjured up a big smile, as if Liam were a tourist in my bookshop who knew nothing about Alaska. "That's life in Southeast Alaska. Planes don't fly in the fog. We don't want to risk a crash. Whenever we want to go somewhere, we prepare to get delayed. We just roll with it." I flung out a hand. "Like this trip, for example. It's fairly typical of traveling in this part of the world— minus the dead body, of course."

"Ugh, I don't know why you like Alaska so much. You could have stayed in Florida with me, you know. White sand beaches and limitless sunshine..."

The fog swirled around me. My clothes were still damp from the rain last night, even with the heat of the fire. Florida was looking pretty good at this moment, I had to admit. But I wasn't going to say so out loud.

Teena picked up a stick from the ground, peeled off some moss and bark, and stuck it in the pork and beans to stir them up. One can shifted and slid to one side, slopping some beans onto the ground.

"Look out!" Flint shouted, jostling Teena's arm as she tried to right the can. More beans slopped out into the fire. They sizzled, sending up a savory scent of food that, unfortunately, was now unfit to eat.

"I've got this," Teena snapped, pushing Flint away. "The beans are almost ready. Did you happen to find any plastic utensils in your search?"

Flint strode a few paces away from the fire, his hands shoved into his pockets. "We'll be eating with our hands," he growled.

Remind me never to go camping with this lot ever again. I tried to keep my frustration from showing on my face. I got up to peek at Lacey and Captain Evan again. I found Lacey awake, staring up at the tarp over her head with a look of despair on her face.

"Feeling any better, Lacey?" I crouched down next to her. "We've got some pork and beans cooking on the fire, and I think you still have half a granola bar with your name on it. Come on out and have a bite to eat."

She reached out and caught my hand. "Did I dream it? Was there a dead man?"

I nodded. "Yes, we found Chuck's dead body. It appears that someone hit him over the head, possibly with his own rifle, which has gone missing. All the rest of us are gathered around the fire, ready to dig into some food. Come on."

I pulled on her hand, but she didn't budge. Her eyes never left my face. "Somebody killed Chuck. But we're the only people on the island. One of us killed him? My bridal party?" I could feel her hand starting to shake, and horror filled her eyes.

In that moment, I knew that Lacey was not the murderer. Nels often chided me for trusting my gut instead of sorting through the evidence and coming up with a logical conclusion. Well, that was why he was the trooper, and I sold books for a living. Books and the people who loved them made up my world, and I knew a thing or two about how people act and react. I was looking down on a vulnerable woman who was paralyzed with terror at the thought that one of her closest friends could be a killer. That dreadful thought wouldn't have crossed her mind if she herself was the killer. There were four people who could have killed Chuck. I just narrowed it down to three.

I tugged on her hand again. "Come on, Lacey, come get some food. It will make you feel better, I promise." She suffered me to help her up. I shook Captain Evan's shoulder but couldn't wake him. I resolved to keep the final granola bar for him.

I led Lacey back to the fire and sat her down next to Liam. He pulled her into a close embrace and kissed her on the cheek. "We were bumbling around in the bushes looking for you, Spacey. Where did you get off to?"

"Spacey." That's what he called her. I wondered what she thought about that pet name.

Lacey relaxed into the safety of Liam's embrace. "I came here to check on Captain Evan. He was fine. Then, I had to pee, and when I got back, nobody else was around. I just tucked up with the captain and went to sleep."

Teena stirred the beans with her stick. "They're ready to eat. Now what?"

We all stared at the three cans, wondering how to get into the hot beans without burning ourselves or wasting the precious food.

"Here's an idea," I said, pulling open a bag of potato chips. Using a soggy stocking cap that lived in my raincoat pocket, I picked up one can and gestured for Teena to shovel some beans into the bag. "We called this 'taco pie' in elementary school— you pour the taco meat over some corn chips and add whatever veggies you want. You just have to eat fast, before the bag bursts." I handed the bag to Lacey and opened up another one. Soon all of us had our individual bags of beans over chips. Not the most elegant food by any means, but tasty. It really improved my mood to get some food in my belly.

"I've found that the hungrier you are, especially when cooking outdoors, the more delicious the food tastes," I said with a smile, noting the raven perched on a branch over my head, his beak swiveling from side to side with a beady eye fixed on our food. "If we're still here by lunchtime, we'll go for a proper Alaska wilderness feast."

Lacey frowned. "We'd better not still be here at lunchtime," she muttered.

Flint wadded up his chip bag and threw it on the fire. "I hate to bring this up, but we need to do something about Chuck's body. There are bears in the vicinity."

All movement and sound ceased. We all stared at Flint, aghast.

"What do you suggest?" Liam downed the last few bites of his food and tossed his bag on the fire as well. The smell of burning plastic intensified.

"We could bury it," Flint said, locking eyes with Liam, almost as if he was issuing a challenge. "Or bring it back here and stash it in his tent."

"When the troopers get here, they're going to want everything undisturbed at the crime scene," I said.

Flint stood up. "Well, they'd probably prefer it if a bear didn't start snacking on his dead body."

Teena turned away, gagging on her mouthful of beans. "You do what you have to do, Flint. I don't want to know about it. I'll be right here by the fire."

I groaned and pulled myself to my feet. Once again, Flint was right.

Liam reached up to catch me by the arm. "Not you, Junie. Flint and I will take care of this." He got to his feet, bent down, and gave Lacey a kiss. "Be back soon."

"Be careful," Lacey said. "Please, Liam, don't try to take on a bear." She didn't add, "or a murderer," but the unspoken words hung in the air long after Flint and Liam had disappeared into the underbrush.

I loaded a few more logs onto the fire. "I'm going to go lie down. I can barely keep my eyes open."

Lacey shot me a look filled with fear. "There's a murderer out there, Junetta. Are you sure you want to be alone?"

I wasn't sure, to be honest. "I think I'll be okay." I threw Lacey and Teena a bright smile and crossed the campsite to get to my wilderness shelter on the edge of the woods, hoping that my mossy bed had dried out a bit since I'd crawled out of it early this morning.

As it turned out, I didn't get to lie down after all.

My wilderness shelter was exactly the same as I'd left it. The branches arched over the cozy bed of moss inside, held securely by the rope I'd used to lash them together. Raindrops glistened on the ferns stretched over the top, but nothing penetrated to the inside. It couldn't be any cozier, except for one glaring thing. Right across the threshold lay a long hunting rifle, its barrel pointed toward the campfire and Chuck's tent beyond. The butt was stained a rusty red in places. Chuck's missing rifle, the murder weapon, lay at the entrance to my personal shelter.

Chapter Eight

I let out a yelp, before I could stop myself. Teena materialized by my side in an instant, with Lacey not far behind. Both women stared at the rifle, their eyes traveling slowly to my face.

"What is this?" Teena said. She hugged her arms around her chest as if protecting herself from a blow.

"It's Chuck's rifle," I whispered. "His blood is on the butt. It's the murder weapon."

Lacey backed away. "Why did you leave it here, Junetta?"

"I didn't leave it here," I cried. "Somebody dropped it here to make it look like I killed Chuck. But I didn't."

"That's what you say," Lacey said, shock deepening her voice. She pulled Teena close to her side. "I knew it couldn't have been my bridal party. I don't know what reason you had to kill him, and I don't want to know. Just stay away from us." She turned Teena around and propelled her toward the fire.

I let them go.

I stood stock still, staring down at the incriminating rifle in my personal space, mocking me. Anyone could see how easy it was to drop the rifle here to frame me. If she stopped to think a minute, Lacey would realize that it would be the height of stupidity for me to leave the murder weapon lying around. Why would I go out of my way to advertise my guilt? The rifle's very presence here seemed like a testament to my innocence, at least to me. I tried to picture Nels's reaction to finding it here. Would he arrest me, based on this evidence? I didn't think so. More likely, he would process the thing for fingerprints and DNA, and he wouldn't find any of mine on it. Case closed. I wished he were here right now, to set Teena and Lacey straight. But he wasn't—that task was up to me.

I turned back to the campsite to see Flint and Liam entering the clearing, their faces grim.

Before I could open my mouth, Lacey flew to Liam, crying out, "It's Junetta! She killed Chuck. His gun is in her shelter. She's the murderer!"

Liam wrapped his arms around Lacey. "Calm down, sweetheart. We all know Junetta's not a murderer. The very idea is ludicrous." He stroked her hair as if she were a small child. "Don't give that idea a second thought."

Lacey pulled out of Liam's embrace. A dangerous edge entered her voice. "You're taking her side over me?"

Flint brushed past Liam and Lacey and advanced on me. "Show me this gun."

I turned my back on the engaged couple, trying to block out the sound of their squabbling. I led Flint to my shelter. Teena trailed along with us.

I pointed to the rifle. "I haven't touched it. I didn't put it there." I bent over to point to the dark smears on the butt. "It looks like traces of blood. I would say it was definitely the murder weapon."

Flint leaned forward as well. He frowned down at the rifle and then raised his eyes to my face, studying me. His closeness suddenly rattled me, and I straightened up and shuffled backward, bumping into Teena. "I don't know how it got here," I babbled. "I could swear it wasn't there when I came out of the shelter at 5:00 this morning. Presumably Chuck was already dead by then."

I could hear Liam's raised voice, "...you don't know her like I do..." followed by Lacey crying, "...we never should have come...I told you it was a stupid idea..."

I closed my eyes, just for an instant. That's what Marcy told me, too. They were both right. Such a stupid idea!

Flint picked up the rifle.

"We shouldn't touch it," I cried. "The troopers can check for fingerprints and DNA when they get here."

He just shrugged. "There's no troopers here now. I'm going to put this in Chuck's tent, so we can all keep an eye on it." He hefted it in his hand. "I'll apologize to your brother, the trooper, whenever he finally shows up. But I'm not going to leave a loaded weapon lying around for anyone to pick up." He stalked back into the campsite and deposited the rifle in Chuck's tent, zipping it up behind him.

Liam and Lacey sat side by side on a log by the fire, both staring into the flames with angry expressions. Clearly, they had quarreled over me—not a great feeling. Normally, I would try to smooth things over, but I hesitated to wade into this dispute. I tried to ignore their hostile vibes.

Liam wasn't about to let it lie. "Sorry about that, Junie. I know you're no killer. So does Lacey, for that matter. She's just overwrought. The best thing we can do is get off this island and back to civilization."

Lacey shot Liam a look of anger. "Don't speak for me! I'm perfectly capable of speaking for myself." She shifted around on the log to turn her back to Liam.

"Too right you are," he muttered. He got up and walked away from her. "We buried Chuck under piles of brush and branches. It was the best we could do." He poked the fire with a long stick. "How about those rescuers? Do you think they're on their way?"

The mist still swirled throughout the woods, and the sky was obscured by thick fog. "Not yet, but soon, I hope. Just as soon as the fog burns off." I flung my hand out toward the underbrush, conjuring up a smile. "There's nothing to stop us from gathering some berries. The blueberries should be ripe for the picking. Just watch out for baneberries. They're red, with a line running down them, kind of like a peach. They grow on tall, upright stalks. They're deadly poisonous."

Lacey turned around to face me. "I don't plan on eating any berries in the woods. They're probably all poisonous. What a great way to get rid of all of us," she snapped.

I bit my tongue before retorting in kind. I went on as if nothing had happened. "There are red huckleberries in the woods, which are delicious. You might also find high-bush cranberries, which aren't quite ripe yet, so they will be sour. Just check with me before you eat any red berries." I headed into the woods before anyone could accuse me again of being a killer.

In the swirling mist, the understory was full of berries. Black and red huckleberries and blueberries practically burst from the bushes. No one had picked them over, except for the bears. The first dozen or so that I picked went straight into my mouth. I reveled in their sharp, sweet taste. Eventually, I paused, ready to pick some for later. I cast about in my mind for a vessel to put them in. My empty water bottle would be just the thing. I walked back to the fireside and rousted out my tote bag. There were still a number of unopened bottles, thank goodness. I fished out the empty one with my name on it. I was about to tip in a handful of red huckleberries when my attention was drawn to a filmy white residue in the bottom of the bottle. I shook the bottle slightly. All the water was gone, leaving behind what looked like some kind of powder dusting the bottom of the bottle. I held the bottle to my nose, but I couldn't smell anything weird. I frowned down at the mysterious mass. There was no reason why bottled water would leave behind a powdery white residue. Was this substance the reason I'd felt so out of it throughout the night and into the morning? Had someone really drugged my water? My fingers shook as I screwed the top back on and dropped the bottle back into my tote bag. At some point, I would talk with Nels, and he could get the powder tested. I could only hope that that time would come soon!

With my water bottle out of the running, I needed something to collect berries in. I cast about the campsite and settled on a curved piece of bark peeled off a log for the fire. It was more natural than a plastic water bottle.

Liam and Lacey entered the clearing as I prepared to go back out. Evidently, the soothing activity of berry picking had helped them to make up. Their fingers were stained purple from picking. They held a big skunk cabbage leaf between them. A lovely mound of berries jiggled on the leaf. The red, blue, and black berries made a pretty picture.

I took a closer look. Among the tasty red huckleberries, I could see the dark red of baneberries. I made a grab at the leaf. "Did you eat any of these red berries? They're the poisonous ones. I've heard that as few as four of them could kill a small child."

Liam gaped at me, but Lacey threw back her head with a sneer. "I don't believe you. Who would know a statistic like that? You're just trying to mess with our minds, to keep us from fixing on you as the killer." She picked up a red berry and popped it into her mouth. "Delicious!"

Hoping fervently that she'd chosen a red huckleberry, I lunged for the pile of berries. I caught the two of them off guard and succeeded in wresting the leaf out of their hands. I pawed through the berries, tossing out the baneberries as fast as I could. I appealed to Liam, "Is it worth it?"

Lacey snatched at the leaf, flipping it out of my hands. All the lovely berries spilled out onto the ground, along with the deadly baneberries.

Lacey and I both scrabbled at the berries on the ground, shoving each other aside like two starving bear cubs fighting over a salmon carcass. Teena wandered into the clearing, her mouth stained purple from the berries. Her sharp eyes took in the pile of berries scattered on the ground. "Watch out for those baneberries," she said. "They could kill you."

Lacey and I froze in our tussle. Liam stared at Teena. "What do you know about baneberries?" he asked.

She shifted the pile with one foot and picked up a baneberry. "This one. It's very poisonous."

Lacey exchanged an anxious glance with Liam. He pulled a half-empty water bottle out of his pocket and handed it to her without a word. She chugged the water down.

"How do you know this?" I said to Teena. "You didn't mention ever coming to Southeast Alaska before."

She shrugged and popped a blueberry into her mouth. "You didn't ask me."

• • •

Liam gritted his teeth. "Okay, we're asking you now. Have you been to Alaska before?"

She shrugged, her hands wide and open. "Evidently. I came up that summer I was backpacking around, about ten years ago. Alaska's not exactly a backpacking trip, since you have to fly, but it was on my list to visit all fifty states before I turned twenty-five. I spent some time traveling around Southeast Alaska at the time."

Lacey's mouth was hanging open. She closed it with a snap. "Did you meet Junetta when you were there?"

I felt as stunned as Lacey. "No, she couldn't have. Ten years ago, I was off to Ohio for college. Did you run into Flint then, or Chuck?"

I watched Teena closely as I said this, remembering the strange, gentle way she'd touched Chuck's cheek after his death.

She threw a handful of berries into her mouth. Mumbling around the edges, she said, "No. I met Flint in Florida, when Lacey introduced us. I never saw Chuck before."

I knew instinctively that she was lying.

What did I really know about Teena Styles? She was an elementary school art teacher with a flair for nature, and she was handy in a crisis. She'd taken very good care of Captain Evan throughout our ordeal. I caught my breath. Had she also caused his incapacitation? Someone had added a substance to my water bottle—a drug of some sort that made me sleepy and sluggish. A sleeping pill, perhaps? Had Captain Evan been drugged in a similar manner, with his own sleeping pills? Was it Teena who had drugged him and then cared for him so he wouldn't die and so we would come to trust her? If she did know Chuck from her past time in Southeast Alaska, maybe she'd arranged to meet him here, using our misfortunes as cover for some other plan. Had she lured him here to kill him? Maybe she was, in fact, a murderer.

"Junie?" Liam touched me lightly on the shoulder. "Are you okay?"

I shook myself, chagrined by the thought that my suspicions might have been evident on my face. "Sorry, I was thinking." I swept my fingers through the berries, pulling out the last of the offending baneberries. I held out a handful of blueberries and huckleberries. "These ones are fine to eat. Let me show you the baneberry plant, so you'll know to avoid it in the future." I clambered to my feet and brushed dirt off my knees.

The whole party trooped after me toward the beach, where baneberries grew among the grasses along the edge of the rocky beach. The aggressive upright stalks with their dense clump of dark red berries screamed danger to me, most likely because I had been taught how deadly they were. I pointed them out to the others, and Teena echoed my warning. Oddly enough, Flint took no part in this botany lesson. How had he managed to live in Ptarmigan Port for a number of years and not learn about dangerous plants in the woods? I supposed he was on the water most of the time.

I found a patch of beach peas among the fireweed and baneberries. The fresh green vines grew in profusion, with pea pods dangling down like edible Christmas tree decorations. "These pods are a little early, but we could eat them in a pinch." I picked a sprig and carried it over to a lupine plant. I loved these wildflowers, with their blue and purple flowers and their swirl of leaves that caught the raindrops in the center like a shining diamond. The tall purple flowers were spent, and the seed pods had emerged along the stalk. "Look here. The beach peas and the lupine seed pods are very similar. While the peas are tasty, the lupine seeds are poisonous. You have to be very careful when harvesting, because they grow in the same environment."

Liam shook his head, a small smile on his lips. "You're a regular nature scout, Junie."

I smiled at him, happy to be able to showcase my Southeast Alaska paradise. Up until now, my beloved homeland hadn't made a very good showing. "Let's go down on the beach and see what sustenance we can find there."

I led the group onto the rocky beach. The mist had lifted a bit, so we could see along the shoreline. "It's always fun to check out the tide pools." I walked over the rocks until I found a tide pool teeming with sea life. Tiny fishes zipped through the still water. A couple blennies swam about, looking like miniature four-inch-long brown eels. I pointed them out to Liam. "We call these 'blennies,' although technically they are something else altogether. I happen to know from experience that, despite their innocuous aspect, these fierce creatures will bite you if you pick them up. Every Alaska kid gets bitten by a blenny before they come to know better."

Teena fished the wriggling creature out of the water. "If you know how to hold it, you're fine." She held it out to Lacey, who yelped and backed away. When she offered it to me, I shook my head, hiding my hands behind my back. "Proceed at your own risk, Teena. I've paid my dues in blenny bites."

She laughed and dropped the blenny back into the tide pool. "Fly and be free," she chanted, as it swished through the water.

I found some sea anemones clinging to the rocks surrounding the tide pool. They showed up as gelatinous round masses. "Check this out." I gently poked an anemone in its center. It squirted a jet of water at me and closed in on itself, protecting its soft underbelly. "This never gets old," I said with a grin.

I led the group down to the tideline, which was alive with seaweed. "I'm not a huge fan of seaweed, but sea lettuce is my favorite." I pointed out the delicate, bright green leaves growing in profusion on the rocks. "You can eat it raw—supposedly it has a lot of protein." I collected a bunch, swirled it in the surf, and handed it to Lacey. "You can photograph it for your magazine," I said to her.

She regarded me thoughtfully, then pulled her phone out of her pocket. "Rats! My battery is dead. Here, Flint, let me use yours." She plucked Flint's phone out of his hands before he could respond.

I stood right next to Lacey and saw Flint's phone screen as it flashed past me. He had the phone open to his text app. I don't know why he bothered. I got a fleeting glimpse of a text that read, 'come alone.' I couldn't tell if it was an outgoing or incoming text, or if it was recent or old. I pulled out my own phone to check if I had any cell service—nope.

Flint made a sharp movement with his hand, as if he were going to snatch his phone back from Lacey. He stopped himself just in time and suffered her to take a series of carefully framed photos of the sea lettuce. It was actually quite lovely to watch her at work. She crouched at ground level, moving from one side to the other to capture every facet of the leafy algae in its natural habitat.

Then, she turned to me. "Hold these bits that you picked, please, while I take a few pictures. Wipe your hands clean first."

Indeed, my hands were quite dirty, streaked with berry juice, slime, and dirt. Mom would send me back to wash up if I ever showed up to dinner with hands like these. I savored the thought of her loving scolding and wiped my hands on my pants. It didn't really improve matters.

I held the little bunch of sea lettuce while Lacey took photo after photo. When she was finished, I handed her the leaves. "Take a taste, so your magazine story will have authenticity."

She accepted the sea lettuce, gave it a sniff, and took a dainty taste. "It's good." She popped the rest into her mouth. She handed the phone back to Flint. "Whenever you can, just text me those photos." Turning to me, she said, "Thank you, Junetta. It was good to find my creative center in the midst of all this madness." She gave me a genuine smile. "I'm sorry for my behavior."

I nodded. "No worries. This trip has been hard on all of us." I caught my breath. "Our challenges aren't finished yet." I pointed behind Lacey's back, to where a small fur ball of a black bear cub emerged from the mist at the edge of the woods.

Chapter Nine

"Cute," Lacey said, starting to walk toward the cub with her hand held out as if she were about to feed a horse an apple. "You look just like a teddy bear I had as a child. Were you peeking in on me in the night?" A second cub frisked out of the woods, just as small and furry as the first one. "Look, here comes another one."

I heaved a sigh and caught Lacey by the arm. "The cubs are adorable—mama bear, not so much." I drew her back from the brink. "She won't be far behind, and she won't take kindly to us messing with her babies. Let's get out of here."

Indeed, a sleek, fat black bear was the next to amble out of the woods. With a slight breeze blowing in from the water, she caught our scent right away. Her head reared up and she let out a loud huff. The noise startled her cubs, who paused to look behind them at their mama. The sight of her open mouth and flared nostrils must have alarmed them, because they scurried back to hide behind her flanks. She huffed again, louder.

"She's gonna charge," Flint cried.

"Get as big as you can," I said, throwing my arms up into the air. The others followed suit. I ripped off my jacket and held it up as high as I could reach, adding a good two feet to my normal stature. I waved it from side to side and held my ground as the bear started sprinting toward us. It was unreal how fast an animal that big could run.

The next few moments swirled past me like the mist on the water, fleeting and unreal. Lacey screamed bloody murder and turned to run. Liam and Teena were right beside her, the three of them streaking away from the angry bear. Flint and I stood firm, trying to block the sight of their fleeing forms from the charging bear.

It was a bluff charge. The bear stopped within three yards of us, blowing hard. I stood rooted to my spot, holding my jacket aloft until I thought my arms were going to fall off. "Go on, then," I said to the bear in a low voice, my breath coming very fast. "Go back to your berries. We're not a threat to your babies."

Flint stood beside me, his eyes darting from me to the bear and back again.

"She's still on all fours," I said to him, never taking my eyes off the bear. "She's not going to attack us."

As if on cue, the mama bear turned away and waddled back to her babies, her dominance over the beachhead established.

I slowly lowered my arms and turned to Flint. I surprised us both by wrapping him in a grateful hug, my arms trembling. I bumped into a solid, angular shape under his coat. "Thank you for standing with me," I said. "If you had run too, she probably would have gone after you all."

He gently disengaged from my embrace. "Cheechakos! Don't they know that you can't outrun a bear?"

Together, we walked to where Lacey, Liam, and Teena crouched behind a tree on the far side of the beach.

"We just saved your skins," Flint said.

Liam responded to this comment with a scowl, rather than the abject gratitude that he should have displayed. Before he could respond, I linked arms with Lacey on one side and Liam on the other. "Survival 101: never run away from a bear. If it's a black bear, you can usually scare it off or fight it off if necessary. If it's a brown bear, curl up and play dead, and hope you won't end up in that state for real."

Lacey wiped a tear from her cheek. "This is probably all old hat for you. I'll bet you get chased by bears on a weekly basis."

"Actually, no. I've never been chased by a bear, mostly because I don't run away. This is only the second time I've been charged. The first time was the same thing—the bear had plenty of room to sense me and charge before turning away at the last minute. The worst is if you sneak up on a bear and they feel threatened without enough time to figure out how they want to react. If they're really close to you, you're likely to get swiped." I led the group in the opposite direction from the bears, toward the clearing to lead us back to the campsite. "We should check on Captain Evan, and make sure the bears didn't disturb his nap."

Nothing had changed at the campsite. Captain Evan still snored under the blue tarp. When I touched his face and neck, it felt cool but not dangerously chilled. I wondered when, if ever, he was going to wake up.

Shaking off that morbid thought, I built up the fire with Liam's help. He drew me aside. "What are we going to do, Junie? We can't search for food on the beach because there's an angry bear waiting to make mincemeat out of us. We don't have a way to get off this island other than a small dinghy, with no navigation instruments to get us back to civilization. We've only got a few bottles of clean water left. We've got an unconscious elder to care for, with no medical supplies or expertise. Oh, and we've got a dead man in a shallow grave, who was killed by one of the five of us in the middle of the night." He balled his fists. "I can't stand it! How are we ever going to get out of this mess?"

I could feel my stress increasing with each item that Liam ticked off his list of dire predicaments that we faced. He obviously expected me to take responsibility for every one of them and magic us out of our troubles.

I took a deep breath, trying to conjure up a feeling of calm and confidence. "I don't think this fog will last much longer." I beat back memories of those three days of solid fog after sunshine had been forecast. "The best thing we can do is relax, conserve our strength, and wait for the rescuers to arrive."

He shook his head. "I think we should send a scouting party off in the dinghy to raise the alarm and bring us help."

"No, bad idea. The alarm has already been raised, hours ago when we didn't come back for supper last night. We weren't planning an overnight excursion, and Marcy knew that. Nels and the troopers are already on the case. Really, Liam, it's just a matter of time." I pasted on a smile. "I'm going to chill out in my cozy shelter for a bit. Maybe you could keep the fire going?"

"I'm going to talk to Flint about the dinghy. We'll see what he has to say."

I really needed to lie down. "Talk all you want. But listen to me, Liam. That dinghy is mine. You need to ask me before you take it away. Don't go off without my permission."

"Permission? Are you in charge here? I don't need your permission to do what I want to do."

"Yes, you do, if you're going to take my property."

Liam stalked away and then circled back to me. "It's your property that got us into this mess in the first place. If your boat hadn't caught on fire with a passed-out captain at the wheel, we would be happily browsing through your bestsellers in your bookshop at this very moment, instead of being marooned on an island with no cell phone service or clean water, inhabited by a maniac who is now dead."

I could only stare at him in shock. I turned and fled to my wilderness shelter. I crawled inside and turned my back to the entrance, curling up in a ball on the bed of soggy moss. My thoughts whirled as tears streamed down my face.

Liam thought all this mess was my fault. He blamed me for everything we'd endured since fire had broken out on the *Northern Dream* and we'd had to abandon ship. All my heroic efforts to get us safely to the island in the dinghy, set up camp under the watchful eye of a paranoid, trigger-happy individual, scavenge food, and even stare down a charging bear meant nothing to him. Liam was probably my biggest supporter in the group. If that's how he felt, I imagined that the others thought the same thing. I felt like the captain of a ship, facing the mutiny of her crew after they lost confidence in the captain's skills.

I knew that if Liam, or both Liam and Flint, went off in the dinghy in the fog and mist, they would regret it. The chance of capsizing, bobbing about in the waves forever, or getting lost and washing up on some other shore was astronomical. When you get lost, you're supposed to stay put until someone comes to find you. I'd had that lesson ingrained in me ever since I could walk. This situation didn't seem to be any different. But I didn't know if I could persuade them to see reason.

I covered my head with my arms, wishing I could just hide out from the responsibility of making more decisions for the group. I pulled out my phone, hoping to find some peace from old messages I'd received from my friends.

I scrolled through some old texts from Marcy. She'd taken to sending pictures of Lisa cradled by one after another of her family members in Ptarmigan Port. I smiled at the infant's chubby cheeks. I longed to cradle her myself, snuggled up in one of my comfortable chairs in the reading nook back at the Shipshape Bookshop. I searched for the latest photo I'd taken of the bookshop to post on social media. I'd homed in on the red door with the wooden sign hanging above it, featuring a line drawing of the *Northern Dream* surrounded by the words, 'Shipshape Bookshop.' The front window display showcased a new novel by our local mystery writer, T.J. Bartlow. I groaned. I was supposed to be hosting a book signing for him this very afternoon. T.J. was a hard man to get ahold of, and we had gone back and forth for weeks before landing on today's date. He would be frustrated at me for standing him up.

I moved on to look at a few texts from Mom. She never wasted words in a text. Her most used phrase was, 'Love you, dear.' I smiled. I could always count on that.

The last text I'd received from Nels said, 'I can't make it after all.' There was no other context. It didn't really matter—that message was a frequent one from Nels. As the agent of law in our small town, he answered the call when needed. I pictured him sending that message to one of his friends who he was going to go fishing with, perhaps, saying, 'I can't make it after all—I have to go get my sister out of trouble again.' I couldn't wait to see his face and take that good-natured ribbing from him.

There were no texts from Uncle Vance. As Owner Emeritus of the bookshop, he might be expected to text me frequently in a professional capacity, even if he didn't want to chat with me, uncle to niece. But Uncle Vance was old school. He owned a cell phone, because Nels and I made him, but he rarely used it, and then only to talk on the phone. He didn't even take photos on the phone. He had a fancy camera that took film, and he would lug that along on hikes and camping trips. Our local grocery kept plenty of film in stock just for Uncle Vance.

Finally, I turned to texts from Angus. He'd texted me yesterday morning, before we set off on our fateful cruise. It wasn't a message, just a link to a news story he thought I would be interested in. I hadn't had time to check it out. I looked at the headline now: 'Iconic Icons on the Rebound?' The accompanying picture was of a Russian Orthodox icon hanging on a bare wall. I couldn't open the story for lack of cell service.

Angus must have found a story about Ptarmigan Port's pair of icons that went missing ten years ago and were rumored to be about to resurface. It was probably the same story that Rachelle Simonson of the *Ptarmigan Times* was so excited about. That was one of the perils of living in a small town—the slightest bit of news took on oversized proportions. I scrolled back to the previous text from Angus.

He'd recently sent me a selfie from New York City with the Statue of Liberty across the harbor in the background. I smiled at his windblown curly hair and the sight of his jacket collar turned up. The photo was from a couple days ago, still summer in New York City, which I knew was quite a bit hotter than here. The accompanying text read, 'Wish you were here—no, wish I were there. There's not a single humpback in New York Harbor, by the way. Have you seen one today?' I'd replied, 'Not yet, but the day is young.' In fact, I hadn't seen any humpback whales that day, but I hadn't felt the need to disillusion Angus as to the wonders of my Alaska paradise. I was hoping to lure him to Ptarmigan Port for good. I wished he were here right now. He wouldn't be much help in finding our way back to civilization, but he would never accuse me of being a killer or tell me that this whole fiasco was all my fault. "I miss you, Angus," I whispered. I wished he could hear me. He was so very, very far away.

I pocketed my phone and snuggled deeper into the moss. I was exhausted but not drugged this time. Maybe I could catch a few winks. I tried not to think of the fact that a murderer still walked among us. Chuck was the one who was killed, and a case could be made that he had asked for it. I didn't want to go so far as to say he deserved to die, but the fact remained that the rest of us were probably safe, as long as we didn't act like jerks. I shelved that thought and focused on Angus. I fell asleep with a smile on my lips, thinking of him.

When I woke up, I could feel his arms around me, pulling my body close to his. I sighed, relaxing into his warmth. It felt so right. Only it wasn't Angus. It was Liam.

"Junie, I'm sorry for fussing at you," he whispered into my hair. "I was freaking out a little bit. I'm good now."

I lifted his arm off my shoulders and twisted out of his embrace. Planting both hands on his chest, I pushed him out of my shelter. "We've got to stop meeting like this," I said lightly. Then, more sternly, "Seriously, Liam, you need to keep your hands to yourself. If this happens again, I'm going to have to tell Lacey. It's not fair to her or to me, or even to you, if you stop and think about it. What you and I had together is over. It's for the best."

He rolled onto one elbow, regarding me. "You were the best, Junie."

"Not anymore." I slithered past him to get out of my shelter. "Where is everybody?"

"They're all taking a siesta. We woke up really early this morning. I came to see if you were awake, because it seems like the fog is lifting."

Indeed, I could see the tops of the trees that had earlier been shrouded in mist. I walked to the middle of the clearing and looked straight up, to see a large expanse of lovely blue sky. A pair of bald eagles circled above us, calling to each other with their high-pitched calls. I pointed them out to Liam. "Eagles always bring good luck. Our rescuers will be out soon, with the weather clearing up. When they see the *Northern Dream*, assuming she's still afloat, they will search carefully nearby. We should build up a fire on the beach to get noticed."

He and I both loaded up our arms with logs and made our way to the beach with cautious glances right and left to be sure no bears were accompanying us. Luckily, the path was empty.

We found a likely spot on the beach and built up a fire. With Chuck's nice, dry wood, there was barely any smoke. "This won't do the trick," I said, wiping some sweat off my face. "Let's gather up some damp moss to make a really smoky fire."

It was the opposite of everything I had learned about camping. Instead of dry, clean-burning wood, we piled on moss, damp leaves, and green shoots from the spruce and hemlock trees. A dark, smelly smoke poured into the sky. "Perfect!"

I was on my way back to the beach with a second armful of moss when Liam shouted, pointing to the bay. "They're here already!"

Wow, that was one successful fire.

Chapter Ten

I hustled back to the beach to see what Liam was talking about. He was right, there was a boat chugging into the bay. It was a substantial boat with an enclosed bridge and plenty of deck room to take on a group of castaways. It steered purposefully toward the beach, following the thick plume of smoke that poured out of the fire.

Liam stood on the edge of the beach. Or rather, he jumped up and down, waving both arms and shouting as loud as he could. He ran up to me and threw both arms around me, lifting me clear off the ground in his embrace. "We're saved!"

I laughed and wriggled out of his grasp. I wanted to go wake everyone up, but at the same time, I wanted to stand firm on the beach and welcome our rescuers in person. I elected to stay put.

The boat came closer, close enough to read her name painted on the bow: *Sea After Sea*. The name evoked images of someone fulfilling their lifelong dream to sail the world. I was grateful that she was in my part of the world at this particular moment.

She dropped anchor close in to shore, and someone set off in a dinghy for the beach. Liam and I had to wait an excruciating twenty minutes before they landed on the beach. I ran out into the surf to grab hold of the line and pull the dinghy up to shore. A man stepped out onto the beach. I'd never seen him before.

He was tall and spare, with a weathered face that made it difficult to guess his age. He wore waders and an oversized slicker with bulging pockets. An old baseball cap covered his head, so faded that I couldn't make out which team it promoted. His grip was strong when he reached out to shake my hand after greeting Liam in the same manner.

"I'm Seth Corliss. I heard an alert about an overdue pleasure craft with six passengers and crew. Are you the only ones left?" He addressed his question to Liam.

"I'm Liam. All six of us are safe. Come on." Liam turned to lead him to our campsite and our sleeping companions.

I forestalled him. "Did you see the *Northern Dream*? What was her condition?"

He shook his head. "I didn't come across your boat."

"How did you know where to find us?"

He pointed at the fire. "You can see that smoke a mile away." He turned to follow Liam through the shore grasses and on to the clearing.

I jogged along behind, wondering. We had only built up the smoky fire ten minutes before the *Sea After Sea* had shown up in the bay. Seth couldn't have seen the smoke from a mile away—it would have taken him much longer than that to reach us. He must have been using the distance as a figure of speech.

Liam burst into the clearing, calling out, "Wake up! The cavalry has arrived!"

Teena and Lacey rolled out from underneath Chuck's sleeping bag. Flint crawled out from the blue tarp next to Captain Evan, who didn't move.

Liam made introductions all around. He seemed to be enjoying his position as leader of our party. Personally, I was glad to cede responsibility to him.

Seth silently took in our campsite, noticing the covered woodpile, the dying fire, and the array of tent, tarps, and wilderness shelter. He indicated Chuck's zipped up tent. "Anyone sleeping in there?"

I froze. The only thing in there was a rifle with blood on its butt. I had no desire to tell that whole story to Seth as an outsider. A quick glance around showed me that the rest of our party had the same reservations. We hadn't agreed on a story to explain the presence of the tent and the well-stocked woodpile, both clearly not the result of a shipwreck. I opened my mouth to say something, anything, but Flint beat me to it.

"We were lucky enough to come across this existing campsite. I don't know whose it is, but we're definitely in their debt."

Seth frowned, looking from one face to another. He strode toward the tent.

I hastened to back up Flint. "We were soaking wet and cold when we made it to shore in our dinghy." I waved a hand at the small watercraft, still upended on the edge of the campfire area. "I don't think we could have made it through the night without this lovely woodpile. When we get back to Ptarmigan Port and find out who camped here, we'll be sure to repay them." I pointed toward the captain. "Captain Evan passed out on board, and he hasn't woken since. Do you have any medical expertise?"

Seth paused at the entrance to Chuck's tent. He turned around and walked over to peer at Captain Evan under the tarp. "He passed out before going into the water? So, it's not simply hypothermia that's affecting him. He should be gotten to medical care as soon as possible."

"Can you take us all back to Ptarmigan Port?" I clasped my hands together, prepared to beg if necessary. Something about Seth's demeanor struck me as off. I couldn't tell if he was really responding to Nels's SOS, or if something else was going on here.

Seth shook his head. "I can't take on six people. Two of you will have to stay behind."

Lacey cried out, seeking shelter in Liam's embrace. "Please, there are bears on the island. Two of us by ourselves can't stay safe from the bears."

Seth cast his eyes around the campsite again. "Do you suppose that's what happened to the owner of this campsite? He was attacked by bears?' His gaze traveled from one of us to the next.

I got the distinct impression that Seth knew all about Chuck. He was playing with us, waiting for us to reveal the truth that Chuck had been killed by one of us. Was he trying to flush out the killer?

I shook off this paranoid train of thought. "We haven't seen any evidence of bear attack," I said. "We were on the beach this morning when a sow and two cubs showed up. She bluff-charged us, and then they went on their way."

Seth swung his gaze around to focus on me. "Tell me your name again."

"Junetta Beale. My family has lived in Ptarmigan Port for generations. My brother, Nels, is a trooper in town. It was most likely him who sent out the alert that you got. Now that the fog has lifted, I'm sure he's got boats and planes out searching for us." I gave him a friendly smile, far from what I was feeling. "It's always nice to have a brother who's a trooper—you feel like you get personalized service." I also had an ace up my sleeve, which I wasn't shy about pulling out when needed. Although Nels was my younger brother, he was very useful as an intimidation factor. I wasn't quite sure why I felt like I needed to intimidate Seth, but my mention of Nels helped to quell the paranoia I was feeling.

Seth didn't react. He was probably a master poker player, unfazed by the ace up my sleeve. He reached over and unzipped the opening to Chuck's tent. He ducked his head inside.

I sucked in my breath. When he found the rifle, Seth would have questions that would be very hard to answer.

He emerged from the tent without the rifle. I looked past him into the tent. The rifle was not there. I could have sworn Flint had dropped it inside and zipped up the tent. Someone must have moved it while I was sleeping. I beat back the alarming thought that it was Chuck's killer who had done so. I almost didn't hear Flint's next words.

"I will stay back with Captain Evan while the rest of you take off with Seth."

"No, bad idea." I knew Flint would take offense at these words, but I needed to stick up for the captain. "Captain Evan needs to get to good medical care as soon as possible. He can't wait for the hours it will take to get Seth's boat to Ptarmigan Port and back for a round trip."

As expected, Flint reddened at my comment. "What do you suggest, then? Who's going to stay behind?"

"We can take volunteers," said Teena. "I volunteer to go with Captain Evan and care for him onboard until we get back to town."

Lacey gave a short laugh. "Nice one, Teena. Way to claim a spot on the boat."

Teena shrugged with a smile, obviously trying to keep her sense of humor throughout this fraught situation.

Liam glanced around our group. "Flint should go with the boat, because he knows about boats. Junetta should stay, because she knows about wilderness survival. I will stay with Junetta and the rest of you should go. The sooner, the better."

Lacey frowned at Liam. I could feel a similar expression on my own face.

Seth cut across our conversation. "I'll take the women and the invalid. The two men will stay here and wait for my return. That's final. Come on."

"Hey!" Liam cried, but Seth was halfway down the path. Liam ran to catch up. He rounded on Seth, blocking his path. "How do I know the women will be safe with you? We don't know one thing about you."

Seth shrugged. "You'll just have to trust me. We're wasting the tide."

Liam took my arm. "Do you trust him? Will you three be safe?"

I heaved a sigh. "We'll be fine. I know a thing or two about boats, like how to operate the ship-to-shore radio. Nels will know where we are before we're thirty yards offshore." I grinned at Liam, raising my voice so all could hear. "Nels gets very protective when there's a threat to his sister."

Liam gave me a hug. "Take care of Lacey for me."

I pushed him off in her direction. "Lacey's the one who needs a hug from you. We'll see you guys soon."

• • •

Flint and Liam lifted Captain Evan into our dinghy and dragged it down the path to the beach. Rather than transfer him into Seth's dinghy, they simply launched the one from the *Northern Dream* and piloted it to the *Sea After Sea* while the rest of us followed in Seth's dinghy. It took the efforts of all three men to sway the captain up from the dinghy into the boat and get him settled in a nest of dry blankets on the seat cushions in the stern.

The boat's stern was crowded with piles of empty crab pots which took up most of the available deck space. With Captain Evan occupying the seat cushions on the port side of the boat, there was only room for a couple people to sit on the starboard side. If we squeezed in or sat on each other's laps, we could probably all fit onboard. Presumably there was space below decks or in the bridge as well.

"Looks like there's plenty of room for all of us," Flint said, with more than a hint of challenge in his voice.

"If not on deck, someone can ride with you in the bridge, Seth, or below decks," I chimed in with a big smile. "That way we can get everyone back to Ptarmigan Port in one trip."

It was a wasted effort.

Seth gave me a lowering frown. "No landlubbers in my bridge, and nobody goes below decks." When Flint started to protest, Seth held up an imperious finger. "My boat, my rules. If you don't like the rules, you can all disembark and wait for the next boat to come around." He pointed at Flint and Liam. "Or the two of you can disembark now and allow the rest of your party to find warmth and shelter in town. Up to you."

Both Flint and Liam bristled at this arbitrary command, but in the end, they had to comply with Seth's directives. They boarded the dinghy and headed back to the beach after a tearful farewell with Lacey, who clung to Liam as if he were marching off to war.

While all this activity swirled around me, I nipped into the bridge, in spite of Seth's random rules. A quick glance led me straight to the boat's radio. I pushed the correct button and delivered the following message: "This is the *Sea After Sea*. We've taken on four of the missing passengers from the *Northern Dream*. Two others remain on Price Island. Headed back to Ptarmigan Port. Over." I clicked the radio back into its holder as Seth materialized in the doorway.

"What are you doing?" he barked. "Hands off my instruments!"

I lifted my hands in the air like a contestant on a cooking competition when time was called. "I was wondering if I could use your radio to send a message to my mom, just to let her know that I'm okay."

He shook his head. "I only use the radio for emergencies. Your mom can wait."

I bit my lip and threw on a smile. "Thank you so much for taking us on, Seth. We were starting to feel like we'd never see civilization again."

He wasn't distracted by my praise. He took me by the arm and basically shoved me out of the control room. "Get out of my bridge. There's a seat for you on deck. We'll be back to Ptarmigan Port in an hour or so."

I went obediently to sit down next to Lacey. She shivered as the boat picked up speed. Tears flowed silently down her cheeks.

I put an arm around her shoulders. "Everything's going to be all right, Lacey. Flint and Liam will be fine. They might even get picked up by another boat before Seth can circle back to them."

She leaned her head in close and whispered, "I don't trust Seth. Something's funny about him."

"Yeah, I don't trust him either," I whispered back. "I grabbed his radio while the guys were getting everything settled. I sent a message alerting the folks back home to our position. Nels will send out a big reception committee to meet us as we come into town. It's all good."

She looked at me with new respect. "I guess Flint's not the only one who knows about boats."

I smiled back at her. "Boats are a part of my daily life—always have been."

We cruised along under mostly sunny skies. Mist rose up from the mountainsides that were still drying out from the heavy rain yesterday. I noticed the streams were flowing full down the steep hillsides, and there was one spot where a mass of dirt and debris indicated a recent landslide. Luckily, it had come down in an uninhabited area.

Suddenly, I saw a boat swinging at anchor. I grabbed Lacey's arm. "Look, it's the *Northern Dream*! She didn't sink or burn up after all."

"That's good luck," Lacey said. "You really do love that old boat, don't you?"

I wiped a tear from my eye. "Absolutely! It's been in my family for generations. My great-grandfather, a pastor, served the surrounding villages from the *Northern Dream*. My bookmobile services are my way of following in his footsteps."

I drank in the sight of the old boat as we cruised on by. It wasn't until she was well astern that it occurred to me that Seth would have passed her on his way to Price Island to pick us up. Was it possible that he simply didn't notice her? Maybe he had approached the island from the north, although there wasn't a navigable channel there. As Lacey said, something was funny here.

Thankfully, the cruise back to Ptarmigan Port was scarcely more than an hour. I whiled away the time searching for wildlife to point out to Lacey. I felt like I owed her at least a humpback whale to make up for our disastrous outing yesterday. The best I could do was to point out a distant puff that signaled that a whale had recently come up for air. She saw it before it dissipated on the breeze.

My close attention to the surroundings served another purpose. I took note of the familiar landmarks, making sure that Seth was, in fact, taking us home to Ptarmigan Port. The specter of kidnappers crossed my mind once or twice, but thankfully, it was a needless worry. The familiar hillsides slipped past, until we entered Havoc Strait and Mom's remote lodge hove into view.

The Sourdough Lady Lodge was always the first human habitation that greeted me on my return from my twice monthly trips to the villages with my floating bookmobile. The channel was fairly narrow at this point, and Captain Evan would steer the *Northern Dream* close to shore so I could greet Mom on the dock. The joy of seeing her every other week across the waves compensated for the fact that she was out of touch most of the time, even if she lived within twenty miles of town. Today, the *Sea After Sea* steamed along in the middle of the channel, and no one stood on the dock to wave at our passing. I knew there was no cell service at the lodge, so I couldn't call Mom to say I was safe and actually in view. Nonetheless, I hung over the rail and waved with all my might as we slipped on by.

Teena looked up from where she sat on the deck of the boat, watching over Captain Evan's prostrate form. "Do you see someone there, Junetta?"

I turned to her with a sheepish smile. "We just passed my mom's remote lodge. Whenever we go by on the *Northern Dream*, she greets me from the dock. She wasn't out today, but it just felt wrong to pass by without waving. There's good karma in keeping to tradition." I held out a hand to Lacey. "Ptarmigan Port is almost in view. Come see."

She took my hand and came to stand next to me on the rail. The wind ruffled through her wispy hair, intensifying her waiflike appearance. She planted one hand on the rail and kept hold of me with the other, whether for security or because she thought I was going to plunge a knife in her back, I wasn't sure. Her hand trembled in mine. Poor Lacey, this trip had taken so much out of her. I could only hope that her engagement to Liam would survive it.

My heart lifted as we approached my beloved hometown. I pointed out the colorful houses as they came into view. Winters were long and dark in this part of the world, and the residents of Ptarmigan Port compensated by painting their homes and businesses a brilliant array of colors designed to chase the winter blues away. "Look, you can see the Tongass Glacier from the water today. The clouds were so low yesterday that the ice was hidden."

Lacey marveled at the massive river of ice flowing down from the Juneau Icefield. "I'd ask you to take us on a tour of it, but I'm afraid we would slip on the ice and tumble into a crevasse."

I forced a smile. "It'll take some time to repair my reputation, huh?"

Teena piped up before Lacey could respond. "As long as we get back in one piece and are greeted with a supersized pot of coffee and about a hundred meatball sandwiches, I'm good."

My stomach grumbled at her mention of food. I was pretty sure we could count on Marcy to take care of us.

The downtown area came into view. I drank in the sight of the Shipshape Bookshop with its teal blue walls and bright purple accents. The cheery red door was propped open to invite the cruise ship tourists inside. There were two large ships in port. The dock bustled with activity, as visitors browsed in the shops along the waterside or connected with the various tour groups that took them out to the glacier or into the beautiful Alaska wilderness.

In addition to the tourists, there was another group milling about on the dock, centered on my brother, Nels. He was dressed in his trooper uniform, hat and all, which indicated how seriously he took this particular moment. A gaggle of tourists snapped photos of him, which usually annoyed him. He paid them no mind. Uncle Vance stood next to him, leaning on his beautifully carved walking stick, his little white dog, Cosmo, frisking at his side. The sight of them waiting to see me safe at home filled me with a deep sense of gratitude for family. I wiped away a tear and waved.

Nels lifted an arm in response and waved for the *Sea After Sea* to pull up to the dock. I peeked in the bridge, to see that Seth was disregarding this direction. He focused on the waterway in front of the boat, ignoring the people on the dock.

I popped into the bridge. "They're waving us in on the dock," I said, pointing to my brother. "Usually boats can't tie up here, but this is a special occasion." I threw him a bright smile. "If the troopers tell you to come, you gotta come."

Indeed, Nels had a bullhorn now, shouting, "Pull up to the dock and tie down your boat."

Seth scowled at me, even as he adjusted his course to pull up alongside the dock. "No landlubbers in my bridge."

I scurried back out, satisfied that he was doing what Nels directed him to do.

It took a few minutes for Seth to get the *Sea After Sea* tied up at the dock. Then Nels came aboard in a rush. He pulled me into a fierce hug. In the strength of his grip, I could feel the anguish of the ten-year-old boy fearing for his dad's life. Then he held me off at arm's length and looked me over carefully. "You all right?"

I burst into tears.

I had held it together through the terror of the fire on the *Northern Dream*, our desperate escape in the dinghy with the rain pelting down, the threat posed by the maniac Chuck once we'd finally found shelter, the grisly discovery of his murdered body and the realization that one of our own party had killed him, not to mention fending off the amorous attentions of my former fiancé, being charged by a mama bear protecting her cubs, and then being rescued by an enigmatic boater who exuded untrustworthy vibes. I had literally reached my limit.

As usual, Nels had no idea what to do with my tears. To help him out, I pulled him back into the hug. I hid my face on his shoulder, just for a moment, while I composed myself. Then I whispered in his ear, "We have to go back and get Liam and Flint. You have to come, too. There's been a murder."

Chapter Eleven

Nels gaped at me.

I nodded and held a finger to my lips.

He closed his mouth with a snap. He held out a hand to Seth, who was watching our reunion closely. "Nels Beale. Thank you for answering the call."

Seth shook Nels's hand. "I'm Seth Corliss. Somehow, you were expecting us just now."

Nels bent down over Captain Evan, his face registering dismay at the condition of the captain. He spoke over his shoulder, "Yeah, we got your radio message. I guess there are two others to go back and pick up."

Seth stared at him. "I sent no message." He glared at me. "But you did, didn't you? Don't you know not to ever touch nautical instruments that aren't your own?"

"Sorry. I wanted folks back home to know as soon as possible that we were safe." It was a half-hearted apology. I wasn't sorry in the least.

Seth abandoned me with an exasperated grunt. He spoke to Nels, "Get the captain and the women on shore, and then I can go back to pick up the strays."

Nels was speaking into his radio, arranging paramedics for Captain Evan. Without responding to Seth, he waved a hand to me, an indication that I should get Teena and Lacey to shore.

"Come on, Lacey." I took her hand. I gestured to Teena. The three of us disembarked, to be swallowed up by the reception committee. Katie Carter, owner of Green's Grocery, wrapped warm fleece blankets around both Lacey and Teena. Uncle

Vance threw a blanket around my shoulders and then enveloped me in a hug while Cosmo romped around my ankles. "Did you sink the *Northern Dream*? She never should have been out in that kind of weather."

"Good to see you, too," I said, clinging to him despite my sarcastic tone. "It wasn't the weather. The engine room caught on fire, and we had to abandon ship. But we passed her on our way back here today, so she's still afloat. I don't know what she looks like on the inside, though."

He shook his head, disapproval rolling off him like water. As former owner of the Shipshape Bookshop, now Owner Emeritus, he took the success of our business very personally. Losing the *Northern Dream*, the boat that had been in our family for generations, would be a heavy blow.

He patted me on the shoulder and released me. "It's good to know that you're safe." He looked around. "Where are the others?"

"They're back on Price Island. We have to go back to get them." I gave Cosmo a good head rubbing before looking over at Nels, who was now talking with Seth while the paramedics strapped Captain Evan to a stretcher to take him to the clinic.

"You don't have to go back yourself," Nels said to Seth. "You've done your Good Samaritan duty. There are other boats out looking, and the Civil Air Patrol is out as well. Now that we know where they are, it's a simple matter to divert someone to Price Island to pick them up."

Seth shrugged. "It's up to you. I'm headed back that way anyway. I didn't get a chance to set my crab pots before I came to the rescue."

Nels glanced over at me. I didn't know the right gesture to alert him to my desire to go back to Price Island in anybody else's boat than Seth's. "Thank you so much for your rescue, Seth," I called to him. "I'm sure Nels can take care of everything now."

Nels nodded. "Give me your contact information, Seth, in case there's any need to follow up with you. And you have my heartfelt gratitude for bringing my sister and her friends back home safely."

• • •

Captain Evan had been whisked off to the best medical care that Ptarmigan Port could provide. Teena and Lacey were safe and warm in the Last Chance Café, tucking into Marcy's tasty food. Nels and I stood side by side on the dock, watching Seth cast off the line and get the *Sea After Sea* underway. Nels inclined his head in Seth's direction. "Is he the murderer?"

"No. It's someone from Liam's bridal party. We have to get back to Price Island, ideally before Seth does. There's something weird about him. It's like he wanted to leave Liam and Flint behind for some reason. He had plenty of room on his boat to take all of us."

Nels turned in a flash and whipped out his radio again. "Mark, bring the cat over to the cruise ship dock. Urgent." He said to me, "Are you coming?" When I nodded, he spoke into the radio again, "Junetta and I have to go back to Price Island to pick up some stragglers." He disconnected and looked at me critically. "Do you want to change or get something to eat?"

All I wanted was to go home, luxuriate in a hot shower until my fingers got all wrinkly, and then fill up on hot soup and tea before sinking into bed even though it was just midafternoon. The absolute last thing I wanted to do was take another boat trip out to that cursed island to lead my brother to the body of a murdered man. "There's no time to change, but I would love some food while Mark brings the cat around."

Nels propelled me in the direction of the Last Chance Café. "We won't leave without you."

I stepped into the sweet and spicy warmth of the café. Lacey and Teena sat at a table together, their hands cupped around steaming mugs. Marcy was busy with a line of tourists who were choosing to forego their onboard buffets for her delicious fare. I caught her eye and pressed my palms together in a beseeching motion.

She abandoned her line, ignoring the annoyed glance of a tall woman with wiry gray hair who looked like she was used to being catered to. Marcy hustled around the counter and caught me up in a big bear hug. "Junetta." She put a lifetime of friendship into that one word. "I'm not going to say, 'I told you so,' at least not yet. Sit down and I'll bring you some food and drink."

I shook my head. "Nels and I are headed back out. If you could give me something to go, that would be awesome."

"Ham and cheese?" She called back to her chef in the kitchen, "Please make a ham and cheese on rye with Dijon mustard for Junetta, Ricky. Top priority." She busied herself fixing me a huge to-go cup of café au lait just the way I liked it.

"Excuse me, miss. I believe I was next in line." The sour-faced woman gave me a withering glare. "You do know about lines here in Alaska, right?"

Marcy ducked into the kitchen without a word. She was usually unfailingly polite to rude customers. I knew she was removing herself from the temptation of telling the woman where to step off.

I flashed a brilliant smile. "I'm so sorry, everyone. We've got a maritime rescue in progress, which is why I'm jumping the line on all of you."

Nels, bless him, popped his head into the café at that precise moment. "Mark's here, Junetta. Ready to go?"

Marcy pressed the sandwich into my hands, tucked several napkins into my pocket, and handed me the coffee. "Off you go, then. No shenanigans this time around."

I almost spilled coffee all over her when I hugged her goodbye. I waved to Lacey and Teena. "Be back in a jiffy!" I hustled out the door after Nels.

Trooper Mark held the line to the catamaran as Nels and I scrambled on board. The Alaska State Troopers maintained a couple of official SUVs for tooling around town, a pickup truck for hauling, and a big 35-foot catamaran for any policing they needed to do on the water. The Coast Guard watchkeepers stationed in Juneau had jurisdiction over the waters of Southeast Alaska, but in a town with no roads in or out, it made sense for the troopers to have water transportation. Mark was very proud of his role as captain of the catamaran.

Seth had a good half hour start on us, so he might get to Price Island before us if that was his intention. The catamaran was likely faster than his boat, however. The race was on!

Between big bites of ham and cheese, I filled Nels in on the events of the last day and a half. I told him about the fire on the *Northern Dream* and how we ended up on the island cold and wet with Captain Evan incapacitated. I described Chuck's paranoid behavior and how we all settled down to sleep in the shelters that we, mostly I, had created. I told him how disoriented I'd felt on awakening, as if I had been drugged. "I saved the water bottle that looked like it had some kind of powder residue in it, in the hopes that you can get it tested."

He nodded, all his attention riveted on my story.

"Then, I went into the woods a bit away from camp, and found Chuck, dead. He'd been hit over the head with something, and his rifle was missing. It turned up later in my wilderness shelter, with blood on the butt. So, we spent the rest of the day running around like chickens with our heads cut off, accusing each other of murder. It's been horrible." I took a big slurp of my café au lait. "The worst part is, one of us really is a killer. If it was purely self-defense, which is totally believable, I feel like the person would have owned up to it."

Nels fidgeted with the handcuffs hanging from his belt, a familiar movement to me. I liked to tease him that he was unconsciously telegraphing his desire to lock up all the bad guys. He usually retorted that he'd be happy to try them out on me. We both knew he never would.

"Who do you think killed Chuck?" he asked me.

"I've been asking myself that question all day long." Had it really been just this morning that I'd stumbled across Chuck's dead body? "I would have pegged Chuck as a murderer with no qualms whatsoever, but I can't figure out who would have killed him."

"Okay, what's the deal with Seth? It seemed like you didn't trust him, and you didn't want to go back on his boat to pick up the rest of your party."

I heaved a sigh, and wiped sandwich crumbs off my chest. "There are a couple of things that don't add up about Seth. He said he saw us from the smoky fire we built, but he showed up only ten minutes after we built it. He said he hadn't noticed the *Northern Dream* at anchor, but we motored right past her on our way back to town. I can't think of any way he could have come where he wouldn't have seen her."

"Maybe he's just unobservant."

"I don't know, Nels. Something just seemed off about him. There was no reason to leave Liam and Flint behind. Plus, I felt like he knew all about Chuck, even though we were trying to keep quiet about that."

"Do you think he could be our murderer? He crept ashore in the middle of the night and whacked Chuck over the head while you all slept?"

"I don't know. All I know is that it wasn't me who killed him." I looked Nels in the eye, beseechingly. "As horrible as this sounds, I hope it was Seth. I hate to think that one of Liam's bridal party drugged my water bottle, fatally whacked Chuck over the head, and then planted his rifle in my shelter to incriminate me."

He gave me a look of compassion, in contrast to his next words. "Take it back a few steps, Junetta. This same person could have drugged Captain Evan as well and set the fire on the *Northern Dream* so you all would have to abandon ship. That couldn't have been Seth."

I dropped my head into my hands. "Plus, the ship-to-shore radio was broken, and I know Captain Evan keeps everything in top working order. He would have checked the radio before we set off, and he would never have undertaken the trip if he knew there was something wrong with it."

"So, one of your passengers planned for you all to have to abandon ship and wash up on Price Island, and they were willing to destroy the historic *Northern Dream* to accomplish that goal. That's pretty dang ruthless, if you ask me."

He'd coldly put into words the suspicions that had been swirling in my mind all day long. One of the four visitors from

Florida: my former fiancé, Liam; his bride-to-be, Lacey; Flint or Teena, best man and maid of honor respectively—one of them had heartlessly set fire to my beloved boat, drugged her Captain, and risked all of our lives to land us on a remote island and then proceed to kill the camper on shore.

Why?

Chapter Twelve

Nels didn't really expect a response. His attention shifted to our surroundings, as we approached the *Northern Dream* at anchor.

"Shall we board her and assess the damage?" Mark said, his hand on the tiller, ready to change course.

Nels shook his head regretfully, his eyes fixed on the boat. "We need to get to the island ASAP. The *Northern Dream* will still be here when we're done." He pointed to her hull. "Look, you can see marks of the fire around all the portholes aft. The glass has been blown out by the heat."

I looked. The black marks fanning out from the rims of the portholes traced the route of the flames that had exploded out of them. The smell of burnt wood wafted across the water from the damaged boat. The strong scent took me back in a rush to the doorway of the engine room with flames leaping in front of me as I tried desperately to beat them back with the fire extinguisher. I started to cough, as if I were still in the midst of the inferno. I turned away from the rail and sank down onto the seat, pulling my knees up to my chest.

Nels tucked the blanket around my shoulders. "You should have changed before coming out again."

I clutched the fluffy folds around me with shaky hands. "I couldn't put out the fire. The fire extinguisher barely made a dent in the flames." My lips trembled. "I didn't consider at the time that it might have been arson."

Nels sat down beside me and put an arm around my shoulders. "We'll have the boat towed back to town for the fire department to go over before we do anything else about it. If the fire was set deliberately, they'll figure it out."

I gave him a quivery smile. His method of comfort was always to try to fix things. "It sure is nice to have a trooper as a brother. I feel like I get preferential treatment."

He patted my hand. "Nah, we give stellar service to everyone who needs it. Nothing special about you."

I grinned at him, strengthened by the bond between us that we rarely acknowledged.

"Price Island coming up," Mark called out.

Nels and I both stood along the rail as the catamaran motored into the bay. I was hardly surprised to see the *Sea After Sea* moored in the bay, with a dinghy pulled up on the beach. "He beat us here," I said.

Nels frowned at the sight. He helped Mark set the anchor and launch the shore boat. Mark loaded in a tackle box that I assumed carried forensic equipment. At the last minute he slung in a flat black bundle. "I've got a body bag," he said to Nels. Both men had their service revolvers handy on their belts. Whether that made me feel more or less safe was an open question.

It was a matter of minutes before we landed on the beach and pulled the boat up above the tide mark. The remains of our fire smoldered slightly. The beach was quiet, with nobody in sight. This fact made me uneasy. Why weren't Liam and Flint waiting for us? Maybe another Good Samaritan vessel had already taken them off the island? I swallowed my reservations and led Nels and Mark along the path to our campsite.

Everything was exactly as I had left it, but no one was there. I caught Nels's arm. "Did another boat or plane come along and take Liam and Flint off the island? I don't know where else they would be. And what about Seth? He's got to be around here somewhere."

Nels cast his eyes around the campsite. He peeked into Chuck's tent, glanced at the blue tarps, and noted my wilderness shelter. "Good job in a pinch," he said to me as he turned away and headed back to the beach. "I'm going to check in with Stella, see if any news has come in. Radio reception will be better on the beach."

I sat down on a log by the fire pit, leaving him to confer with Stella Turner, the dispatcher back in town. A friendly woman in her mid-thirties who addressed everyone, even the troopers, as 'honey,' Stella had her finger on the pulse of Ptarmigan Port like no one else did. If someone had picked up Liam and Flint, she would know.

I heard a rustling in the bushes on the far side of the campsite. Mark was fully occupied taking pictures of everything in sight, but it wasn't him who made the noise. "Do you hear that, Mark?" I called. "There are bears in the vicinity. It could be them."

Mark straightened up from his position in the entrance to Chuck's tent. He unclipped a can of bear spray from his belt. He and I waited in silence to see who or what would emerge from the underbrush.

Just when I couldn't stand the suspense for one more second, a fat porcupine waddled out of the bushes, its quills trailing behind like a king's royal cloak. Mark and I stood as still as statues while the porcupine dawdled across the clearing and disappeared into the brush on the far side. We could hear it swishing through the bushes, making no effort at concealment. Why bother? No one would mess with a porcupine.

Mark eased the can of bear spray back into its holster. "My dog, Monty, took a noseful of porcupine quills last fall. I had to get the vet to put him under to get them all out. He's a little more careful about hassling the wildlife these days."

I exchanged a smile with him, but the lighthearted mood didn't persist. Nels came back into the clearing, his radio still in his hand. "Nobody's been in contact with Stella to say they've made a rescue. My best guess is the guys are still here. Come on, Junetta, show us the body."

I gulped. "I don't actually know where the body is right now. I can show you where I found him, but Liam and Flint went back and buried him or at least covered him up so no animals would get to him. It might not be easy to find."

Nels shrugged, picking up the body bag. "Show us where you found him, and we'll take it from there."

I led the two troopers through the underbrush to the smaller clearing where I had discovered Chuck's body. Like the campsite, this clearing was empty and deserted. I pointed to the spot on the ground where the body had lain.

Mark leaned down, camera at the ready. "I can make out a bit of blood here, Nels." He fired off a series of pictures.

Nels examined the ground, the broken branches on the underbrush, and the flattened grasses where the body had been. "There are a number of footprints, as you would imagine if two men came and moved the body." He turned to me. "Did you get the impression that they moved it far away?"

I thought back to earlier today. "They said they covered it up. I would have thought it would be right here where it happened."

"Okay. Junetta, you stay here—don't wander off. Mark, let's search the area."

I bristled at the thought that I would wander off like some bored child. But as I watched Nels and Mark casting about in ever widening circles radiating out from the spot where Chuck's body had lain, I did begin to feel bored and tired. There were no logs to sit on, and I didn't fancy sitting on the damp ground. I started to pace around the small clearing, taking care to stay out of the way of the troopers at work. That's the only reason I saw him.

Lurking on the edge of the clearing, obviously trying to keep out of sight, was a person wearing dark green waders. He might have thought they would serve as camouflage, but I could tell the difference between slick vinyl and living leaves. He kept on the edge of the troopers' ever-widening circle, so as to evade detection. I knew it was neither Liam nor Flint, because neither of them had been wearing waders. It had to be Seth. What was with that guy?

I realized that I didn't want to find out on my own. He had shown nothing but disdain for me in every interaction I had with him. I had no desire to provoke that scorn alone in a deserted clearing, even if the troopers were within earshot.

I adjusted my trajectory, pacing in the opposite direction from Seth. When I reached the underbrush, I dropped the leisurely pace and pushed through the devil's club and blueberry bushes as if that mama bear was after me. "Nels!" I called out. "Mark!" I cringed at the sound of fear in my voice, but I couldn't help it. I thought I heard footsteps coming up behind me.

I pushed past a rotting tree stump and careened into Nels. I grasped him with both hands, panting.

"Geez, Junetta, what part of 'don't wander off' do you not understand?"

I clung to his arms. "I'm not a little child, you know." Okay, maybe I was acting like one. I lowered my voice. "There's a man in waders lurking on the edge of the clearing, taking care to stay out of your search perimeter. Neither Liam nor Flint have waders. It has to be Seth." I took a deep breath. "I guess he kind of freaked me out."

Nels frowned. "That guy is starting to get on my nerves. I thought I was pretty clear that we could handle things from here. Now, he's hanging around while we look for a dead man." He bit off his next words and sloughed my hands off his arms. "It would be better if you stayed out of it, but I get it if you don't want to be left alone with all the weirdness that seems to be going on here. Stick close to me and be ready to duck if I pull out my gun."

I could tell that he meant that last part. It was equally clear to me that he wasn't going to share with me who or what he thought he might have to shoot at. I had to be content with being allowed to remain in his presence.

I followed one step behind Nels for the next twenty minutes, while he searched the ground, occasionally conferring with Mark when they crossed paths. I could sense his growing frustration. At one point he turned back to me, "What were those big city lawyers thinking, stashing a body so far away from the crime scene?"

Good question.

Suddenly, I picked up on a rustling in the bushes off to my left. I stopped to listen, then I grabbed Nels's arm to stop him too. Last thing I wanted was to be left behind in this tangle of underbrush with bears and weird guys floating around.

Nels started to say something, but I shushed him. "Hear that?"

We stood still, listening. "It's not Mark," Nels whispered. "Come on. Quietly." He trod stealthily in the direction of the rustling, with me hot on his heels. I didn't like the thought that we were likely stalking a mama bear with two cubs, or a murderer. Still, the existence of Nels's gun gave me some comfort.

Nels paused behind the shelter of a massive hemlock tree. He held out a hand behind his back to stop me. "Two guys, dark hair, one's got a goatee," he breathed.

"That's Liam and Flint," I whispered. "Are they doing anything suspicious?"

He didn't answer. Instead, he pushed through the tangled branches, calling out in a deep voice, "Alaska State Troopers. Halt."

I followed close behind, calling out on my own part, "Liam, Flint—it's Junetta with my brother. We've come back for you."

Liam answered in a weary voice, and the two men stood still until we came up to them.

"Where were you?" I said, failing to keep my exasperation out of my voice. "We said we'd come back. Why weren't you waiting on the beach?"

Liam held out his arms for a hug. "Junie."

Nels watched in silence as I walked over and embraced him. I turned to Flint but decided against giving him a hug.

"We figured it would take time for you to get back, so we did a bit of exploring," Flint said. "There's another beach with a sheltered harbor on the other side of the island."

My attention quickened. Maybe that was where Chuck had stashed the boat that had brought him to the island. "Were there any boats in the harbor?"

Liam shook his head. "Why would there be?"

I didn't feel like trying out this theory on him. Instead, I waved a hand to Nels. "This is my brother, Trooper Nels. His associate, Trooper Mark, is around somewhere. They're looking for Chuck's body that you took care of."

Nels held out a hand to Liam and then Flint. "Good to meet you. I'm sorry it's under these grim circumstances. Can you show me the body?" He phrased it as a request, but it resonated like a demand, to be disobeyed at one's peril.

Flint and Liam exchanged glances, and then Flint turned to lead us back the way we had come, back to the little clearing where I'd discovered Chuck's body. We followed without a word. Along the way we picked up Mark, who joined the procession without comment. Flint led us all the way back to the spot where Chuck's body had lain. He turned to the north, walked ten paces, and stooped over a fallen log covered with moss that looked like it had come down fifty years ago when Uncle Vance used to come to Price Island as a young boy to swing on the rope swing out over the water. Together, Flint and Liam heaved the log over, revealing the disturbing sight of Chuck's cold, dead face.

I turned away, not at all interested in watching the troopers go over the body. I knew that they wouldn't be able to come to many conclusions after the body had been moved in such a fashion. I closed my eyes and hummed to myself, trying to block out the sights and sounds of the troopers loading the body into the body bag. I was relaxing into serene thoughts of the tide washing gently onto the beach when Nels's loud voice shocked me back into the moment. My eyes flew open.

"Come out, Seth! I know you're there, watching us. Show yourself!"

My first thought was to marvel at my little brother's courage. He had no idea what Seth was up to or if he was armed, which seemed likely. I remembered the bulging pockets of his windbreaker. But Nels didn't care. He called him out with every expectation that Seth would comply with his directives. In fact, Nels was right.

Seth materialized from behind a convenient clump of devil's club. He strolled over to our little group and looked down at the body bag which now hid Chuck's remains. "Well, well, what have you got here?"

Nels folded his arms on his chest. "What are you doing here, is the question. You were headed back to set your crab pots, as I recall. I'm sure you didn't set them among the brambles, so why the lie? Just what exactly are you up to, Seth Corliss?"

Wow, Nels remembered his full name. If he knew Seth's middle name, I'm sure he would have trotted that out as well, the way Mom used to call the both of us out when we were in trouble.

Seth wasn't fazed by Nels's tone. "As soon as I saw the castaways on the beach, I knew something funny was going on here. So, I came back to see what it was. A dead body concealed under a rotten log sure smells funny to me."

"What is it to you? Was he a friend of yours? Or maybe you killed him?"

Seth drove his hands into his pockets.

"He might have a gun," I shouted, getting ready to duck.

Nels calmly pulled out his revolver. "He might. I do." He gestured toward Seth. "Hands where I can see them."

Seth pulled his hands out of his pockets and held them warily by his hips. "In fact, I do carry a gun. I have a concealed carry permit. I'm not interested in a gunfight with you."

"Perfect," Nels said. He holstered his weapon. "What are you interested in, Seth?"

My gaze flicked from Nels's stern face to that of Seth. I wasn't quite sure why Nels put his gun away, or why he assumed that Seth wouldn't try to attack us. Nels seemed to think that he was coming out on top in this power struggle. I wasn't so sure.

Seth gestured at the body bag. "Who is the deceased? Why was his body concealed? How did he come to die?"

Suddenly, Nels broke eye contact with Seth. He turned to Mark and said, "Let's get the body back to the cat." As Mark grasped the body bag's handles, Nels turned back to Seth. "Follow us back to the station, and we can talk there. We just need to gather up Junetta's things from the campsite and we'll be on our way." He grabbed his side of the body bag with one hand and took my elbow with the other as if I were an old lady who needed to be helped across the street. "Let's go break camp."

I suffered him to lead me by the arm until I felt sure that Seth was innocently following behind us. Then, I pulled my arm out of his grasp.

He gave me a quick, amused glance with no comment.

When we arrived at the campsite, I asked, "Did Mark get all the photos he needs?"

Nels nodded. "Let's get everything loaded up as quickly as possible." He pulled out a utility knife and cut down the tarps, instructing Liam and Flint to fold them neatly and pile them on the ground with my tote bag on top. I gathered up the blanket and folded it as well. Nels and Mark collected Chuck's tent, sleeping bag, and all his belongings.

"Where's Chuck's rifle?" I said to Liam in a soft voice. "Last I saw it, it was zipped up in his tent."

Liam gave me a surprised look. "You're right, it wasn't there when Seth peeked in. I don't know where it got to." He grabbed Flint's arm on the way by. "Flint, do you know what happened to Chuck's rifle?"

"I threw it in the tent, to keep it away from everyone." Flint frowned, looking at the spot where the tent had stood. "Now it's gone. I don't know where it went."

Both Nels and Seth were following this conversation, despite my efforts to keep it quiet.

"Missing rifle, huh? Could that be the murder weapon?" Seth glared at each of us in turn, as if we were all responsible both for the death and for the missing rifle.

"All right, load up the gear in Junetta's dinghy and the body bag in our shore boat," Nels said. "Seth, you're on your own getting off the island. Come check in at the station when you get back to town. Feel free to take care of your crab pots on the way, though. We might be awhile." He pointed to Liam, Flint, and I. "Fan out and look for that rifle. We're not leaving without it."

I stifled a groan and started looking around. If Flint or Liam had hidden it, maybe they would pull it back out again, pretending to find it, just to get us out of here. That was my hope, anyway. The men started shuffling through the bushes, searching the ground. If that's where the rifle was, we would be here forever. I paused a moment, to think. Where would someone hide the murder weapon?

The first place I looked was in my wilderness shelter, where the rifle had turned up once before. There wasn't anything in the shelter, but the structure looked different than before. I opened up my phone and checked the proud picture I'd taken. The sheaf of ferns that had stretched across the branches forming the roof were now missing. I scanned the area to see where they had ended up. There was a pile of brush not ten paces from the shelter, topped with an armful of dying ferns. I swept the fronds to one side and sifted through the hemlock branches until I saw a gleam of metal. Then, I called Nels over.

He carefully swept the remaining branches aside, revealing Chuck's rifle. He pulled out a handkerchief to grasp the rifle by the barrel, taking note of the bloodstains on the butt. He wrapped the handkerchief around the butt and cradled the weapon in his arms. "Ready to get out of here?"

"Yes, please." I glanced over my shoulder, to see that Seth had lingered on the edge of our search. He pulled out his phone and snapped a photo of the rifle in Nels's arms. What was the deal with that guy?

It took another forty-five minutes to get everything transported to the catamaran. We were able to tie my dinghy to the stern, even though the extra drag would cause us to keep our speed down on the return trip. I wanted to drop it off at the *Northern Dream*, but Nels brushed aside this suggestion. "I want to take a quick look at the harbor on the other side of the island, if you all can stand a short detour before getting back to town." He spoke softly to Mark, "Take note of how long it takes to get from here to there."

It was a small island, so it only took us fifteen minutes to get there. We motored into the bay and Mark cut the engine. I had never been to this side of the island. It looked pretty much identical to the other side, only lacking the rope swing. There was no boat in the bay. If Chuck came to the island by boat, it wasn't in his own boat. Maybe he came with Seth?

Nels turned to Flint. "What did the two of you see when you hiked over here?"

He shrugged. "Nothing. Although, it did look like people have come this way recently. There was a faint path that led across the island from one side to the other. But there was no one other than us."

Nels nodded. He glanced over at Liam, who held his arms wrapped around his chest, shivering. "We'll leave it for now."

The wind picked up as we motored back to town. The catamaran was fast and handy in the water, but she was stuffed with gear and a body bag, leaving very little in the way of shelter. I stood at the rail wrapped in Uncle Vance's fleece blanket, focusing on the hot shower that I hoped awaited me on our return.

Liam came to stand next to me, still shivering. Was he genuinely cold, or was he hoping for a cozy cuddle before getting back to his fiancée? I pulled the blanket close around me and then paused to reflect. If that's who he was, that was his problem. I wasn't going to let him change who I was, which I hoped was a generous and helpful person to a friend in need. I lifted the blanket to allow him to slide in under its warmth.

He snuggled up to me, his arm snaking around my waist to pull my body close to his. He was legitimately shaking, so I let him share the warmth of my body. But when he snuggled a little too close, I slipped out from under the blanket and tucked it carefully around him. "Lacey is waiting for you at the Last Chance Café, relaxing with a hot cup of Marcy's best coffee. I'll ask Nels to radio ahead so they'll know when we're going to arrive."

He watched me walk away with such a mournful, puppy dog look on his face that I almost burst out laughing. Oh, Marcy, you were so right! This trip was a bad, bad idea.

When I made my request to Nels, he threw a glance over his shoulder at Liam. "This guy is your ex, now engaged to one of those other two women? Seems like he's a little addled from being marooned on an island with a dead guy."

I shook my head. "Yeah. Hopefully when he gets back to Lacey, he'll realize that she's the only one for him. Unless one or the other of them is a killer, of course."

Nels glanced sideways at Liam again. "I can run him off if you want."

I punched his arm. "Now, that sounds like preferential treatment, if you ask me."

He laughed, and reached for the radio to let Marcy know to put the kettle on.

Chapter Thirteen

It was such a relief to walk into the Last Chance Café without having to head back out immediately. The sweet warmth enveloped me like a blanket. Marcy sat me down with a steaming cup of herbal tea before I could even say a word to her. She returned with a deep bowl of savory chicken soup which she placed in front of me. "You're staying to eat this time, right?"

I staggered up from the chair and folded her into a big bear hug. "Marcy, you're the best."

She smiled and patted me on the back. She waved Liam and Flint to some chairs, and ladled soup all around.

I tackled my soup like a hungry bear just emerging from hibernation. The bowl was empty and I was holding it out for seconds before I even noticed that Lacey and Teena were not in the café. "Where have the others gone?" I asked Marcy, as she ladled more steaming broth into my bowl.

"Lacey and Teena went back to their rooms at Clarissa's Bed and Breakfast to wash up and rest. They said to meet up at the Grizzly Bar around 9:00." Marcy glanced over at Liam and Flint, who were diving into their bowls with the same ravenous attention as I was. "I should let those guys know as well."

"Are you coming too? We could challenge them all to pool."

She shook her head. "Grandma has been watching Lisa all afternoon, so she needs some time off. With Rob up on the slope, Grandma's babysitting is a lifesaver."

Marcy's husband, Rob, worked two weeks on, two weeks off in the North Slope oil fields. The two of them were used to the biweekly rhythm, but the new baby changed everything. I knew

Marcy hoped that Rob could find a job in town so he could be with his family on a daily basis.

"Plus, I need some baby time, after all this drama," Marcy went on. "But when things settle down, we can take on your friends and show them who owns the pool tables of Ptarmigan Port."

I grinned at her. "Mostly you, if truth be told."

She inclined her head like royalty accepting her due and turned to speak to Flint and Liam.

• • •

My car was still in the alley behind the Shipshape Bookshop, where I had parked it yesterday morning. The bookshop was closed for the evening, so nothing was stopping me from heading straight home. Still, I unlocked the door and stepped into the dark space. I could tell by the diminished pile of mysteries on the front counter that Uncle Vance had hosted the book signing in my absence. I should never have spent a single moment worrying about it. Feeling reassured, I inhaled the clean scent of shelves full of books. Even in the semi-darkness, I could see the myriad of colors shining from the book covers. I felt like I was surrounded by old friends who would never let me down. I caressed a couple of solid hardbacks, straightened a display of new mysteries, and peeked in on my glass case of first editions before slipping back out the door and locking it behind me.

It was a five-minute drive from the downtown strip to my house on the hillside. The road zigzagged up the hill, with my house standing on the topmost zig. It had started out as a log cabin with a loft for sleeping, until it was renovated in the last century, resulting in an addition that boasted two roomy bedrooms and an up-to-date bathroom. It was a sanctuary in the midst of the tumult of life.

I felt much better after a luxuriating shower and a bit of a nap. When my alarm woke me at 8:45, I would have been happy to roll over and sleep straight through until morning. But the group was gathering at the Grizzly Bar, and I didn't want to miss out.

I decided to walk down the hill this time, so I could have a drink or two and not have to worry about driving back home. The trail through the woods was lovely as always. The dense overstory of hemlock and Sitka spruce covered the trail completely, creating a twilight feel to the wooded space. A red squirrel chattered from its perch on a branch laden with pinecones. One after another, the squirrel dropped cones onto the ground after munching the seeds inside. The resulting tattoo vied with the tapping of a woodpecker circling the trunk of a gnarled tree. Everybody was looking for something to eat. I was headed for something to drink, myself.

The party was in full swing at the Grizzly Bar, like always. I shouldered past the glass case displaying a nine-foot-tall brown bear with claws outstretched to sober up the boisterous clientele. I touched the glass with my fingertips in gratitude for keeping one step ahead of a menacing bear. The walls of the bar were papered with expired hunting and fishing licenses, some dating back to the early days of statehood. The magnificent moose head mounted over the bar was draped with fishing nets today, complete with a brightly colored quilted salmon tucked into a fold of the net. This whimsical fish in the midst of the rugged Alaska décor made me chuckle.

"Junetta, it's great to see you here, babe." Kirk Dunbar greeted me in his usual expansive manner, following up his words with a foaming beer. He leaned on the bar and beamed at me. "They said you were lost at sea, but I was sure that wasn't the end of your story."

I took a swallow of the cool beer. "Thanks for your faith in me, Kirk. It was touch and go there for a while." I heaved a sigh. "You heard the *Northern Dream* caught on fire? We had to jump ship and leave her behind."

He reached out and patted my hand. "You brought them all safe to shore. Can't say fairer than that."

His wholehearted compassion nearly overwhelmed me. If he had dropped to one knee and pulled out the ring box that I suspected he carried around in his pocket, I might have even said yes.

Happily, Kirk refrained from playing on my fragile state. Marcy liked to tease me about the torch he was carrying for me ever since we'd broken up after graduating from high school. She called him a sweetheart and predicted that I would make him a happy man one day. Her teasing had cooled once Angus came onto the scene to tickle my fancy, but she continued to maintain that Kirk was a sweetheart. In fact, that's exactly what he was today.

Before going too far down this perilous road, I scanned the rowdy space for Liam and his party. I found them just settling down at a large round table in the far corner. Liam approached the bar.

"Junie, you made it!" He gave me a side hug and waved for Kirk. "Can we get four local beers over in the corner, please?"

I laid a hand on his arm to arrest his movement. "Liam, this is Kirk Dunbar, owner of the Grizzly Bar. Kirk, this is Liam Blackwood, who I knew in Florida."

Liam grinned. "We knew each other in Florida," he said, managing to put all kinds of suggestive overtones into the simple phrase. He shook hands with Kirk, who flicked his gaze from my reddening face to Liam's and back again.

"It's nice to meet you, safe and sound after your adventures," Kirk said.

Liam rolled his eyes and took my hand. "Come sit with us, Junie."

Kirk leaned across the bar. "If you need a peanut butter sandwich, babe, just let me know."

I was touched. Kirk had set me up with a safe word, "peanut butter," in case I felt like I needed to be rescued from harassing men. I had yet to request a peanut butter sandwich, but it was great to have the option. I gave him a big smile. "I don't think I'll need one tonight, thanks. But we could sure do with your finest assortment of bar snacks. Marcy fed us all soup a few hours ago, but I feel like I could eat an entire smoked salmon without sharing one bite with anyone else."

Kirk laughed. "I can't give you a whole one, but I'll fetch you some crackers and salmon dip, and one or two other things."

Liam pulled on my hand, his eyes on Kirk. "Come on, Junie."

I followed him to the round table in the corner.

Everyone looked much better after a wash and a rest. Lacey's wispy curls cascaded onto her shoulders, smooth and shiny. Her pallor had receded—she looked like she was firmly back in the land of the living. Teena's eyes sparkled as she sipped her beer and took in the rugged Alaska atmosphere. Flint leaned back with one arm thrown across the back of his chair, at ease.

Liam sat down next to Lacey, patting an empty chair on his other side for me. I sat down.

"The bartender's going to bring over our beers," he said to Lacey. "Junetta's arranged for some food as well." He turned to me, waving at the moose head on the wall. "So, have you seen a moose like this out in the wild?"

I smiled. "Not one with a quilted salmon in its rack. But I did see a cow with her calf one time, along Color Creek. They don't usually come into town—too far south for them. The calf wanted to come and say hello—I had to climb a tree to put a halt to that conversation."

At Lacey's questioning look, I launched into a discussion of how dangerous mama moose can be, with their huge, stomping feet and their natural desire to protect their young.

Kirk walked up to our table; a large tray balanced on one hand. "We had a moose munching in our garden when I was a kid. If you think a mama moose is bad, you should see a mama Dunbar. My mom raided my dad's secret stash of fireworks and lit up the night. Mama moose never showed her face again." He handed out the beers amid the general laughter and placed a plate of crackers and salmon spread on the table, followed by savory pretzel bites, spicy chicken wings, and little twists of fried dough sprinkled with cinnamon that looked like they belonged in the Last Chance Café rather than the Grizzly Bar.

"Kirk, meet Liam's bridal party. Lacey is the bride, Flint is the best man, and Teena is the maid of honor," I said.

He rested the tray under his arm and beamed down on us. "Yeah, I remember Flint from school. You were a couple years ahead of us, right? I remember you were the leader of that epic prank, where we shoveled snow in front of all the doors of the school on the eve of the standardized tests." He laughed at the memory. "As far as the state was concerned, Ptarmigan Port had a class full of failing students. But Ms. Hampton congratulated us on our ingenuity and gave us all extra credit in Physics."

Flint chuckled. "Yeah, I remember that prank. It was a good one."

Lacey laughed and poked him. "Flint Sands, the model lawyer, instigating mayhem in high school? I would have loved to see that."

Kirk went on serenely, "I remember Teena too. You were here a few years later, maybe ten years ago? You were going out with that guy, Chuck What's-his-name. He was big into geology, as I recall. Whatever happened to him?"

He got no answer. Four of us were stunned speechless, while Teena sat still as a stone, clutching the silver Celtic knot around her neck. Lacey found her voice first. "You were here ten years ago? You went out with Chuck? Why didn't you say?"

Teena ignored her. She addressed Kirk, "I lost touch with him over the years."

He smiled at her. "It happens. But everyone we meet becomes a part of our story, right?"

"Yes," she whispered. She got up from the table. "I'm pretty tired. I think I'm going to call it a night."

Lacey grabbed her arm and pulled her back down. "Hang on a minute. Tell us about your relationship with Chuck."

Kirk melted away from our table, perhaps sensing that he had set something in motion that he hadn't intended.

Teena tossed her head. "I went out with a guy named Chuck ten years ago."

"Here, in Ptarmigan Port?" Lacey said. "Why didn't you say you'd been here before?"

"You knew I'd been to Alaska, along with all the other states on my country-wide odyssey. What does it matter if it was Ptarmigan Port that I came to?"

Lacey gripped her hands together. "It matters if you were dating that horrible Chuck. Was it the same guy? Tell us about your relationship with him."

Teena stood up. "That was ten years ago. Why don't you tell us about your relationship with Flint? That's going on even as we speak." She stalked out of the bar.

"What?" Liam cried. "What's your relationship with Flint?" He looked from Lacey to Flint. "What is she talking about?"

Lacey looked back at him, wide-eyed. "I have no idea what she's talking about. Flint is a friend. Teena's trying to blow our friendship out of proportion to deflect attention from her and Chuck, of all people." She took Liam's hand. "You're my fiancé, Liam."

Flint stared at the table, shaking his head slowly. "Can we go back to the story of the snow in front of the school doors?"

Liam rounded on him. "What are your intentions toward my fiancée, Flint?" He sounded like an offended noble about to issue a challenge to a duel.

"Lacey is my friend. She was my friend before she ever met you, if you recall." Flint's brows lowered. "Maybe we should ask you what are your intentions toward Junetta? You've done nothing but canoodle up to her ever since we set foot in this town."

I jumped up. "Leave me out of this! I broke it off with Liam a year ago and I haven't looked back once. I'm happy for him and Lacey, really, I am."

Kirk materialized at our table. "Peanut butter sandwiches, anyone?"

I burst out laughing, a touch of hysteria evident in my voice. The rest of the table gaped at me like I was off my rocker.

"I feel like I stirred up some smoldering embers," Kirk said. "Sorry about that. Do you need a tissue, babe?"

I nodded and accepted the cocktail napkin he handed me. "Sorry to make a scene in your bar, Kirk."

He threw up his hands with a grin. "What's the use of having a bar if you don't get a good scene at least once a night? It's all good, babe."

"Stop calling her 'babe.'" Liam was on his feet. "It's 'Junetta' to you, dude. Who do you think you are?"

Kirk didn't rise to the bait. He just winked at me, mouthed 'peanut butter,' and sauntered back to the bar. I could be sure he had my back. Yep, he was a sweetheart.

I turned back to the group. Liam had sat back down, his face red. Beside him, Lacey shredded a cocktail napkin between her fingers. Flint scowled at the tabletop. I sat down without a word.

"So, you and Kirk, huh?" Liam's words came out reluctantly, as if he was afraid to pronounce them for fear they might come true.

I glanced over my shoulder, to see that Kirk continued to watch our table closely. I leaned in and said to Liam, "Kirk and I dated in high school, like I mentioned when I first met Flint yesterday morning. I broke it off when I left for college. Today, he's a dear friend, and that's all."

"Is he married?" Liam persisted.

"No." I refrained from detailing Kirk's dream wedding, which featured me in the starring role. I planned to stick with 'dear friend,' or 'sweetheart.'

"Well, it looks to me like he's putting some serious moves on you, Junie."

Lacey laid a soft hand on Liam's arm. "Darling, you've got nothing to worry about. Junetta has a different guy she's seeing; a guy named Angus. Isn't that right, Junetta?"

"That's right. He lives in New York City. We've known each other for about a month." I reached for my phone to show them a picture.

"Angus?" Liam drawled out the name with a chuckle. "Sounds like a beefsteak."

I sucked in my breath. Liam had been hurt when I handed him back his ring and scampered back to Alaska. He'd stopped short of following me, but his frequent texts and phone calls over the next few months had continued to remind me that he was unhappy with my choice. Supposedly, he had moved on, although he sure wasn't acting like it right now.

I glared at him, tight-lipped. "Seriously, Liam, my relationships are none of your business. Neither is Teena's relationship with Chuck, if it comes to that." Okay, so I was deflecting attention. I could play with the best of them.

"Not true," Flint said. "If Teena had a history with Chuck, that could give her a motive for killing him. We need to figure out who the killer is, right? I'd say she just stepped into the number one spot—and the fact that she walked away and isn't willing to talk about it makes her even more suspect." He turned to Lacey. "What do you know about Teena's past relationships?"

She twisted her hands together. "I've known her for five years. She'd already completed her country-wide trek by that time. When we met, she was dating a musician who played acoustic guitar in bars on the beach on the weekends and lounged around the house playing video games the rest of the time. She dumped him after a few months and moved on to a respectable doctor who made a lot of money. Everyone thought she had hit the jackpot, but he was secretly manipulating her all the time, trying to isolate her from all her friends. It was really hard for her to get away from him. Lately, she's been hanging out with another teacher at her school. They're not supposed to date their colleagues, so they have to meet on the sly. She asked me if he could come along on this trip, but I wanted it to be a bonding experience just for my wedding party." Her eyes filled with tears. "Some bonding experience this has been!"

We sat in silence for a minute, reflecting on this fiasco of a bridal trip. Unless they're lucky enough to live in Alaska, most people who come here are on a once-in-a-lifetime dream trip. There are no second chances or 'next times.' Weddings fall into the same category, with brides and grooms hoping that they will only need to have one. The pressure to create the perfect experience for a lifelong memory is practically overwhelming. No matter how this murder investigation turned out, Lacey's lifelong memories of her wedding trip would be forever tainted.

I shook off the gloomy thoughts. We should be celebrating the fact that we were alive! I took a deep breath and conjured up a smile for the group. "We have a tradition here in Ptarmigan

Port. I'm sorry Teena's not here to share in it, because she was a big part in our journey." I stood up and lifted my beer, calling out to the whole crowd, "A toast, to the travelers' safe return." The assorted bar patrons all joined in with gusto. Kirk saluted me across the bar and downed a drink of his own. Liam and his party all lifted their drinks, first in silence and then with a lightening of the mood.

My phone dinged. It was Nels, telling me that Captain Evan was being medevaced to Seattle for more advanced medical treatment than Ptarmigan Port could provide. Not all of the travelers returned safely, at least not yet.

Liam poked me. "What was that?"

I slipped my phone into my pocket. "Nels let me know that Captain Evan is being sent to Seattle for medical treatment." I looked around the table. Had one of these three caused the captain's incapacitation, or was it Teena, the very one who had nursed him so diligently throughout the entire time we were marooned?

"I'm sorry to hear that," Liam said, reaching for my hand. I slid it away before he could make contact.

"They'll take good care of him in Seattle." I forced a smile. "What are your plans for tomorrow?"

Lacey looked up from her beer. "My preference? I want to jump on a plane back to Florida first thing." She shot me a defiant glare, as if I was poised to stand in her way.

I was, in fact. "I'm sure Nels is going to want you all to stay in town until he can sort out what happened to Chuck. Might as well plan to enjoy the sights that Ptarmigan Port has to offer."

Liam and Lacey both exclaimed in dismay. "He can't force us to stay here, can he?" Lacey said. "You're the lawyer, darling. Tell him he can't hold us here without charging us with a crime."

He squeezed her hand. "I'll talk to him in the morning, dear. If you want to leave, we'll leave."

I tried to hide a smile. Nels was fully prepared to run Liam off if I said the word. I was sure he could hold his own in a battle of legal wits.

I stood up. "Well, if you find yourselves still in town and looking for amusements, stop by the Shipshape Bookshop for Junetta's special tourist tips."

"You're leaving?" Liam stood up as well. "Shall I walk you home?"

"No, I'm good."

Ignoring my words, Liam grabbed his jacket and took my arm.

"No, really, Liam, please don't feel like you need to come with me." I shook off his hand. "I'm just going down the sidewalk to pop into the public safety building and chat with Nels. You would probably prefer to wait until tomorrow when you're fully sober to talk to him about your next steps." I shrugged into my jacket and held up a hand toward Liam, palm facing outward in the universal sign for 'Stop.' "See you all tomorrow." I bolted across the room, but then stopped at the bar to say goodbye to Kirk.

"Thanks for everything. The food was just the thing." I handed him a wad of twenties and held both hands behind my back when he tried to hand them back to me. An occasional beer on the house was fine with me, but Kirk shouldn't have to foot the bill for a large group of people who weren't even his friends. I glanced over my shoulder to see Liam's eyes on me. I leaned in close, pushing the bills onto the floor behind the bar, and said to Kirk, "If Liam gets up to leave, please stop him from following me. Bring him a peanut butter sandwich or something."

Kirk grinned and pulled a plate out from under the counter. On it sat the loveliest peanut butter sandwich anyone could desire. "I got your back, babe."

I laughed and waved a cheery goodbye on my way out the door.

Chapter Fourteen

I wasn't really headed to the public safety building, which was bound to be closed at this time of night. But I did want to talk to Nels. I texted him, 'Can we talk?'

He got right back to me, 'Just finishing work. Stop by.'

So much for the building being closed.

The public safety building, which housed Nels's Alaska State Troopers as well as the local police, fire department, and animal control, was down the sidewalk at the edge of town. Its dingy corrugated metal roof and gray walls created a dreary atmosphere. It wasn't hard to conjure up pictures of criminals lurking in the shadows, hoping to evade the long arm of the law. I shook off the macabre image and pulled on the door. It was locked, but Nels answered when I rang the bell.

He grabbed his jacket and closed the door behind him. He led me to the dock. "What's up?" he said.

We walked side by side on the wooden boards of the dock in the waning daylight. "I just wanted to check in with you, see what you found out about Chuck."

He gave me an enigmatic glance. "You know I can't share information about a case with a civilian."

"Okay, call me a witness, or you can deputize me and put me on the case."

He shook his head. "You are a witness. I took notes on everything you told me on our ride back to Price Island. I may need to question you further, so plan on staying in town."

I rolled my eyes. "I might be able to help you out with some more information, but not if you're going to shut me out like that."

I paused to watch a fishing boat steaming into the harbor. The setting sun sent a shaft of light across her bow like a benediction.

Nels folded his arms across his chest and frowned at me. Before he could say anything, I went on, "Pretend I'm a newspaper reporter. Just tell me what you would tell the press. That can't hurt."

Suddenly, he laughed, dropping the stern pose. "We're playing pretend, now, are we? How about you pretend that I know what I'm doing and can be trusted to get to the bottom of this case?"

Without wasting time commenting on his willingness to play along, I said, "I just want to know what you found out about Chuck. What's his last name? Off the record?"

He sighed. "Off the record, we didn't find any identification on the body."

I gasped out loud and rooted through my coat pockets. "I found these on him when I discovered his body. I forgot." I handed him Chuck's billfold and pocketknife, and the piece of paper with a phone number on it.

He stared from my face to the items and back again. I had a hard time keeping eye contact. "Jeez, Junetta, you're not a trooper! What did you do, go through his pockets looking for loose change?"

"Sorry. It just seemed to happen before I thought about it. I was trying to keep things safe from a murderer. I had every intention of turning them over to you, but I forgot. I'm sorry."

If ever I wanted to disarm Nels's anger, an apology was my best weapon. As always, he looked so surprised that I would say I was sorry that he dropped his scolding. He flipped open the billfold and extracted a driver's license. "Charles Melvin Woodhouse. Thirty-six years old, with a Washington state address." He flipped through a pile of bills. "Looks like several hundred dollars in cash and multiple credit cards. How did he come to be camping alone on Price Island in Southeast Alaska?"

"Here's the thing, Nels. He's been here before."

Nels sat down on a bench on the dock and motioned for me to sit beside him. I looked out at the sunset sparkling on the moving water and breathed in the scent of the sea.

"We all met up at the Grizzly Bar this evening. I introduced Kirk to the group, and he said he remembered Flint from when he went to high school here, and he also remembered Teena from ten years ago when she was dating Chuck What's-his-name. Teena looked shell-shocked. She said she'd lost touch with Chuck and refused to tell the group about her relationship with him or even if he was the same guy. I'll bet he was, though. She stroked his cheek after he was dead, just like you would if you cared about the dead person. I found it very strange at the time."

"Okay, this is useful information. I'll need to talk to Teena."

"She took off after this confrontation, saying she was tired. She's probably asleep by now."

"All right, I'll talk to her in the morning. Do me a favor, Junetta. If any of this group tries to leave town, let me know. I want them here until I figure this out. Don't take it upon yourself to stop them, but let me know. Okay?"

I inclined my head. "I'm miles ahead of you. I already told them that you'd want them all to stick around. Lacey wants to fly back to Florida first thing, and Liam is going to show up tomorrow and try his lawyer schtick on you to allow them to leave."

He stood up and stuck out his hand in mock respect. "Good job."

I jumped up and shook hands solemnly. "There's another thing. What did you find out about Seth Corliss?"

He resumed our stroll along the dock. "Do you have any secret information about him, too?"

"No, nothing. I just don't trust him, and I can't even tell you why I feel that way."

He gave me that sidelong glance again. "Maybe because he's a bit of a mystery. I checked the registration of his boat, the *Sea After Sea*. His name's not on it. The boat is registered to a Norman Oliver out of California. We're tracking that down now." He stopped and looked me in the eye. "Don't take it upon yourself to sweet talk Seth into revealing his backstory and motivations to you."

I flung out my hands with as innocent a face as I could conjure up. "Whatever do you mean, Officer?" I dropped the facetious tone. "It wouldn't work anyway. Seth has nothing but contempt for me. He won't even speak to me unless there's nobody else he can talk to." I looked out at a disturbance in the water. A harbor seal popped his head up and then dipped below the surface again, leaving behind a widening circle of ripples. "How did your conversation with him go when he stopped by the station?"

"Yeah, he never stopped by. I've got him on my list to follow up with tomorrow."

"Did you see him taking a picture of Chuck's rifle when you pulled it out of the underbrush?"

He shook his head, a frown on his face. "I'll check on that detail when I talk to him tomorrow." He turned to me. "Go get some sleep, Junetta. I'll keep you posted with whatever news I would routinely give to the press, okay? I'm not expecting any breakthroughs at this hour."

"Okay." I turned to go, but Nels caught my arm and suddenly pulled me into a hug. It lasted no more than two seconds, then he let me go. "Stay safe, Junetta. It sucks having to worry about you." He cleared his throat and accompanied me back along the dock. "Did you call Mom?"

"I haven't had a chance. My phone was dead when we got back, and then I crashed. I'll call her tomorrow."

We were approaching the Grizzly Bar on my way to the path up the hillside to my house. Through the swinging door I saw Liam's party getting ready to head out. The last thing I wanted was to encounter them again this evening, with the looming specter of Liam insisting on walking me home through the woods.

"Bye, Nels, gotta go!" I ducked into a darkened doorway as Liam opened the door to the bar to usher Lacey out. Nels stood stock still on the sidewalk, looking at me as if I'd gotten a touch of snow blindness in the middle of summer. I pointed at the bridal party and crouched down so as not to be seen.

I saw the light dawn on his face, and then he turned to walk back to his car at the public safety building. I wondered if Flint or Liam would call out to him, but neither of them did. Just as well—Nels was not that skilled at pretending.

I slid out of my hiding spot once the bridal party had gone and headed for the trail leading up to my neighborhood.

I could have asked Nels to spin me home, but I really wanted to walk. Something about the peaceful wooded trail winding up the hill calmed my soul. Old man's beard dripped from the spruce and hemlock trees, shining pale and mysterious in the dusk. Similar to the Spanish moss that hung on live oak branches in Florida, this lichen dangled like Christmas tinsel on the evergreen trees. I breathed in the fresh air laden with scents of good, clean dirt and sweet blueberries ripe for the picking on the bushes. I caught the sharp scent of high bush cranberries that tasted sour straight off the bush, but wonderfully tangy when boiled down with the right amount of sugar.

I knew I should make noise while walking through this wonderful smorgasbord for bears. I preferred to walk quietly, however, listening to the subtle sounds of the approaching night. I kept a sharp eye out as I rounded the bends in the trail. When I saw a dark shape near the base of an old-growth spruce tree, I froze, thinking I had stumbled upon a black bear. A second glance showed me that it wasn't a bear, but a person, crouching down among the tree roots. I took a few tentative steps forward, until I was sure.

It was Teena.

She hadn't noticed me coming up on her. I stood quiet for a moment, watching. She fiddled with something on the ground among the roots, and then she stood up and reached for a bit of old man's beard hanging down from a low branch. She squatted back down and resumed whatever it was she was doing.

"Hey, Teena," I called.

She yelped and jumped up, spinning around as if she was going to run headlong down the trail to get away from me. The stark fear on her face shocked me.

I took a step closer. "That was a big mess back at the Grizzly Bar, huh?"

"Are you following me?" She peered past me as if I was the leader of a posse out to apprehend her.

"No, not at all. This is the path to my house." I took another step closer and looked down at the tree roots. She had arranged bits of leaves, sticks, and moss in the hollow of the roots. "What are you doing?"

She sighed and crouched back down. "I'm making a fairy house." She looked up with a sheepish smile. "We've been making them at school with the kids. I find it relaxing and a great way to interact with nature." She pointed at her creation. "This leaf is the roof, the moss makes a soft place to sleep, and this corral of sticks shows the way to the stream."

"Marcy and I loved to build fairy houses when we were young. I haven't made one in a long time." I knelt down next to her and picked up a bit of bark. "Our only rule was, we couldn't take anything that was still living. We had to scavenge for broken-off twigs." I beamed at her. "I still remember the one time when I really wanted some ferns for a canopy, but there was nothing lying on the ground. I 'accidentally' tripped over a magnificent fern, breaking off a number of shoots. Marcy wasn't fooled for one second."

Teena smiled, brushing away a bit of dirt to make a tiny walkway.

I positioned a trio of twigs. "You must have been surprised to see Chuck on the island, after all these years."

She sighed. "I didn't even recognize him at first. He'd changed a lot." She concentrated on the pile of sticks she was building. "Something was weird about him. That whole 'I'm the boss' vibe? That wasn't really him. He was putting that on, for some reason."

I sat back on my heels and gazed at her. "You just said he'd changed. Maybe what we saw was the new Chuck."

She looked me in the eye. "No. I talked to him in the night, after everyone had gone to sleep. That conversation was completely different, like old times. It was like he had a split personality or something."

I opened my mouth to respond, but she held out a hand to stop me. "You want to know the whole story? We met in Ptarmigan Port when I was traveling through Alaska ten years ago. I was young and single, looking for every experience I could have during that magical year of wandering. I was having a drink in a bar, chatting with some fishermen who wanted to take me out the next day to pull their crab pots. Chuck walked in and called for drinks all around. He sat down next to me and offered me a red licorice stick from a bunch he clutched in his hand. That was the tastiest licorice I've ever had." She glanced sideways at me. "You probably don't believe me, but he bowled me over. There was this sense of elation about him that was intoxicating. I never did find out what he was so pleased about." She sighed again and fussed with the leaves she was arranging.

"I hung out with him for a couple weeks. We spent four nights in Ptarmigan Port before visiting other Southeast Alaska towns on the ferry system. Your buddy, Kirk, has a phenomenal memory."

"Wow." I dusted my hands together. "Why did you leave him?"

She gave me a quirky glance. "Why did you leave Liam? He clearly wishes he was still with you."

"I'll tell if you will."

"Okay. I was ready to move on. My time was running out and I hadn't been to Hawaii yet. Chuck said he couldn't afford a jaunt to Hawaii. So, I took off. It was never supposed to be a lasting thing—more of a fling in the best sense of the word. Truly, I rarely thought about Chuck after I left, but whenever I did, it was with fondness. I was shocked to see how different he was." She stood up. "Your turn."

I stood up too. "Liam was incredibly romantic, and I fell in love. Problem is, he's a hockey fanatic. When he proposed, he gave me a ring in the shape of the Stanley Cup. I knew I would always come in second to the hockey puck, so I called it off. You laugh, but I wasn't ready to be a hockey widow."

Teena gasped with laughter. "You've described him to a tee! He must have learned his lesson from you because he gave Lacey a regular diamond, but he'll never give up hockey for her."

"Well, I'm happy for them to get married and live happily ever after. I hope this trip to Alaska isn't a relationship breaker for them."

She plucked a bunch of old man's beard and pulled the rough strands through her fingers. "Then you should stay away from Liam. He looks like he's fixating on 'what might have been.' Don't give him reality to go with his daydreams."

I dusted some dirt and leaves from my knees. "I'm trying, really I am." I turned away from her to watch a woodpecker knocking on a nearby spruce tree. If only Liam wasn't so attractive! I pulled out my phone for a quick peek at the photo of Angus at the glacier.

"What did you and Chuck talk about in the night?" I asked.

Teena's sprig of old man's beard shredded under her fingers. "Old times, mostly. He asked me how Hawaii was. He remembered that I was headed there, after all these years." She raised her eyes to my face. "Do you think I killed him?"

I held her gaze. "Did you?"

She stared back at me, unblinking. It was a staring contest, where the first one to blink loses. I was just about to lose when she broke off and turned to start striding back down the hill at a rapid pace.

I scurried after her. "You brought it up. Did you kill Chuck?"

"No! But they all think I did, don't they?" She tossed her head, her thick brown hair tumbling around her face. "I had no reason to kill him. We were close, ten years ago. We parted on good terms. Yeah, he was acting weird on the island, but that's not a reason for me to hit him over the head with his own gun."

I caught her by the hand, arresting her indignant walk down the hill. "Teena, you ran away from your friends at the bar, leaving them to imagine the worst. Go tell them what you told me. I'm sure they'll listen, and everything will be good."

She raised plaintive eyes to my face, looking like a child in need of comfort. "We're all staying at Clarissa's Bed and Breakfast. If anyone's still up, I'll tell them tonight. Otherwise, there will be time enough tomorrow morning."

I dropped her hand. "When I started up the hill, it looked like they were getting ready to head back to Clarissa's. Do you need a ride? My neighborhood isn't much farther, and I can spin you over."

She accepted, and we hiked in companionable silence the rest of the way up the hill. I almost offered her my spare room, but it made more sense for her to stay in her bed and breakfast room.

It was a short drive to Clarissa's. I kept my eyes fixed on the road to give Teena some space to answer my next question. "What's up between Lacey and Flint? Do you think she's cheating on Liam?"

She snorted. "They're not married yet, so 'cheating' might be a strong word. The two of them were very close before Lacey met Liam. I think Flint was planning a lavish proposal, but he waited too long. She met Liam, and the rest is history." She gave me a sidelong glance. "That's what Lacey thought, anyway. But now, Liam is wavering in his devotion, and Lacey doesn't want to lose him." She chuckled at my quizzical look. "Come on, it's the oldest trick in the book. She's trying to make Liam jealous by cozying up to Flint. If he feels threatened, maybe he'll snap his attention back to her. Alternatively, he could dump her altogether and try to win you back. It's a risky game that she's playing."

I was sorry I asked. I was beginning to feel the crushing weight of sleeplessness and stress bearing down on me. The tangled relationships between Lacey, Liam, Flint, and yes, me, would have to wait for another day. I dropped Teena at the door of the B & B and zipped back to my home.

Darkness was settling in as I checked the locks on my doors and windows. It was too late to try to call Mom, and way too late to talk to Angus. The four-hour time difference between Ptarmigan Port and New York City was always frustrating, and even more so tonight. I scrolled through my photos for what seemed like the hundredth time and then turned to the article Angus had texted me with the headline, 'Iconic Icons on the Rebound?'

As I had suspected, it told the same story that Rachelle Simonson of the *Ptarmigan Times* was so excited about. The two icons that went missing from Ptarmigan Port ten years ago were rumored to be about to hit the market. The author of the article seemed to think that their appearance would rock the art world. I thought back to the news of the theft ten years ago. I was away at college in Ohio at the time, and Nels was deep in his rebellious phase at the age of fifteen. He and Mom were at her remote lodge most of the year, so my family didn't share much information with me about the icon theft. All I remembered was that there was a fire at the manse of the Orthodox church which brought out an army of volunteers to help. Then, at a church service the next day, the community realized that two out of three historic icons had gone missing.

I stashed my phone for the night. I had to wonder how the thief expected to remain anonymous if they put the icons up for auction. Wouldn't that just bring the law down on their head? I also wondered why Angus felt the need to text me this article. True, he was an historian. I didn't know if he was interested in Russian history, iconography, or just anything that had to do with Ptarmigan Port, which he (and I) hoped to make his adopted home.

I snuggled under my covers, safe and dry at last. As I dropped off to sleep, I realized that I didn't know whose phone number was on the piece of paper I'd given to Nels. I would have to ask him tomorrow.

Chapter Fifteen

I slept soundly all night and woke up stiff and sore from my adventures. I rolled over and checked the clock. I had time for one phone call before I headed down the hill for the day. After a quick calculation of time zones and other people's schedules, I called Angus. I knew Mom would forgive me.

He picked up on the first ring. "Junetta! You're back on dry land? Marcy told me you were overdue on a boating excursion."

A thought flicked through my mind, that I hadn't told Angus about Liam and his bridal party and my plan to take them sightseeing on the *Northern Dream*. If not for Marcy's intervention, Angus would have never known I was in danger. I didn't stop to examine my reasoning for not telling him about Liam's presence in Ptarmigan Port. "It's great to hear your voice, Angus. What did Marcy tell you?"

"She texted that you were out with some friends, and you hadn't come back before bad weather set in. She said she'd singlehandedly mobilized the National Guard, the search and rescue people from Juneau, and that the President of the United States was flying in at a moment's notice to coordinate the rescue attempt."

I started to laugh. "She did not! But she did set Nels in motion, and that was how we got rescued. We spent the night on Price Island, where we ran into a freaky guy who ended up getting killed by morning." I shuddered, even though Angus couldn't see that. "It was actually pretty horrible."

"Wow," he breathed. "Tell me everything."

I took him through the entire story, from the moment we found Captain Evan passed out at the wheel to dropping Teena off at Clarissa's B & B last night. The only thing I omitted was Liam's continued efforts to, as Flint put it, 'canoodle' with me at every opportunity. But I did reveal that he was my ex-fiancé. I could only hope that Angus would understand.

"Wow," he said again when I was finished. "So, you don't know which one of these folks from Florida is a murderer?"

I shook my head, and then remembered that Angus couldn't see me. "No. I think I've ruled out the two women, but then I wonder if I might be wrong about that. It's a horrible feeling to know that one of the people I'm hanging around with is a killer, and I don't know which one."

He blew out a gusty breath. "No kidding. I wish I could help you."

"You actually did, even if you didn't know it. There was no cell service on the island, so we couldn't communicate with anyone. But I kept checking my phone, reading your old texts, looking at your pictures. It made you seem a little bit closer and helped to keep the panic at bay."

"That's sweet." I could hear the pleased smile in his voice. "In fact, truth be told, I did the same thing with your pictures. There's one in particular that I took on our shipwreck boat tour, when you were just an enticing new acquaintance." A note of shyness crept into his voice. "We were coming back into harbor, and I didn't know if I would see much of you again. I wanted to capture the moment in case it was the only one I got. You were standing at the bow rail as the town came into view when I took the picture. Here, I'll text it to you."

In a moment, his photo appeared on my phone. I stood at the bow rail, my face turned toward the colorful town of Ptarmigan Port, my red hair blowing behind me. Looking at the picture, I was struck by the peaceful expression on my face as I drank in the sight of the town I loved, clearly unaware that I was being photographed.

"I'm not a big religious person," Angus went on, "but I lit a candle for you, and focused on that picture of you returning to Ptarmigan Port over the waves, hoping that I could manifest that return journey in reality."

"I'm touched," I said, wiping away a tear that Angus couldn't see.

"Just a side note," he said. "It's important to blow out the candles, even the manifesting ones, before going to bed. I woke up in the night to the sound of the glass candle holder shattering after the candle had burned down to the bottom. The flame was a good six inches high. I had to snuff it out with a bowl full of spent popcorn kernels from my bedtime snack the night before. I woke up this morning to dozens of charred popcorn kernels all over the floor."

I was laughing again. "What, you were munching on popcorn while you were manifesting me home safe and sound?"

He chuckled. "I confess. But I didn't burn my apartment down, so it's all good."

Talking with Angus was like a breath of sweet air after a torrential downpour. Much as I would have loved to chat with him all day, I had a business to run. I was about to say goodbye when he changed the subject.

"So, as you were looking through my old texts, did you take the time to read the article I sent you about your missing icons?"

"I looked at it last night. What's the big deal?"

"I have a friend at Columbia who's really into the art scene. When I told him I had a connection to Ptarmigan Port, he practically flipped out. He remembers when those icons went missing and has been kind of an armchair sleuth over the years, trying to figure out where they went. He follows the careers of these two big art dealers, Ernie Fleming and Norm Oliver, who always try to outbid each other at auctions. He says they are bound to want the missing icons if they show up on the market."

"Huh." I started gathering my things together for the day.

"So, what's really interesting," Angus went on, ignoring my noncommittal response, "is that those two are both headed to New York City even as we speak. My friend says they're both posting enigmatic messages on social media about some fabulous art find that they hope to capture. Each one is hoping to beat the other to the finish line. These messages are feeding speculation that one or both of them might know something about the missing icons that are rumored to be about to hit the market. It's all very exciting."

"Well, keep me posted on the great icon mystery. We're focusing on a murder here in town, so art theft is kind of taking the back burner."

"Of course. Great to talk to you, Junetta. Steer clear of that murderer."

"I will. Bye, Angus." I sat still for a moment with a smile on my face, savoring my connection with Angus. But only for a moment. Duty called.

• • • •

I scrambled to get ready for the day and headed out within a short fifteen minutes. Even in my haste, I paused for a deep breath of fresh air when I stepped outside. The sky was full of clouds. I referred to it as 'high overcast,' which simply meant that it wasn't raining but I couldn't see the sun. It still counted as a lovely day in my book. I drove down the hill, parked behind the Shipshape Bookshop, and slipped through the door of the café with time enough to sit and enjoy my coffee before it was time to open up the bookstore. Marcy greeted me with a brimming cup of café au lait and a chocolate croissant.

"My favorite!" I motioned to the chair across from me. "Can you join me for a minute?"

She glanced over her domain. There were three tables with customers enjoying coffee and sweets, and no one in line at the moment. She fixed herself a cup of ginger tea and sat down. "What's the news on the murder? Last I heard, it had to be one of Liam and Lacey's bridal party. Have you fingered the guilty party? 'Cause I know you're on the case, Agent Beale."

I laughed at her sleuthing nickname for me, even though there was nothing funny about trying to pinpoint a murderer among a group of friends. "I'm pretty sure it's not Lacey and it's not Teena, which just leaves the two men."

"What makes you let the two women off the hook?"

I took a big, flakey bite of croissant. "I feel it in my gut," I mumbled with my mouth full.

She pointed to the sweet treat. "Don't be maligning my good cooking. You mean you have a hunch?"

"Sure, we'll call it that." I grinned at her ferocious scowl and went on. "On the island, I had a conversation with Lacey that convinced me that she wasn't a killer. She just seemed so shocked that one of her friends could have committed murder and so heartbroken and lost over the whole thing. I don't think she could have been faking that. Then last night I talked with Teena. She knew Chuck from ten years ago and liked him. It didn't seem like she would have any motive to kill him. She seemed genuinely sad about his death. I could see her showing up at the funeral to say a few words."

A smile was growing on Marcy's face. "So, your hunch is based on your feelings about the emotions of two people who you only met the day before yesterday?"

"Stop—you sound like Nels."

Her smile grew. "Don't pull me into your pre-existing sibling issues. I'm not judging, just clarifying things for you."

I took another bite, savoring the burst of gooey sweetness. "Okay, that's clear enough, then. I'm trusting my gut feelings." I faked a cringe at her grimace. "I believe that Lacey and Teena are innocent. That leaves Liam or Flint as the killer. I'm hoping it was Flint."

"Because you still harbor romantic feelings for Liam?" Marcy knew me almost better than I knew myself.

I took a long, slow drink of coffee. "Think about that word, 'harbor.' That's where a ship goes to take shelter for the night. The engine is turned off and the ship doesn't move. Maybe I do still have romantic feelings for Liam. They're not moving. The power has been turned off. As long as they stay in the 'harboring' stage, it's all good, right?"

Marcy reached out and patted my hand. "The struggle is real. I have faith in you, that you're up to the task. I'm happy to be your shadow for as long as those guys are in town, ready to pop up at a moment's notice so you won't find yourself alone with him."

"Time to activate Operation Boyfriend Befuddlement?"

She burst out laughing, causing all the café patrons to swivel in their chairs to gape at us. "I remember when we used that on Joey Sampson in ninth grade," she said. "He really wanted to go out with me, but you were always on the scene. He hated you with a passion by the end of that year."

I laughed along with her. "He sure was persistent, wasn't he?"

"He would always ask me, 'What are you doing Friday night?' I would have to come up with one creative reason after another as to why I couldn't go out with him. Then, if I really wanted to go to the party that he asked me to, I couldn't go, or he would know I was lying to him. Everything got so much easier after the launch of Operation Boyfriend Befuddlement. I could just say that you and I had plans, and he had to live with that." She smiled at the memory. "Here's a thought. If I'm not in the vicinity to break up a tempting twosome, you can always tell Liam that I'm counting on you to babysit Lisa. Day or night, I'll let you come over and watch her."

I downed the last of my coffee and stood up to give her a big hug. "Once he's gone and everything gets back to normal, we'll have to initiate Operation Auntie Junetta, where I really do show up for you and Lisa in a meaningful way."

She hugged me back. "I'm not gonna say no to that." She looked over my shoulder. "Oops—looks like Patrick is looking for you. Plus, my customers need more coffee." She gathered up our dishes and carried them into the kitchen before circulating with a fresh pot of coffee.

I turned to see Patrick waving at me from the other side of the groovy beaded curtain that separated the bookshop from the café. I rustled through it. "Good morning, Patrick."

"Ready to open the doors?" he asked, his voice catching.

I checked the time—yep, it was time to open, according to the sign on the door. But I wasn't sure Patrick himself was ready. A closer look revealed that his normally pale face was flushed, and his thin hands twisted together in a gesture that was more pronounced than his habitual anxious state of being.

"How are you doing today, Patrick?"

I just released the floodgates.

"Someone was in my car overnight. It could have been the murderer. I'm kind of freaking out."

"Maybe it was the bear from the other day? Did you leave food in your car again?"

He shook his head vigorously. "I'm super vigilant about it now. No food, nothing scented at all. No, I know it wasn't a bear." He leaned in close and whispered, "The car was driven. I'm sure of it. No bear could do that."

A chill ran down my spine at his conspiratorial tone. "What makes you think that?"

He grinned sheepishly. "I'm a big fan of two-minute mysteries. There's always a clue that points to the answer. One of the staples is the radio station being changed in the car, or the seat being moved to accommodate a taller person." He looked at me earnestly. "That's exactly what happened. Nobody else drives my car, so I never have to adjust the mirrors. But this morning, I did. Somebody took my car overnight, adjusted the rear-view mirrors to their height, and then brought it back to the same spot."

I tried to shake off the fear sparked by his words. "Maybe the bear knocked into the mirror, which is why it was off."

He just shook his head. "Somebody took off in my car and then brought it back, hoping that I wouldn't notice. But I noticed."

"You know what they say, if the ferry is in town, it's car theft, but if not, it's just joyriding. Have you notified the police?"

He shook his head, churning a hand through his bright purple hair. "Let's just open up the bookshop, and I'll worry about the car later."

"Sure." I flipped the sign to 'Open' and unlocked the door. "Why don't you have a cup of tea in the café and then get to work. Boss's orders," I said, as he started to protest. I shooed him through the beaded curtain and called out to Marcy, "Please give Patrick a soothing cup of tea, on me. Make sure he relaxes and doesn't gulp it down all at once." I smiled at Patrick and then took my place behind the counter in the bookshop.

• • •

Maybe I should have insisted on a soothing cup of tea for myself, as well. I only managed to help three customers before Liam and Lacey burst through the door. Seriously, they pushed the door so hard that it banged against the wall, startling a baby in a stroller, who promptly began to wail. The mother glared at me, as if I was responsible for allowing a ruckus to erupt in my bookshop.

I pasted a professional smile on my face. "Hi guys. What's on your itinerary for today?"

They rushed to the counter. Liam slapped both hands on the glass and leaned in close. "Teena's run off," he said breathlessly. "She must be the killer."

I stared at him, barely comprehending his words. "What do you mean, 'run off?'"

Lacey answered impatiently. "She didn't come down to breakfast. When I went up to call her, there was no answer. Her door was unlocked. Her knapsack was gone, and her bed hadn't been slept in. We don't even know if she came home last night."

"Of course she did. I ran her back myself in my car. She didn't say anything about leaving. She was going to tell you guys her story in the morning. I can't believe she would run off like that." I frowned, remembering her earnest question, 'Do you think I killed him?' No, I did not. I'd ruled her out based on our conversation last night. Now she was gone, and Liam and Lacey took her absence as an admission of guilt. For the second time that morning, I said, "Have you called the troopers?"

"Not yet." Liam squeezed Lacey close to his side. "We wanted to check in with you first."

I pulled out my phone and dialed the troopers' number. "Hi, Stella. Is Nels in?"

After a hearty 'Hi, honey' greeting, I heard Nels come on the line. "What's up?"

"Lacey and Liam are here at the bookshop. They say Teena took off in the night. I know you wanted everyone to stick around."

"Okay…?"

I could hear the question in his voice. "They think she ran off because she's the killer." I glanced over at Liam and Lacey, who were watching me closely. "Maybe you could send out a search party or something."

"Well, today's Thursday, so she couldn't have left by ferry. It shouldn't be too hard to find out if she hopped on a different boat or got someone to fly her out of town. I'll look into it."

"Maybe you should pop on over to Clarissa's and take a look at her room. I can meet you there."

I heard an ironic chuckle. "I'm sure you can. Okay, be there in ten minutes. I've got a phone call I need to make first."

I hung up before he changed his mind. "Nels wants to have a look at Teena's room," I said to Liam and Lacey. I turned to Patrick, who looked more grounded after his cup of tea. "Can you hold down the fort for an hour or so? Uncle Vance will be in by noon today."

He rubbed his palms on his jeans. "Sure, no problem."

"Want me to mention your car to Nels?"

"Would you? That would be great." I could see relief wash over his face. For some reason, Patrick was intimidated by Nels and his uniform. I was happy to run interference for him. Nels's position as trooper failed to inspire awe in me. He was, as always, my little brother.

"Come on," I said to Liam and Lacey, "I'll drive you back to Clarissa's and you can tell Nels what he needs to know about Teena."

Chapter Sixteen

It was a short drive to Clarissa's Bed and Breakfast. As the only establishment in town that catered to independent travelers, as opposed to cruise ship tourists, the B & B was usually hopping during the summertime. Today was no exception. A young family gathered on the expansive front porch held up by varnished tree trunks, with two kids rocking madly on the bentwood rockers strewn with patchwork pillows and fluffy crocheted throws. Mom and Dad hovered over a succession of daypacks. A teen boy lingered in the foyer, intent on looping his lasso over the antlers of the magnificent moose head mounted on the wall above the stone fireplace. His efforts had knocked the daisy chain encircling the antlers askew. Hopefully, he didn't have the strength to pull the whole thing off the wall if he did succeed in lassoing it.

Clarissa emerged from her office as we walked inside. As usual, she was dressed in a long, flowing calico gown with a deep ruffled border that tickled the ankles of her brown rubber boots. Her graying hair was swept up into a pompadour worthy of the finest models of the 1890s. The flyaway hairdo was augmented by tiny sprigs of forget-me-nots to create a whimsical Alaska cozy vibe.

"Good morning, Junetta. Your guests from Florida are lovely." She beamed at Lacey and Liam.

"Hi, Clarissa," I said. "We haven't seen Teena today. Did she check out, by any chance?"

She screwed up her face in thought, then consulted her hefty leather-bound ledger where guests signed in the old-fashioned way. "No, she didn't check out or turn in her key. Maybe she went out for an early hike or something."

"Okay, thanks." I followed Liam and Lacey down the hall to the Fireweed Room. Lacey pushed open the door and we all went in.

The décor fit the name of the room. A quilt printed with magenta flowers covered the bed, and a photograph of a field of fireweed with the Tongass Glacier in the background hung on the wall. It was all a bit frou-frou for an adventurous spirit like Teena.

Lacey was right, the bed was neatly made as if it had not been slept in. At first glance, it looked like the room was ready for a new occupant.

"You said her knapsack is gone?" I said. "Is that all she brought?"

Liam nodded. "She was a seasoned traveler, unlike Lacey, who checked two suitcases for the trip."

Lacey's cheeks reddened, but she didn't respond.

I checked the closet and pulled open the dresser drawers. When I got to the bedside table, I hit paydirt. Tossed in next to the Gideon Bible was a black leather cord with a Celtic knot hanging from it. I'd seen that necklace before, dangling around Teena's neck.

I gazed at the necklace for at least a minute before I slid the drawer shut again without touching it. I knew Teena would never pack up and leave without her cherished talisman. Yet, she was gone. Her absence suddenly struck me as sinister.

"So, is your brother coming to take a look around or what?" Liam's words shocked me back into the moment. I stared at him in a bit of a daze before pulling myself together. "I'll check my phone," I said, but there wasn't any message from Nels. I shrugged and slipped it back into my pocket. "Where's Flint?"

"He said he wanted to see if he could go fishing today. I think he went down to the harbor or something." Was there a furtive note in Liam's voice? Could Flint be missing as well? I was starting to feel freaked out, just like Patrick.

Lacey tossed her head. "We have a big lead in a murder case, and the troopers can't be bothered to come and check it out! Do they think we're going to sit around all day waiting for someone in authority to deign to look at our evidence?"

A knock on the open door startled all three of us. Nels popped his head in, his uniform hat in hand. "You've got some evidence to show me?"

I compressed my lips in what was probably a vain attempt to hide a smile. I could see that Nels knew how to intimidate if he wanted to.

For the second time that morning, Lacey's cheeks burned. But she managed to say, civilly enough, "Teena has run off in the night. Her bed wasn't slept in. We think that's an admission of guilt. She must be the one who killed Chuck."

"Okay. Why don't you all have a seat in the lobby while I take a look at the room? We can talk after that." Nels made a small shooing motion with his hand that included me. I waited until Liam and Lacey were headed down the hall before saying softly, "I don't think Teena left of her own free will. I think something bad happened to her."

He held out a hand to stop me from leaving. "What makes you say that?"

I watched Liam and Lacey disappearing into the lobby. "I came across Teena on my walk up the hill last night. We talked about her relationship with Chuck here in Ptarmigan Port ten years ago. She liked him and they hung out together for a couple weeks. She says they parted on good terms. I can't think of any motive she might have for killing him." I drew Nels into the room and shut the door. "All her things are gone, so Liam and Lacey think she ran off. But look here." I pulled out the bedside drawer. "She wore this cord around her neck." I fumbled with my phone. "Look, here it is in the picture Marcy took before we set out on Tuesday. I can't imagine her leaving without it."

He peered at the photo and then pulled out a little spiral notebook. "What are you saying: that somebody killed her and hid her body?"

I cringed from his bald words. "I hope not. Maybe they kidnapped her? I just don't think she'd up and leave like that. She said she was going to tell the others her story in the morning."

Nels leaned over to take a picture of the Celtic knot before scooping it into a plastic evidence bag. "So, the others haven't heard her story? Only you?" He ranged around the room, checking the drawers and cabinets just like I had.

"She said she was going to tell them, so I assumed that they didn't know. I could be wrong about that. You'll have to ask them."

He completed his circuit around the room and stopped to face me. "You might be interested in this." He pulled a piece of paper out of his pocket and unfolded it to reveal the phone number I had recovered from Chuck's pocket. Nels dialed the number and held out his phone for me to hear the voice mail message: "Hi, it's Teena. Leave a message and I'll call you back." That was all.

He pocketed his phone. "She didn't pick up when I called earlier. There was no phone on Chuck's body. You don't happen to have it, do you?"

"Very funny," I said. "So, Teena intended for Chuck to be in touch with her later. I just can't believe that she killed him."

He made another note in his notebook. "Let's go talk to your friends."

He led me to the lobby where Liam and Lacey sat side by side in silence, scrolling through their phones.

Nels didn't waste any time with niceties. "When did you notice Teena was missing."

"I went up to fetch her for breakfast when she didn't come down," said Lacey. "She was gone, and her room was cleaned out. It looked like her bed hadn't been slept in. Junetta said she brought Teena home last night, but none of us actually saw her." She put the faintest of queries into her voice, inviting me to defend my story.

I just nodded to Nels. "That's right."

"So, you found out last night that Teena was here in Ptarmigan Port ten years ago, where she met Chuck Woodhouse. Kirk Dunbar remembers her from this time. Did she know anyone else in town that you're aware of?"

I watched the two of them closely. Liam looked nothing if not confused. He mouthed the name, 'Woodhouse.' Lacey just shrugged. "I didn't know she had been here before until last night. How could I know who she knew here?"

"All right. Did she ever mention people she knew from Alaska?"

They both shook their heads. "Teena's a kind of live-in-the-moment kind of person," Liam said. "She doesn't really tell a lot of stories about her past."

I lost the thread of Nels's questions, distracted by a furtive movement outside the big bay window. Clarissa had the side panes open to let in the damp summer air as a misty rain began to fall. I caught a glimpse of a dark blue jacket sleeve. I couldn't say how long the person had been lurking by the open window, taking in every word.

"Where's Flint?" Nels was saying.

"He's headed back here," Lacey said. "I texted him. He got his hands on a rod but hadn't gone out to fish yet. He sounded annoyed about having to postpone his excursion."

I opened my mouth to alert them all to the listener's presence when Flint walked into the room. As Lacey said, he held a fishing rod in one hand. He wore a dark green jacket that looked like it could stand up to whatever rain Southeast Alaska had in store for him. He couldn't have been the person lurking outside.

"What's going on?" Flint asked. He propped the fishing rod against the stone fireplace and sat down on the couch next to Lacey. She made the slightest move to take his hand, then clasped her own hands together in her lap. I didn't know if anyone else noticed.

"When was the last time you saw Teena?" Nels asked Flint.

"Last night, just before she ran out of the bar. She was pretty upset that we found out about her knowing Chuck from a long time ago. What was that all about, anyway?"

"His last name was Woodhouse," Liam said. "Apparently."

Flint shrugged. "And?"

"You were also here in Ptarmigan Port ten years ago, am I right?" Liam glared at Flint. No one could mistake it for a friendly gaze between best friends. I wondered, not for the first time, if

Liam's friendship with Flint would survive this trip. Liam went on, "Did you know Teena then, or Chuck?"

Flint scoffed. "I was fully occupied on a fishing trawler. I didn't have any free time to hang around with random people in a bar."

"Which boat did you crew on?" Nels positioned his pen over his little spiral notebook.

"It was the *Western Star*. Captain's name was Roger, I think. It was a long time ago now."

"Roger Gannett? I'll have a word with him."

Flint shrugged. "It might have been Gannett. I'm not sure anymore."

Nels glanced at me. "You said Kirk recognized Teena last night. Maybe he knows of other people she knew in town ten years ago. I'll have a word with him, too."

I nodded. "If there's anyone who knows what went on in Ptarmigan Port ten years ago, that would be Kirk."

Nels made another note in his notebook, then snapped it shut with a flourish. "That's all for now. Thank you for your time."

He turned to go, when Liam spoke. "We're planning to head back home today. This trip has been a disaster, and we can't wait to be on our way." He didn't say, 'shake the dust of this place off our feet,' but the sentiment was there.

Nels turned back to face him. "I'm sorry, I need you all to stay in town until we've sorted things out." He held up a hand when Liam started to protest. "I'll check back in with you at the end of the day. Maybe we'll have more answers by then. In the meantime, please try to be in contact with Teena, in case something untoward happened to her. I'm sure you wouldn't want to leave your friend behind."

They all stared at Nels striding out of the room.

"What is he talking about?" Lacey said. "How could we be leaving Teena behind if we went home? She's the one who took off without telling anyone." She looked wildly around the room. "She's the murderer!"

I opened my mouth to explain my theory that maybe Teena was actually innocent and perhaps someone had abducted her, but I left my words unsaid. If I was right, then one of the three people sitting in the room with me might be the killer. Maybe now was not the time to speculate on their possible actions and motivations.

Liam put an arm around Lacey's shoulders. "It looks like we're stuck here, darling. Junetta, you offered tourist tips last night. What have you got for us?"

I forced a smile. "It's a pretty day, even with a bit of rain. We have some lovely beaches in Ptarmigan Port, but maybe you'd like to try something different. How about a hike out to the glacier?" I could take them on the well-traveled Creek Trail and hope that in broad daylight nothing would happen to another member of this group.

Flint made some noises about his desire to go fishing, but in the end all three of them agreed to go for a hike out to the glacier. The level Creek Trail was only a half hour walk through the woods, but Liam's party turned it into an expedition. They all retired to their rooms to gear up, while I agreed to arrange for a picnic lunch and return in a bit to pick them up.

As I headed out to my car, I spied a furtive movement in the woods behind Clarissa's. I tried to look closely without seeming to be looking at all. I saw a glimpse of blue, like the jacket I had seen earlier, as well as the glint of binoculars. Clearly, someone was spying on us. If it wasn't Flint, it had to be Seth. I got in my car and pulled out my phone to text Nels, 'Bring Seth in for questioning. I think he's stalking us.' There was no immediate response, so I set off on my picnic procuring task.

I collected a feast of smoked salmon and sourdough bread and went back to Clarissa's to pick up the group. It was another half hour before they were all ready to go, even though there were only three of them. Finally, we all piled into my car and drove to the trailhead.

Chapter Seventeen

The Creek Trail was a gentle, well-groomed trail leading to the face of the Tongass Glacier, that towering river of ice that overlooked our town. I didn't see any vehicles at the trailhead, but that didn't mean that the trail was empty. The two tour buses in town, driven by seasonal workers, would collect tourists at the dock and deposit them at the trailhead, and then circle back to pick up the next load. In the early afternoon, I was sure there would be plenty of people about.

A gentle, misty rain was falling as we set off down the trail. There was good tree cover to prevent us from getting wet. The rain intensified the bright green of the moss and the deeper green of the spruce and hemlock trees.

Lacey squealed, pointing to a perfect circle of mushrooms growing on the side of the path. "Look, a fairy ring!" She bent down to take a close-up picture while Liam, Flint, and I watched. It made me think of Teena and her fairy houses. I wondered where she was right now.

Lacey stood up, smiling. "Have you been on this trail before, Flint, when you were living here?"

"Of course. It's the most accessible trail in town, with an awesome payoff at the end."

She smiled up at him as the two of them walked down the trail together, side by side.

Liam hung back to walk beside me. "Thanks for bringing us out in the fresh air, Junie. At least this time we're not marooned on a desert island."

"I don't think you could ever use the word 'desert' to describe the terrain around here, but your point is well taken.

It's possible we could encounter a bear on our walk, but other than that, it's quite tame."

Then, a chattering group of tourists passed us headed back to the trailhead. They smiled and greeted us as they walked by. I recognized one of the customers who had purchased a pile of thrillers at the bookshop this morning. When I paused to say hello, he looked surprised, and then realization dawned. "You're from the bookshop. I didn't know that locals liked to hike on these trails."

"We live for it," I called out cheerily as he passed on by.

In this brief pause, the rest of my group went on ahead, and the person hiking behind me caught up to me. I was surprised to hear him speak.

"Well, well, if it isn't the castaways. I didn't expect to see you out braving the elements again so soon."

It was Seth Corliss. He wore rugged hiking boots and that same indistinguishable baseball cap, along with a dark blue jacket. I was ninety-nine percent sure that he was my mystery stalker.

He matched his stride to mine. "Looks like there's only four of you out today. What happened to the others?"

I decided to play dumb and let him reveal himself. "Captain Evan was medevaced to Seattle. He hadn't regained consciousness by the time they flew him out. Thank you for asking about him."

"Poor guy. I hope he makes a full recovery. What about the other one? There were two other women, right?"

"That's right. She's not hiking with us today." I paused to take a photo of a perfectly ordinary stream trickling down the hillside. I lingered over it as if it were Niagara Falls.

As I suspected he would, Seth lingered alongside me. "I heard your other companion has left town. What's that about?"

I pocketed my phone and looked him in the eye. "That's what you heard, is it? Was that when you were eavesdropping outside the window at Clarissa's Bed and Breakfast? I hope we spoke clearly enough for you."

At the surprised look on his face, whether real or assumed, I went on, "Yeah, we saw you. I'm guessing that you heard the whole conversation, so you know as much as I do. Or maybe you know more? What do you know about Teena taking off?"

He chuckled ruefully. "All right, you got me. I was outside the window. Would it surprise you to learn that I am staying at Clarissa's B & B while I'm here in town? I did hear you talking about Teena skipping town because she's the murderer. Is that true, do you think?"

I resumed walking down the trail. By this time, my companions were out of sight. "I couldn't say. What I don't understand is, why do you care?" I thought back to the conversation when Nels was questioning the group. Had he or I revealed anything about the Celtic knot necklace that would compromise his investigation?

"Why do I care? I was cruising along, minding my own business, setting my crab pots, when I was called upon to rescue some people stranded on an island. Come to find out, one of them was dead and there were suspicious efforts to conceal his body. So, I'm curious. Now one of the remaining castaways has vanished, and you're wondering why I'm asking questions."

"You're curious. Is that all?" I couldn't really fault him for that. Curiosity was one of my stronger qualities. "How many crab pots did you set, Seth?"

He looked genuinely startled, although he tried to cover it up. "Actually, I never did get back to them. Another day, I guess."

"What's your quota, coming from California like you do?" I kept a steady eye on him.

He bristled. "What makes you say I'm from California?"

I merely smiled. "I told you, my brother is a trooper. It's his job to check up on people like you." I shot him a superior glance. "Nels likes to consult with me on his tricky cases." This was completely untrue, so much so that I had a hard time saying it with a straight face, but Seth didn't know that. "He's waiting for you to drop by the station, by the way." I picked up my pace, hoping to reconnect with Liam and the group before Seth got too annoyed with me.

Too late for that.

He stepped in front of me, bringing me to a halt. "Do you mean to tell me that Ptarmigan Port's state trooper shares confidential forensic information with his sister, the local bookseller?"

I just shrugged and made a move to go past him. "It's all in the family, I guess."

He planted himself in my path again. "Okay, if you know so much, tell me why Chuck Woodhouse was murdered."

I pulled out my phone and took a picture of his angry face. I've found that to be a good ploy in getting rid of annoying men. "If you want to know about the case, you should ask the guy in charge—Trooper Nels." I fiddled with the buttons on my phone. "I just texted him your picture, so he can come pick you up since you're ignoring his explicit instructions to stop by the station."

That gave him pause. He lifted both hands in the air in a gesture of concession and stepped out of my way. "All right, you can text him that I'm on my way to check in with him. I'll tell him he should hire his sister as gatekeeper."

Nels would get a kick out of that one. I gave Seth a dazzling smile, to underscore the fact that I'd won our little tussle, but I held no hard feelings toward him. "Maybe I'll see you again, Seth."

He merely grunted and turned away to retrace his steps along the trail.

I watched him until he was out of sight. I wasn't sure if I'd learned anything more about Seth Corliss today. It seemed like he was genuinely wondering who killed Chuck and why, which might indicate that he wasn't the killer himself. But I had never really suspected Seth of being the murderer. It had to be someone on the *Northern Dream* at the time that the fire broke out. What I didn't understand was, why was Seth trying to find out who the murderer was? What was his stake in the matter? It had to be more than simple curiosity.

Suddenly, I wanted to talk with Kirk, to pick his brain about what he knew about Seth or about Teena when she was here ten years ago. Maybe he knew something about Chuck, himself, that would be useful. Usually, I tried to steer clear of Kirk, for fear he would come out with yet another marriage proposal at the most inopportune moment. But I felt like it was worth the risk. Maybe Marcy would come with me, in the spirit of Operation

Boyfriend Befuddlement. I chuckled to myself. Why did I ever think that particular game should be relegated solely to my high school existence?

As if on cue, Liam appeared from the trail ahead of me. "What are you doing, standing there laughing to yourself? We're almost to the glacier, but Flint said we should wait for you so we can all have the breathtaking view moment together."

"Good job, Flint! He's right, there is a spectacular view that springs out from nowhere." I hustled down the trail with Liam.

"So, what were you doing lagging back like that?"

I didn't know if he saw me talking to Seth or not. "I ran into someone I know, and we stood chatting for a few minutes." I grinned at him. "That's one of the perks of living here—you can't go anywhere without seeing at least one person you know. You're never alone."

"Sounds a tad overwhelming to me." He glanced in all directions. For this one moment, we were alone. He reached for my hand, but I shied away from him.

"Let's catch up to the others," I said. I speed-walked down the trail with Liam jogging to keep up.

"Okay, I get it," he said, when he came abreast of me.

"Good."

• • •

We caught up to Flint and Lacey at a fork in the trail. Both paths were clearly marked for visitors. The left fork led to the Fireweed Meadows, which were in full bloom today and well worth the diversion, and the right fork led to the face of the Tongass Glacier. Up to this point the trail had meandered along under heavy tree cover, which hid the glacier from sight. But, as Flint knew, this was about to change.

"Sorry to hold you all up," I said cheerfully. "What'll it be, the Fireweed Meadows or the glacier?"

"Are you kidding?" Lacey said. "We've come all this way for a look at the glacier."

I managed to hide a smile. The hike had been gentle in the extreme, and no more than half an hour from start to finish. But I couldn't argue with a desire to see the glacier.

We set off on the right fork. Within minutes, the path led out of the forest, opening up a magnificent vista. The Tongass Glacier lay before us, a massive river of ice flowing between its two matching nunataks. These sharp mountain peaks were once the only things that protruded above the ice field. As the ice melted and the glacier retreated, the pyramid-shaped nunataks emerged. Local artists loved to paint or photograph the glacier framed by the two mountain peaks with such startling symmetry.

Liam and Lacey exclaimed over the beautiful sight. We paused for a long moment for them to take photo after photo. The misty rain and overcast skies brought out the deep blue of the glacier that got washed out closer to white on a sunny day. I joined in on the photo session, posing all three of them in the foreground with the mighty river of ice behind them. "I just wish Teena was here to complete the picture," I said.

Lacey tossed her head. "She's gone. Good riddance, I say. If she shows up again, all you have to do is call your brother to come arrest her."

So much for the lasting bond of friendship between bride and maid of honor.

When everyone was finished taking photos, we continued on to the face of the glacier itself, where it melted to become Seven Mile Creek. Unlike the tidewater glaciers in Glacier Bay that flowed into the ocean, the Tongass Glacier didn't calve very much. Rather, it melted, becoming a rushing stream that tumbled through the rocky terrain left behind by the retreating glacier.

I picked up a flat stone to skip in the stream. It gave a satisfying four skips before it sank. If everyone could spend half an hour throwing rocks into the water, the world would be a happier place.

"Can we touch the ice?" Lacey asked, framing the glacier for at least the hundredth photo.

"Of course!" I led them along the creek's banks to the terminus of the glacier. Along the shores of the creek, there were a few places where visitors could walk onto the glacier or venture into the magical ice caves underneath. We hadn't brought the proper gear for either of these activities, so I decided not to even mention them to the group. I hoped Flint would exercise similar restraint.

Nope.

"Look, here's an entrance to ice caves," Flint said, pointing to an innocuous looking overhang of ice. He glanced at our shoes. "We should be okay going in. Come on."

"Not me, not today," I said hastily. "I tend to avoid certain situations prefaced by 'should be okay,' or 'try to land safely.' Personally, I don't venture into the ice caves without ropes, ice cleats, and a confident guide."

Flint rounded on me. "You don't consider me a confident guide?"

I pressed my lips together and held my ground. Last thing I wanted to do was go into ice caves unprepared in the company of a potential murderer. "Not today, Flint. We don't have the proper gear. With all the slick ice, there's a real chance of breaking a leg or two. I don't think Lacey's wedding dress would go nicely with a cast."

Lacey tossed her head, her wispy hair tumbling around her shoulders. "You haven't seen my dress, have you?"

"No, I haven't. I'd love to. Do you have a picture?"

Flint rolled his eyes as Lacey pulled out her phone. Liam reached out and put his hand over the screen. "I'm not allowed to see this, remember?"

She looked up at him with a sweet smile on her face. "Don't look, then." She turned her phone on and started scrolling through her photos.

Flint poked her. "Are you coming into the ice caves or not?"

She ignored him, seemingly fully intent on her photos.

Flint turned to Liam. "What about you?"

I shook my head at Liam.

He looked from me to Flint and back again. "How about if we come back tomorrow with all the proper gear? We can make it a high adventure Alaska excursion. You'll take us in with the proper preparation, right Junie?"

"If I can. I can't promise it a hundred percent, though." I bent over Lacey's phone as she scrolled through her photos. Maybe I could ignore this conversation just like she did.

Lacey scrolled quickly, but I was able to get a glimpse of her photos. There were seemingly hundreds of pictures of food, all delectable. Surprisingly, there were many, many photos of Flint. Lacey had photographed him at table with some of the food, as well as on the beach, browsing in a museum, and dancing at an outdoor venue sparkling with hanging lights. She made no comment as she scrolled, and neither did I.

Finally, she landed on a photo of herself in front of a triple full-length mirror, wearing a stunning wedding gown. I had expected a sophisticated style, but she had chosen a gown with a bodice covered in lace and sequins and a wide chiffon skirt. The overall effect was of a fairy princess. I almost expected to see a sparkly wand in her hand. I had to wonder if Liam was her Prince Charming, or was it Flint?

"How beautiful," I gushed. She smiled and scrolled through a dozen different views of the dress. Liam put his hands over his eyes, and Flint stood with his arms crossed on his chest, glowering.

Finally, Lacey closed her phone. She caught my eye with a shy glance. "Sorry, I got a little carried away."

I grinned at her. "Thanks for sharing those photos with me. You'll be a beautiful bride."

She turned away from the two men, drawing me along with her. "You don't mind?"

"Mind? Why would I mind?" Then, I realized that she was fishing to see what feelings I still harbored for Liam. I called up an image of a strong sailing ship resting peacefully in harbor. "Are you talking about me and Liam? I was the one who broke up with him. He's a nice guy, and I want him to be happy, and I knew that he and I would not have been happy." I locked eyes with her. "Will he be happy with you, Lacey?"

"I hope so," she whispered. She turned back to the two men, who were now arguing.

"You don't trust me," Flint snapped.

"I think we should listen to Junetta. She's the one who lives here. You haven't been from Ptarmigan Port for the last ten years."

I slung the backpack off my shoulders and plopped it down on a boulder. "Lunch, anyone?"

I had just gotten the sourdough bread and smoked salmon unloaded when my phone dinged. It was a text from Marcy: 'Fire at the Grizzly Bar. Where U?'

I yelped, causing all three of them to stare at me. I ignored them. I fired off a quick text to Marcy, 'Is everyone okay?'

Her prompt response, 'Not sure,' was definitely not reassuring.

"We have to go." I started throwing the food back into my backpack. "The Grizzly Bar is on fire."

Chapter Eighteen

If Lacey thought the hike out to the glacier was long, she was about to be challenged by the return. I jogged down the trail, ignoring the sights and pushing my way past a group of tourists who strolled and chattered in front of us. I longed to sprint rather than jog, but then I would just have to wait for the three of them to catch up at the trailhead, since I was their ride back. "Come on," I urged, pulling Lacey along with me. Flint and Liam ran alongside, trying to keep up.

We burst out of the woods at the trailhead, to see a large group of tourists milling about, waiting for their ride back to town. A couple of them leaned against my car, as if it was put there for their express convenience. I was about to shoo them all away when a spry elderly woman bustled up to us. "There's a bear in the trees on the other side of the parking lot. It's not safe at the moment."

"Okay. Thanks for letting us know." I unlocked my car and ushered the others inside. "Get a quick glimpse of the bear in the far tree, there. We can't stay for a better look." I cranked the engine and pulled out, regardless of the woman's warning. Dodging the gaggle of tourists, I drove as quickly as I could without actually speeding. "Do you guys want me to drop you at Clarissa's, or are you coming downtown with me?"

"We'll come downtown," Liam said. I saw him in the rearview mirror, opening up my backpack and rooting around inside. I was about to demand what he thought he was doing, when I realized he was rousting out the nice picnic lunch I'd prepared. It was nothing more than fast food, now. I waved him off when he held out some bread to me. There would be time enough for eating once everyone was accounted for.

In addition to Kirk, who really was a sweetheart, there were any number of townspeople who could have been caught up in a fire at the Grizzly Bar. Marcy liked to go there to play pool—although her text to me seemed to indicate that she wasn't in danger. Uncle Vance and his buddy Davey Harper were regulars. I sped up on the last stretch of road before entering town. A coil of thick smoke rose up from the main drag.

I pulled up in the alley behind the Shipshape Bookshop and abandoned my guests to their makeshift lunch. I ran through the back door, which was unlocked although the bookshop was empty. "Anybody here?" I called out into the eerie silence. I poked my head through the beaded curtain, but the café was similarly abandoned.

I ran out the front door to see a large crowd assembled on the sidewalk. Uncle Vance and Patrick stood side by side, staring in dismay at the bar. Marcy saw me run out the door and came over to greet me with a hug. "You and your crew are safe!" She looked around. "Your crew is safe, right?"

"You mean Liam and them? Yeah, they're having our picnic lunch in my car." I waved a hand vaguely in the direction of the alley. "What happened? Is Kirk okay?"

She totally refrained from teasing me. "I haven't seen him. The fire department just got here." She pointed at the volunteer fire fighters uncoiling a massive hose and hooking it up to water. "Nels got here first. He's inside." As a wave of panic broke over me, she grabbed me by the arm. "He's a smart guy, Junetta. He'll come out before he's in any danger. Look, Vance isn't worried."

The sight of Uncle Vance leaning impassively on his richly carved walking stick steadied me, as Marcy had known it would. She and I stood side by side, ignoring all potential customers, heedless of the misty rain, watching smoke pouring out the saloon door of the Grizzly Bar as the fire hose got to work.

Marcy poked my arm. "There's Davey. Go ask him what happened inside."

I threaded my way through the crowd of chattering tourists taking pictures to add to their Alaska photo albums. They weren't the only ones. Rachelle Simonson of the *Ptarmigan Times* hovered on the sidewalk, taking pictures for the newspaper with a ghoulish energy that revealed her enthusiasm for news, even if it was bad news.

Davey's face was smudged, and his long, white Santa Claus beard was streaked with smoke. He coughed and accepted a bottle of water handed to him by a random tourist. "Are you all right, Davey?" I asked, laying a hand on his forearm.

"Oh, yeah, I'm fine." He looked around in a bit of a daze, taking in the crowd on the sidewalk and the fire truck in front of the bar. "This looks a lot worse than it is. A fire started in the back room, and some cases of whiskey went up before we knew anything was wrong." He patted my hand. "Alcohol's a pretty powerful accelerant. But Kirk has a big old fire extinguisher hanging behind the bar, and he wasn't shy about squirting it everywhere. It got pretty exciting there for a while. Then, the fire department came along and told me to get out, and here I am." He grinned. "Some of that whiskey was top notch. Shame to see it go up in flames."

"Is Kirk okay, and everyone else who was in the bar? And Nels?"

"Yeah, yeah, everybody's good. Like I said, it looks worse than it is." He looked over my shoulder. "Here's your friends."

I turned to see Liam, Lacey, and Flint coming up behind me. I gave Davey a hug. "I'm glad you're okay, with only a little whiskey to mourn."

A grin split his grimy face. "Any spoiled whiskey is cause for sorrow. But we'll get over it, somehow."

I laughed, as a huge wave of relief rolled over me. I flashed a big thumbs up to Marcy, and greeted Liam, Lacey, and Flint on the sidewalk. "Sounds like it was a fire among the whiskey, and no one was harmed."

"Well, that's a relief." Liam took me by the elbow. "Come get some food, Junie. There's nothing you can do here."

I gently pulled my arm out of his grasp. "I'm not hungry. I'll be here until the fire's out and Kirk and Nels come out." I tore my eyes away from the smoke billowing out the saloon door to face the three of them. "You guys don't need to hang around here. Go enjoy the wonders of Southeast Alaska while you're still here."

Liam and Lacey exchanged a glance. Flint said, "Maybe I'll get that fishing trip in after all. Want to come?"

I left the three of them to figure out their next moves.

I made my way through the crowd to Marcy's side and told her Davey's assessment of the situation. We had a chuckle over the thought of Kirk's good whiskey burning down his bar. Thankfully, it wasn't going to come to that.

Finally, it seemed like the smoke was dying down. The firefighters turned off their massive hose and started coiling it up for the next time.

Kirk emerged through the dwindling smoke, clutching a fire extinguisher in both hands. His face was grimed black, and ashes clung to his hair like a spritzing of snow on an evergreen tree. He took one look at the crowd and held the fire extinguisher aloft, spraying out a triumphant stream of foam to a rousing cheer from the crowd. Marcy and I joined in wholeheartedly.

He was mobbed by well-wishers pounding him on the back and grabbing his hand, as he forged his way over to us. Before he could say a word, I engulfed him in a huge hug. "I'm so glad you're safe!"

His face broke out in a grin. "You weren't worried about me, babe?"

I let him go in some confusion. "I...I couldn't tell how bad things were."

Marcy tapped me on the shoulder, breathed "Boyfriend Befuddlement" in my ear, and threw her arms around Kirk in a hug to rival my own. "Rumor has it that your whiskey stash is the culprit, Kirk."

He chuckled. "It was the most expensive stuff that went off. The perp must have known his whiskey."

My hands went cold. "Perp?"

He gave me a helpful smile. "It means 'perpetrator.' The fire department thinks the fire was deliberately set."

I punched his arm. "I know what 'perp' means. What makes them think it was arson?"

He rubbed his arm, still grinning. The smile faded as he took in the smoldering interior of his bar. "You'll have to ask them."

Nels was just coming out, accompanied by Wally Monahan, chief of the volunteer fire department. At the sight of Nels's drawn, smoky face, I abandoned Kirk. I threw my arms around my brother and pulled him in close for a hug. "I'm glad you're safe," I said, for the second time in a matter of minutes.

He squeezed me tight and then pushed me off. "More work to do here." He turned away, and then swung back around to face me. Suddenly, all his attention was focused on me. "Where are your out-of-town friends, Junetta?"

I gaped at him. Lowering my voice, I said, "You don't think one of them set a fire in the Grizzly Bar, do you?"

"Where are they?" he repeated in his official trooper voice, the one that told me he was not about to share any information with his lowly, bookselling sister.

"We all went hiking out to the glacier, where we were just starting lunch when Marcy texted me about the fire. They couldn't have had anything to do with this. They've gone off sightseeing, or fishing, or something."

"And Teena? Did she turn up, by any chance?"

I shook my head. "Did you find out if she left by plane or boat?"

He rubbed his nose with a blackened finger that left a dark smudge behind. "There's no indication that she left, which means she might still be here. While you were all out at the glacier, she might have been lurking in the storeroom of the Grizzly Bar, setting the whiskey on fire."

"But why?"

He shrugged wearily. "It's just a theory." He shook himself and pinned me with his eyes. "Please don't spread this theory around, Junetta. Especially to your other Florida friends."

I drew my fingers across my mouth in a zipping motion. "My lips are sealed."

Satisfied, he turned back to Chief Monahan.

I looked around for Marcy. She was waiting for me to finish engulfing smoke-covered men in massive hugs. She took my arm and ushered me to the door of the Last Chance Café. "The café is closed, and Ricky's gone home for the day, but I'm sure I can find us a quick bite to eat before I head home to my baby."

Bless Marcy. Her answer to all of life's challenges was to provide some comfort food of one kind or another. I could see nothing wrong with this approach to life. I pitched in to help her gather the ingredients for a skillet full of cheesy scrambled eggs with chili peppers thrown in for some zing. In a matter of minutes, we were seated at one of her café tables, digging into the savory treat.

"So, Agent Beale, anything new to report in the case since we talked this morning?" Marcy asked.

I took a deep drink of my herbal tea, settling into my 'Agent' persona. "This morning, I told you that the murderer wasn't Lacey or Teena, but I might be wrong. Teena took off in the night and is now missing. Nels says there's no evidence that she left either by air or boat, so she's still around." I almost went into Nels's theory that Teena might have set the fire in the Grizzly Bar, but my promise to keep it under wraps stopped me. I've always shared everything with Marcy, so it felt really wrong to keep this thought from her. "So, that's weird," I finished lamely.

She frowned, a forkful of eggs occupying her focus for a moment. Then, she said, "You don't think she set the fire, do you?"

Okay, she said it, not me. "I don't know why she would do such a thing. Kirk says the fire was arson. Who would want to go after Kirk? The guy is everybody's best friend."

She poked me. "Even yours?"

I rolled my eyes. "No. You're my best friend. Keep up!"

She laughed, maybe a bit too hard for my silly comment.

"Kirk is a sweet guy," I went on, choosing to ignore her teasing. I picked up my cup for a sip of tea. "Teena doesn't even know him…" I froze, my teacup dangling in the air like a hummingbird looking for a bit of nectar. I put it down slowly. "Teena said something to me last night about Kirk having a phenomenal memory for remembering that she was together with Chuck ten years ago when she passed through Ptarmigan Port. His comments last night caused her to stalk out of the bar, and her party hasn't seen her since."

Marcy stirred another spoonful of sugar into her tea. "So, you think that maybe Teena was mad at Kirk for outing her relationship with Chuck, thus exposing her motive for murdering him, so she took out her anger by attempting to burn down his bar?"

I blew out a gusty sigh. "Maybe." I took a few bites of scrambled eggs in silence. "It doesn't feel right, though. I just don't see her as the murderer. From what she told me, she really liked Chuck back then and bore him no ill will when they broke up. Why would she kill him?"

She frowned down at her empty plate and then jumped up from the table. "We need some chocolate to get our creative juices flowing." She rattled chocolate chips into a large bowl and returned to the table. We both dived in.

"Then there's Seth Corliss," I said, "the guy who mysteriously knew where to find us when our signal fire was only minutes old. He was lurking outside the window at Clarissa's and heard the whole story of Teena going missing. He's stalking us, Marcy. He was following us on our walk out to the glacier this afternoon. He says he's interested because he witnessed us pointing Chuck's body out to Nels. He thinks there was some effort to conceal Chuck's death on the island. But the thing is, he would never have been there to witness that if he hadn't gone back to Price Island after dropping us off in town. Why did he think there was something to see there?"

"He is our mystery man, isn't he." She closed her eyes for a minute, thinking. "Maybe Seth set the fire at the Grizzly Bar." She held up a hand to stop me from speaking. "Here's how it went down. Seth overheard how Kirk recognized Teena from ten years ago. Maybe Seth also knew Chuck ten years ago, and now he knows that Kirk will remember him too. He sets fire to Kirk's bar, hoping to either kill or injure Kirk to prevent him from mentioning Seth's connection to Chuck."

"No, that can't be it. Seth was on the trail to the glacier this afternoon at the time of the fire." I stopped, remembering that

Seth had turned back toward the trailhead after talking to me. "On second thought, he could have gotten to the bar while we were exploring the face of the glacier. Was he in the crowd watching the fire? I didn't notice."

Marcy shrugged. "Everyone in town, including a whole boatload of visitors, was watching the fire. I'm guessing he was there, although I didn't actually see him. Then again, I don't know what he looks like, so I can't really help you." She glanced at the clock. "I need to get going." She gathered up our plates. "It seems to me, Agent Beale, that you need to talk to Kirk about Chuck's time in town ten years ago. What did Chuck do in Ptarmigan Port all those years ago that got him killed this week?"

I groaned. "Will you come with me?"

She sat back down. "I can't, not tonight. Sorry."

"That's okay, you have a cutie pie to take care of." As we both got up to leave, I paused. "Ten years ago, I was off to Ohio for college, but you were here in town, Marcy." I glanced around to make sure no one was lurking outside the windows spying on us. "Do you remember Teena or Chuck or even Seth in town at that time?"

She stopped, lost in thought. "Ten years ago, in 2005, I was working in the kitchen at the Orca Inn, missing my best friend, and wishing I was hanging out with Rob George and his friends. That was the year after we graduated, the year the Orthodox church caught on fire."

I gasped and caught her hands. "Another fire, Marcy! Ten years ago, Teena and Chuck were in town, and the Orthodox church caught on fire. Then, the *Northern Dream* caught on fire on Tuesday and we got washed up on Price Island, where Chuck was killed. Now, Teena is missing, and there's an arson fire at the Grizzly Bar this afternoon. Maybe all these fires are connected." I pulled her back down to her chair. "What do you remember about the fire at the church ten years ago?"

She pulled out her phone and checked the time again. "I gotta go, Junetta, really. Lisa is ready to nurse, I can feel it. Come with me, and we can talk on the way."

I jumped up. "No, I don't want to talk anywhere where someone could overhear. Seth's an eavesdropper and we don't know what's up with Teena. I don't want to put you or your family in danger in any way. Seriously, don't talk about any of this stuff until we figure out what's going on."

"Now you're making me paranoid." She turned out the lights, heightening the eerie mood.

"Wait, before you go…" I pulled out my phone and called up the picture I'd taken of Seth on the trail. I held it out to Marcy. "This is what Seth looks like. He has a concealed carry permit and carries a gun. I would say he's very dangerous. If you see him lurking around you, call Nels right away."

She studied the photo. "Text it to me, okay? I'll be on the lookout, and I won't be shy about calling Nels." She gave me a quick hug. "I'm the mama bear—I'll do anything to protect my baby bear cub."

"Give her a kiss for me. I'm going to tidy up in the bookshop before I head out." I bolted the café door behind her before rustling through the beaded curtain to check on the bookshop.

Uncle Vance and Patrick had left things in good order, even though they did leave the back door unlocked when they ran out to watch the fire. I bolted that deadbolt and then checked every door and window to be sure they were locked. Then, I systematically checked every nook and cranny, including the back room, the bathrooms, and the hidey hole under the front counter where I used to squirrel myself away and reach out to tickle Uncle Vance's ankles when I was little. Nobody was lurking in my bookshop tonight.

I gave a gusty sigh of relief and settled down on an easy chair in the fiction section. Time to give Angus a call.

Chapter Nineteen

He answered on the first ring. "Junetta! I was hoping you would call. Any news in the murder case?"

"Well, one of the suspects is now missing. The maid of honor, Teena, turned up missing this morning, and she hasn't been heard of since. Then, someone set the Grizzly Bar on fire—it might have been her."

"Oh no! Is everybody okay?"

"Yeah, but the whiskey is a total loss, evidently."

He chuckled. "What about the big stuffed bear? Riley? Did he survive?"

"Riley? You named the bear in the Grizzly Bar? I didn't know you had such a soft spot in your heart for him. I'll have to check on his status and let you know tomorrow."

"I guess I'll have to settle for that." The light note faded from his voice. "Do you think that the bar fire has to do with the murder?"

I told him how Liam, Lacey, and Flint were with me at the glacier while Teena was at large, as well as how Seth had been stalking us. "I think it's weird how many fires there have been: the bar fire today, the fire on the *Northern Dream* on Tuesday, and then there was a fire at the Orthodox Church ten years ago when the two icons were stolen. Ten years ago seems to be the magic number when everything was happening. It's weird."

"Ten years ago. Sounds like you need the services of an historian."

I chuckled. "If only there was an historian in Ptarmigan Port…"

"Oh well, you might just have to settle for an out-of-town consultant. I might know someone who could help you out, someone who has become very interested in the events that took place in Ptarmigan Port ten years ago."

"I'm hoping his name is Angus Montgomery."

"The very fellow!" He dropped the playful tone. "My friend at Columbia who is waiting for your stolen icons to magically reappear has piqued my interest. I did some digging into national accounts of the crime at the time. They mentioned in passing that there was a fire that was set as a diversion to cover up the theft of the two icons."

"There were actually three icons in the church, as a triptych," I said. "There was one large one in the middle and two smaller ones on either side. One of the smaller ones is still hanging in the church."

"Is it?" Angus's voice sharpened. "Have you laid eyes on it recently?"

"What do you mean?"

"Well, let's say for argument's sake that the story of the icons coming onto the art market is somehow linked to the murder on Price Island. Let's further suppose that there is one criminal who sets fires to get what he wants, and all three of these fires are related. What does this person want?"

"You think he might want the third icon? The person who set the fire in the manse in 2005 might be lurking in town right now, ready to set another fire after already setting two this week?"

"I don't know," he said. "It sounds pretty far-fetched when you put it like that. I wish I had access to the local news reports of the fire and icon theft at the time. I imagine the local newspaper has archives, but they're not online. I've already looked."

"You can hop on a plane and be here by tomorrow or the next day and root through the *Ptarmigan Times* archives to your heart's content."

"I wish." I could hear the smile in his voice. "Failing that, maybe you could stop by the archives tomorrow and call me, and we can look through the news accounts together."

"Sounds like a date."

We fixed a time to talk at the archives tomorrow and then moved on to talk about more general topics. All too soon, Angus said, "Time for me to head off to bed. Talk to you tomorrow, Junetta. Don't forget about the update on Riley."

I promised to find out Riley's fate for him and said goodbye.

Now, I had two reasons to go to the Grizzly Bar and talk to Kirk. I felt reluctant to go there, however. My cheeks colored when I thought about how enthusiastically I had greeted him coming out of the smoky building. He was bound to read more into it than was really there, despite Marcy's valiant efforts to match my greeting with her own. I heaved a sigh. No time like the present.

The sidewalk was crowded along the one block stretch between the Shipshape Bookshop and the Grizzly Bar. Tourists milled about, taking in every last bit of their day in our little corner of paradise. Locals lingered outside the bar, talking in small groups, evidently waiting for Kirk to open the doors for the evening. I wondered how much damage needed to be cleaned up inside first. Maybe now was not such a great time to interview him about nefarious goings-on from ten years ago.

I walked past the Grizzly Bar without stopping. I didn't see Liam, Lacey, or Flint around anywhere. I hoped they were having a great time fishing and planned to fend for themselves for the rest of the evening.

Suddenly, I felt a sharp sense of loneliness. Everybody had somebody to be with, except me. Marcy was fully occupied with her darling baby, Kirk was at work cleaning up his beloved bar and storing up stories to tell, my friends from Florida were enjoying themselves without me, Nels was probably hard at work trying to solve a murder case as well as a missing person case, and Angus was so far away that he was headed off to bed when it wasn't even dark yet in my part of the world. I could call Mom, but I doubted that she would be close to her radio phone at this hour.

I found a dryish bench on the dock and sat to enjoy the evening for a bit. There was a slight breeze rippling the surface of the water, bringing forth a shimmer worthy of an impressionist painter's brush. The tide was ebbing, leaving the briny smell of the sea in the air. A pair of seagulls quarreled over their chosen spot on the rail. When I closed my eyes, a peaceful feeling crept over me as I drew strength from the scents and sounds of my dear coastal Alaska hometown. With a deep cleansing breath, I opened my eyes and pulled out my phone to look at the photo of our boat trip together that Angus had shared with me. He had truly captured the feeling of love and anticipation on my face as I enjoyed the journey and looked forward to a sweet homecoming. Ptarmigan Port was my center. It didn't matter if I sat alone on a bench at the moment. I was surrounded and enveloped by a lifetime of friendships and experiences that made me who I was. Nothing could take that away from me, not even a killer who needed to be unmasked.

I hopped up from the bench, energized. I decided that I didn't need to talk to Kirk this evening, while he was busy with cleanup and greeting well-wishers from town. Instead, I could visit the Russian Orthodox church and take a look at the remaining icon. I knew the church was open every evening in the summertime to allow tourists to visit and marvel over its beauty.

St. Michael's Russian Orthodox Church stood on a small hill overlooking town. A winding stone walkway led up to the church, giving visitors the feeling that they were making a sacred pilgrimage. The brass onion dome, weathered green over the course of the church's 120-year history, topped the small wooden structure. The double doors stood slightly ajar, inviting the visitor in while keeping the weather at bay. The circular interior shone with gold. Even though Ptarmigan Port was a small fishing town, the Russian Orthodox church was richly appointed. A large iconostasis stood at the front of the church, separating the altar area reserved for the priest from the larger area for the congregation. There were no pews, only an open space where the faithful traditionally stood throughout the service. A number of rich paintings of saints adorned the iconostasis, painted on canvas and ensconced in lavish gold frames. They didn't include the icon I was interested in. I knew it was a small icon painted on wood and touched up with gold, that was gifted to the church by the Russian tsar in 1912, along with the other two that were now missing.

I wandered through the sanctuary, admiring the banners hanging from the domed wooden ceiling, the faded but still beautiful icons on the iconostasis, and the gold candelabras resting on several pedestals throughout the space. I didn't see a lone wooden icon anywhere.

A docent sat on a wooden folding chair by the entrance. A young woman with long, dark hair braided in two braids, she knitted quietly while keeping an eye on her domain. When I wandered in her direction, she greeted me, "Welcome to Alaska. Would you like to light a candle and make a donation to our church?"

I gave her a big smile. "I actually live here." I held out my hand. "Junetta Beale. I own the Shipshape Bookshop."

She laid her knitting in her lap and took my hand. "Nice to meet you. My name's Amanda. I'm here for the summer from Texas. Sorry for taking you for a tourist."

"No worries. I have a question. You obviously weren't here ten years ago when it happened, but two out of three wooden icons were stolen. I was wondering what happened to the third one. I don't see it anywhere in the sanctuary."

She gave me a strange look. "You're the second person today who's asked about those missing icons."

My pulse quickened, but I tried to hide it. "Who else was interested in them?"

She busied herself with her knitting. "Uh oh, I shouldn't have said that. I'm not supposed to share information about the people who come through here." She looked up with a smile. "Would you like to light a candle?"

"Sure." I took out my wallet and dropped a dollar in the donation box. "I would love to talk with the priest about the icons. Do you know when I might be able to connect with him?"

She handed me a votive candle and a long utility lighter that contrasted with the opulence of the church. "Father Thomas always comes by to close up the church at 7:00 pm. He should be here any minute."

"Perfect." I flicked the lighter to light the small candle and then placed it gently in the tray with a few dozen other candles.

Sure enough, Father Thomas showed up at the stroke of 7:00. He looked like he couldn't be anything other than a Russian Orthodox priest. He wore a long black robe knotted at the waist with an ornate tasseled cord. He had an unfashionably long salt and pepper beard and long hair that brushed his shoulders. He bade Amanda a farewell and turned to me. "The church is now closed."

I held out my hand, marveling at the fact that he and I had never met, after all these years. "I'm Junetta Beale, owner of the Shipshape Bookshop. I'm hoping I could talk with you a minute."

He took my hand. "Are you related to Trooper Beale, by chance?"

Hoping that Nels had never run afoul of the Russian Orthodox church in his rebellious youth, I said, "Yes, he's my brother."

Still holding my hand, he said, "That makes Vance Peterman your uncle, right? I thought he was the owner of the bookshop."

I smiled even wider, noting that Amanda had lingered in the doorway and seemed amazed by the depth of my family connections to our town. I could go back a few more generations, if necessary. "Uncle Vance sold me the bookshop last November. He's still at the shop every day, as Owner Emeritus."

He chuckled, patting my hand with his free hand. "Things do change, don't they."

"They sure do." I beamed at him. "In fact, I wanted to ask you about something that happened ten years ago. Do you have a minute?"

He finally released my hand. "Sadly, no. I have an appointment in just a few minutes. Perhaps we could talk tomorrow, say, midafternoon? I have a busy day tomorrow, but I could sit down with you at three thirty, if that works?"

"That would be great." I hastened to leave the church before he could change his mind. As I walked down the winding stone pathway, I met Seth Corliss on his way up. Seth was the person who Father Thomas was meeting for an appointment!

It was too late for either of us to hide. I stopped in the middle of the path, waiting for him to come up to me. "Seth. How's my brother?"

He shook his head slowly. "Junetta Beale. Why do I keep running into you? Are you following me?"

I laughed. "Come on, Seth. I'm on my way out, and you're just arriving. If anyone's doing any following, that would be you." Before he could respond, I repeated, "Did you have a nice chat with Nels?" I really wanted to know.

He flung his hands out in a gesture of innocence. "Oh, you know, police investigations seem to be shrouded in secrecy and mystique, even in small town Alaska. I wouldn't want to spoil that vibe." He took a step closer to me. "Excuse me…"

I moved aside to let him pass. As a parting shot, I said, "I'll give your regards to Nels."

He strode past me without a word.

My mind was working furiously. Amanda said someone else was asking about the missing icons. It must have been Seth, who had made an appointment to talk with Father Thomas about them. If Seth was the arsonist, and had already set fire to the manse years ago, did he pose a danger to Father Thomas tonight? I wasn't sure, but it seemed plausible enough for me to conclude that I needed to pass this information on to Nels. I pulled out my phone and dialed his number. As usual, it went straight to voice mail. I left a quick message and headed down the main drag toward the public safety building. At this time of evening, it was likely to be deserted, but it was worth checking to see if Nels's car was there.

I walked past the Grizzly Bar. The sidewalk was now clear of both tourists and locals waiting to get in. I could see why. The saloon doors were shut, with the 'Closed' sign hanging from them. A piece of paper was taped to the door underneath. I stepped closer to see what it said: "A trooper, a firefighter, and an insurance adjuster walk into a bar. The trooper asks for fingerprints, the firefighter looks for scorch marks, and the insurance adjuster asks for a shot of the finest whiskey…" I started to laugh. Good old Kirk, he couldn't come up with a real punch line, but that didn't stop him from finding humor in his situation. I chuckled all the way down the street to the public safety building.

As expected, the building was closed and deserted. Nels's car was not in the parking lot. I groaned in frustration. What good was it to have a trooper as a brother if he wasn't available when I wanted to talk to him?

I turned around to walk back to my car when an idea hit me. I could practically see the lightbulb shining over my head. If Seth was chatting with Father Thomas, that meant that he wasn't at his boat. I could have a quiet look around while he was otherwise occupied. I hustled back to the alley behind the bookshop and jumped in my car to drive down to the harbor.

Chapter Twenty

I found the *Sea After Sea* right away. She was peacefully tied up to the dock, with no sign of current occupancy. With a cautious glance around the harbor, I stepped on board. I wasn't sure what exactly I was looking for, but I wanted to take a look at the spaces on the boat that Seth had prohibited us from accessing. Why was the bridge and below decks off limits in an emergency rescue?

I started with the bridge, which Seth had kicked me out of as we made our way back to Ptarmigan Port. I thought back to his imperious command for me to keep my hands off his instruments. Was he just possessive, or did he have something to hide? I found the handheld GPS on the center console and checked its historic data to see if I could find out where the boat had been recently. As best as I could tell, the *Sea After Sea* had been moored in a harbor north of San Francisco until she began her cruise through the Inside Passage to Alaska two weeks ago. She stopped in Juneau overnight last Saturday, then made straight for the back side of Price Island and moored there for a couple days before proceeding around the island on Wednesday, when she picked us up. She cruised to Ptarmigan Port for the first time on this voyage, returned to Price Island, and then headed straight back to Ptarmigan Port. I couldn't find any evidence of pausing long enough to set crab pots.

I switched off the GPS, lost in thought. According to its history, Seth had come directly from California to Price Island by way of a brief stop in Juneau. He had lingered in the small harbor on the far side of Price Island for a few days before responding to our signal fire. He had obviously lied about how he came to be our rescuer. He could have crept ashore in the night, traversed the small island, and whacked Chuck over the head while we slept. I shivered at this sinister scenario. In terms of motive, means, and opportunity, I would say that Seth absolutely had means and opportunity. But what was his motive?

I abandoned the bridge and regarded the deck. The crab pots were still piled up, seemingly untouched. As I suspected, Seth's story of needing to go back to set crab pots was a ruse. I passed over the storage compartments built into the seats, conscious of the need for haste. How much time could Seth spend talking with Father Thomas, who would be ready to head home for his supper? I probably had a matter of minutes before Seth might show up. I needed to go below, another area that we were forbidden to access. What was down there that Seth wanted to hide?

I clattered down the ladder to find a small kitchen area with miniature appliances fitted into the smallest space. I always loved to explore the efficient use of space on a boat, especially in the kitchen, but now was not the time. I found the door to a cabin in the bow. I slipped inside to see what I could find.

The tiny cabin held nothing but the necessities for a two-week cruise up the coast. The bunk was neatly made, a few clothes hung in a miniscule closet, and a couple of books lay next to the pillow. A firm believer that you can learn a lot about a person by what they were reading, I investigated the little pile. On top was a detective thriller, which covered up a paperback history of Russian America. I picked up the history book, curious. We carried the same title in the Shipshape Bookshop. It was published in 1978, written in a scholarly style that was not favored by modern non-fiction writers, and was considered the definitive word on Russia's colonization of Alaska. A bookmark kept Seth's place in the book. He was deep into the chapter on the distribution of Russian Orthodox churches throughout Alaska. I noted the page, 247, so I could read along at my leisure back at the bookshop. As I replaced the bookmark, I noticed that it was a business card from Oliver's Art and Antiques in the name of Norm Oliver, Proprietor. I took a picture with my phone before sticking the bookmark back in the book and arranging the little pile exactly as I had found it.

Time to get out before it was too late. I slipped out of the cabin, closing the door behind me. I couldn't remember if I'd opened the door to get in or if it had already stood ajar. I guessed that Seth was a tidy, particular individual who wouldn't leave a door hanging open on his boat. Then I froze. What if he had rigged the door, so he would know if it had been opened in his absence? What if he had cameras on his boat, and he would know immediately who it was who had sneaked on board? I glanced wildly around, looking for the telltale signs of surveillance cameras. I couldn't see anything right away. Then I froze again, at the sound of footsteps walking purposefully down the dock. I needed to get off this boat, and fast.

I ran up to the deck and then ducked down when I saw Seth's nondescript baseball cap come into view. Too late to disembark onto the dock! I groaned without making a sound and slung my legs over the rail on the far side of the boat. I let myself into the water without a splash, trying to contain my gasp when the cold water hit my body. But I had no choice. Holding my phone above water in the hopes of keeping it from being ruined, I swam around a boat or two until it seemed like Seth wouldn't notice me getting out of the water. I had just about decided it was safe for me to climb out when I heard my name.

"Junetta, are you okay?"

It was Annalisa, Marcy's grandmother. She had a liveaboard that she kept tied up at the harbor. I had never been happier to see her face.

I held a finger to my lips. "Shh. I'm hiding." I paddled around to where I could get out of the water and still be hidden by Annalisa's boat. "Can I come aboard?"

She nodded and disappeared into her houseboat while I clambered onto the dock. She reappeared with a couple of thick towels to dry me off before I stepped onto her boat.

I'd been to several of Marcy's birthday parties on this boat, the *Water Ways*. It was nothing more than a wooden box-shaped structure on a deck attached to two pontoons, but Annalisa's personal touches made it homey. There was a full garden in the window boxes attached to one wall, and cheery red and white checked curtains adorned the few windows. The front of the house featured a sliding glass door that was rarely covered. A flowery curtain inside provided privacy for her sleeping quarters. The living space, consisting of a tiny kitchen and an ample table where all the good stuff happened, was usually open to anyone who wanted to look in. Annalisa lived on the boat in the summer by herself, and then in the winter she moved into the home of Marcy's cousin, Nathan. He had told her numerous times that she could live with his family year-round, but she always refused. She loved her houseboat.

She sat me down at the table and had a steaming cup of tea in front of me before I could say a word. Clearly, Marcy took after her grandmother. "Who are you hiding from?" she asked, adding a plate of fresh-baked cookies to the table.

I smiled in some embarrassment. "You shouldn't be so nice to me, Annalisa. I was snooping on somebody's boat without their permission. I should probably turn myself in to Nels for breaking and entering."

She sat down across from me with her own cup of tea. "Did you break anything?"

I grinned at her. "No, but I did enter."

She shrugged, her eyes twinkling. "It can't be breaking and entering if you didn't break anything." She shot me a searching glance. "Did you steal anything?"

I shook my head, feeling like a little kid being grilled on my lapses in proper behavior.

"I took a photo, is all." I wiped my phone off on the towel and switched it on, rejoicing when it turned on with no issues. I showed Annalisa the picture of Seth's bookmark, feeling like I needed to fully confess my transgressions.

She peered at the photo and then looked at me. "Nothing here to display in an art gallery, is there?"

I laughed and turned off my phone. "No, it's just to jog my memory." I downed the last of my tea. "I should head on out, Annalisa." I started to get to my feet.

She laid a hand on mine, arresting me. "Whose boat was it, Junetta? What were you looking for there?"

I sat back down. "It was Seth Corliss's boat. He's the one who rescued us from Price Island. It seems like there's something funny about him, but I just can't put my finger on it." I picked up my phone again and called up my photo of Seth. "Do you know anything about him, Annalisa? Have you ever seen him in town?"

She studied the photo. "I've seen him around here these past couple of days." She closed her eyes and sat in complete silence for a moment. "I don't recall seeing him in town before this week." She opened her eyes and looked at the photo again. "He looks quite angry. Is he a threat to you, Junetta? Is that why you went into the water to avoid running into him?"

I nodded. "Yes. Well, I don't really know. He was angry during that conversation, which is why I took his photo, to tell him I was letting Nels know that he was bothering me." I grinned at her. "It's nice to have a trooper in the family." I looked at the photo again. "I don't know what part he plays in Chuck's murder—the guy we met on the island who was killed. I think Seth is mixed up in it somehow. That's what I was looking for—some evidence of what his relationship is to Chuck. I didn't really find anything, though."

Annalisa stood up, signaling that our conversation was finished and I could head out now. "I will watch over him and let you know if I see anything suspicious." She wrapped one of the towels around my shoulders. "Bring it back when you no longer need it," she said.

I squeezed her hands, in lieu of a hug that would only get her wet. "Thank you for the tea and the shelter. Gunalchéesh."

She smiled, pleased as always when I spoke in her native Tlingit language.

I looked carefully around me before disembarking from her houseboat. Seth was out of sight. He could have been observing me from the shelter of his boat, or he could have recognized my car from all the time he'd spent following me around. I couldn't help that. I just hoped that he would leave me alone if he discovered that I had snooped on his boat.

I turned the heat all the way up on the short drive back to my house. Time for another long, hot shower followed by snuggling on the couch for the evening. I was done with sleuthing for the day.

My phone dinged on the way home. It was Liam, asking me to join them for dinner out at the Orca Inn. After my recent drenching, the last thing I wanted was to get all dressed up and go out for an expensive dinner with a group of people that may or may not include a murderer. I texted back, 'Thanks, but I'm in for the night. Enjoy the Orca Inn—the food is superb. Tell Lacey to take lots of photos for her magazine.' I turned off my phone and put Liam and his party out of my mind.

After the long, hot shower, I settled down on the couch with a fuzzy blanket and called Mom. Finally.

My timing was good—she picked up on the fourth ring. "Junetta, how are you sweetie? Katie told me you'd been rescued after sinking the *Northern Dream* and spending the night in the wild on an island."

Katie Carter and her husband, Mike, owned the local grocery. She was second only to Kirk as the most well-informed person in town. She served as Mom's source of all news and gossip from Ptarmigan Port. Whether she got all the details correct was another question, however.

"I'm fine, and I didn't sink the *Northern Dream*. She caught on fire, and we had to abandon ship. But she's still afloat, although I haven't had a chance to take a look at the damage. Sorry I didn't call earlier—it's been a rough couple of days." I told her all about my adventures, from the moment of abandoning ship to the discovery of Chuck's murdered body, Teena's disappearance, the fire at the Grizzly Bar, and the mysterious coincidence of the story of the missing icons. I glossed over our desperate journey through the driving rain in the dinghy searching for safe harbor before it was too late. Mom had a good imagination, and I didn't want to take her back to that dreadful time when we found out that my dad's boat had gone down. I knew she was haunted by the thought of her beloved husband drowning in the icy waters of Havoc Strait.

I shook myself before I let my own mind go too far down that terrible road. "Have you talked to Nels, Mom? He's on the job, as always."

"No, he hasn't called. As you say, he's likely preoccupied with the pursuit of justice." The phone crackled, cutting off the beginning of her next question. All I heard was, "…hosting your former fiancé and his wedding party. Liam, right? He moved quickly, didn't he?"

My heart warmed. I could always count on Mom to take my side, even if battle lines had never been drawn. "It's okay, he's allowed to get engaged again. I'm the one who didn't want him."

"Speaking of," she said, the hint of a smile in her voice, "have you been in touch with your new guy, Angus?"

My 'new guy.' I told her about my conversation with Angus and his sweet effort to manifest me home safe and sound. "But don't think that I chose him over you, Mom. I had to make time zone choices with my phone calls."

She laughed. "I chose a life off the grid, and I have to live with the consequences. But I have faith that my children can handle themselves in the world and will fill me in when they get the chance."

We talked for a few more minutes, mother to daughter, before Mom said, "Now, I have to make hostess choices. I have a group coming in from Chicago tomorrow morning for the weekend, and the laundry's not all done yet. Take care of yourself, sweetie. I love you."

"Love you too, Mom." I ended the call and snuggled deep under my blanket. No more thinking about fire, or murder, or stolen icons tonight! I flipped on the TV and fell asleep on the couch before the boy even had a chance to meet the girl, much less get her.

Chapter Twenty-one

I woke up the next morning energized. I threw open my blackout curtains to greet the day—and what a day it was! Sunshine beamed from a clear blue sky, illuminating the raindrops clinging to the tips of the spruce needles on the trees outside my window. They looked like tiny holiday lights twinkling all over the trees. The sun would dry them up in a matter of minutes. I was glad to have been a witness for this fleeting moment.

The rooftops in my neighborhood steamed in the sun as I headed down the hill to the bookshop. I could see mist rising from the channel as a cruise ship sailed into town. The day could unfold in one of two ways: we could get glorious sunshine and blue skies, or we could get a dense fog obscuring everything. I threw out my arms when I got out of my car, embracing all possibilities. Whatever this day had in store for me, I was ready!

By mid-morning, it was clear that the fog had won out. Angus and I had arranged to meet by phone at 11:00 at the newspaper archives to learn as much as we could about the missing icons and the fire at the Orthodox church manse. I left the bookshop in the capable hands of Uncle Vance and Patrick and made my way through the deepening fog to arrive at the *Ptarmigan Times* office at 10:45.

The *Times* occupied a large storefront next door to the Ptarmigan Port Historical Society. This housed the 'new' printing press dating back to 1965 that Rachelle Simonson, editor and publisher, used to singlehandedly put out a semiweekly newspaper for our small town. The *Times* used to be a daily, but Rachelle had gotten involved in so many other aspects of life in town that she wasn't able to keep up with a daily paper. As Father Thomas said, things do change. Of course, Rachelle could modernize her printing process and then she would be able to keep up, but she loved the clanking of the old press. It emphasized the urgency of the news, she would always say.

She greeted me now with an energy that almost took my breath away. "Junetta! I'm glad you got here early. I'm headed out in a sec. Let me show you the boxes to look at." She led me past the hulking printing press to a door marked, 'Archives.' When she threw open the door, a wave of mustiness billowed out. I followed her into the small, windowless space crammed with floor-to-ceiling steel shelves laden with cardboard boxes stuffed with newspapers. The boxes were clearly marked by date, but the sheer volume of them was overwhelming, and the smell of mold and mildew was almost overpowering. I pulled out a tissue to hold over my nose.

Rachelle saw me. "We had some water damage three years ago when the roof caved in from all the snow we had that winter. Luckily, the papers weren't lost, but some of them did get wet. I had a heck of a time drying them out, and we were left with some mustiness. You'll have to do the best you can." She pointed out the boxes from ten years ago. "You can take them with you if you want, but you'll have to bring them back in the same condition. Otherwise, feel free to use my desk. Gotta run!" She was gone before I could respond.

I dragged the first box off its shelf and pried off the lid, grimacing at the smell I had liberated. I didn't want to introduce mustiness into my house, car, or bookshop. A quick glance at Rachelle's desk was enough to show me that there was no way I could use it for my task. She had piles of manila folders, random stacks of closely written notebook paper, and an array of sticky notes in all colors scattered across her desk. A pile of old newspapers sat on her desk chair. There was no way I could move things out of the way and then return them to their places. Luckily, the floor was relatively clear.

I pulled a pile of newspapers out of the box and checked the time. My phone rang at the exact same moment.

"Hi, Angus, are you ready to get to work? I want you to know that these newspapers are stinky with mold and mildew, by the way."

"Alas, historical documents often are. I'll be mindful of your sacrifice in pawing through them and try to keep my historical curiosity to a minimum."

I chuckled and started laying out page after page of newspaper stories from 2005, ten years ago.

Since I knew the date of the fire, it was easy to focus on the correct pages. I pulled them out and read the text to Angus. The initial article on the fire detailed the chaotic scene in the middle of the night when Father Thomas awoke to find his house on fire. It said the priest was able to get out with his dog and three rabbits, but the manse was a total loss. There was a dramatic photo of the manse fully engulfed in flames, with numerous firefighters wielding their hoses while a crowd of onlookers comforted the distraught Father Thomas. An accompanying photo showed a young boy hugging a soot-covered bunny, with the caption, 'Rabbit Rescued from Ravaging Conflagration.' I took pictures of both newspaper photos and texted them to Angus.

The next article detailed how the townspeople gathered at the Orthodox church that Sunday to give thanks that the priest had been spared, and that was when the theft of the icons was discovered. There was a trio of historic Russian icons dating back to the early twentieth century. The largest one depicted the Virgin Mary cradling the Christ Child, with two smaller ones for the Archangel Gabriel on one side and the Archangel Michael on the other. Gabriel was the only one left. The journalist, whose name wasn't listed but was most likely Rachelle herself, departed from her strictly factual style to decry the sacrilege of stealing the icons. I imagined she echoed the thoughts of most of the townspeople at the time.

A subsequent article told how, when the flames were finally out and the forensic fire investigators from Juneau came to take a look, they found that the fire had been deliberately set in a pile of discarded wooden pallets under the kitchen window of the manse. The investigators concluded that the fire was merely a diversion, and the icons were the real target. Since that time, no trace of them had been found, and no one was ever charged with the arson or the theft.

I searched through a few more editions, but that was all the coverage of the fire and the stolen icons. "That's the end of it, Angus."

"Take a close look at those photos, Junetta. Crowd scenes are often good sources of historical information. I can't see much when I zoom in on the images you sent me, but maybe you can see something in the originals."

I spread out the papers again and peered at the crowd. I could pick out some people I knew, like Davey Harper, who was always on hand when something was happening in town, and Uncle Vance, looking noticeably younger. Wait a second… "Angus, look at that guy by himself on the edge of the crowd, the one wearing a dark sweater. That could be Chuck." I scanned the crowd to see if I could see Teena anywhere, but there was no one who could possibly be her. "I'm almost positive that's Chuck. He must have somehow been involved with the fire and robbery."

"There are a lot of people assembled, which always happens with an event like a church fire. It doesn't mean that any one of them is the perpetrator. All we can conclude is that Chuck was present at the crime scene. How about Seth—do you see him in the crowd?"

I scanned the sea of faces, but I couldn't pick out Seth. "No, Chuck is my only suspect who I can place at the scene of the church fire. Now, Chuck is dead. His death is definitely linked to the icons. I can feel it!"

"That's hardly historical proof." I could hear the smile in his voice. "What do you remember about this event, Junetta? It sounds like it affected the whole town."

"Not much. I was off at college. I remember Marcy called me. She was shocked—her voice shook when she told me about it. Her family have always gone to the Orthodox church, so she really took it personally. I remember feeling very far away from my hometown at that moment. Then, I went out to a dance at college, even though I felt guilty for enjoying myself when the people of my town were hurting. There was a whole gamut of conflicting emotions. I was nineteen years old."

"That's the age of conflicting emotions, isn't it. When I was nineteen, I was torn between thinking I should join the Marines and wanting to write poetry for a living. I ended up with neither."

"The Marines? What made you think that was your path in life?" I didn't mean to laugh at him, but the thought of Angus in the Marines was more than my imagination could manage.

He chuckled. "If I told you that impressing a girl played a large part in it, you might think the less of me. Let's just say that her father and his father before him were proud members of the Marines, and she knew that was the hallmark of a real man. I struggled with the thought that I might not prove to be a real man, but in the end, I've reconciled myself to that reality. I never made it as far as ROTC, much less boot camp."

"Lucky for the rest of us," I said heartily. "Your historical talents would have been wasted in the Marines. Poet, on the other hand…that would be interesting to see."

"Yes, I still have my poetry from that era. I'm an historian, and historians, as you well know, never throw anything away. But they know when to bring items to light and when to shroud them in the mists of time. My poetry definitely falls into the shrouding category."

"Well, if you ever change your mind, at least you know someone who knows a lot about books."

He gave a mock groan. "That would make things so much worse. If impressing a girl is my goal, and I'm not saying it is or it isn't, my poetry from ten years ago would definitely have the opposite effect."

I laughed and said goodbye, promising to fill him in on what I learned from my interview with Father Thomas later in the day.

I got back to the bookshop to find Liam browsing in the true crime section. He came up to me as I took my place behind the front counter. "Hi, Junie. We're getting a slow start today. Do you have some time this afternoon to hang out with us?"

I smiled at him. "I'm pretty busy this afternoon. What did you have planned?"

He shrugged, leaning on the counter in an intimate pose. "Got any suggestions?"

I pulled out a trail guide that I kept handy for just such inquiries. "It's a lovely day to go hiking. You can find long or short hikes in this book."

He thumbed through the slim volume. "Actually, you said you would take us to the ice caves today. How about it?"

The fog was finally burning off, and the sunshine was magnificent. There was a tradition in town where shopkeepers would hang out a 'Closed for Sunshine' sign and head for the hills, literally. The question was, did I want to find myself under the glacier exploring the wonders of the ice caves in the company of a murderer? If only I could believe that Teena was the killer!

"I have some things I need to do today, so I can't take you to the ice caves. Sorry. How was your fishing trip yesterday?"

He fiddled with a pile of bookmarks on the counter. "We didn't catch anything. I think Flint wants to try again today. I don't know if Lacey and I will go with him."

An elderly woman approached the counter with an armful of Alaska picture books. "I hope you all have a lovely day in the sunshine," I said to Liam, and turned all my attention to my customer. He got the hint and ambled off.

I grabbed a quick lunch and a brief word with Marcy at the café. Her tables were full, so she couldn't sit down with me, even for a minute. As she dropped off my sandwich, she said, "Any news, Agent Beale?"

I looked around the café, making sure nobody was lurking to eavesdrop on me. "I saw your grandma yesterday evening. She helped me out of the water at the harbor after I sneaked onto Seth's boat for a quick look around."

She shook her head at me. "Most people can visit the harbor and even go onboard a boat without ending up in the water. What is it with you?"

I grinned ruefully. "I'm after the complete experience, I guess."

She leaned closer. "So, any new developments?"

"No. I'm going to talk to Father Thomas this afternoon about the fire and icon theft ten years ago. I'm sure those events are somehow connected to what's happening today."

"Well, be careful when you talk to Father Thomas. If you bring up anything that has to do with fishing or subsistence, it's all over. He can talk about salmon until the last fish is spawned out and the snow is halfway down the mountainsides."

"How about you come with me? You can keep me on track, Agent George." I took a big bite of roast beef on rye and smiled around the edges.

She grinned back at me. "Are you inviting me to go sleuthing with you? You're on!"

Chapter Twenty-two

It was a slow afternoon in the bookshop, with the tourists all out enjoying the rare sunshine, not knowing how lucky they were. They only got one day to enjoy our little town. Most days were rainy or cloudy, so this glorious sunshine was a gift.

I collected Marcy just before 3:00. We made our way up the winding stone pathway to the Russian Orthodox Church. Father Thomas met us in the doorway.

"Good afternoon, Father," I said. "You know Marcy George, of course?"

He twinkled his eyes at her. "Of course. How's that new baby of yours doing, Marcy?"

She couldn't help herself. She pulled out her phone and showed Father Thomas the latest picture of Lisa kicking her legs on a blanket in the sunshine. It might have been taken as recently as two hours ago.

Father Thomas cooed over the photo. "And your husband, Rob? I haven't seen him in church in a while."

"He's up on the slope right now. It's the first that he's been gone since Lisa was born. He hates missing out." She flashed a brave smile. "It helps him when I send baby pictures every day."

Father Thomas nodded sympathetically and then led us to a stone bench in a little garden alive with forget-me-nots, shooting stars, and monkshood. The delicate wildflowers blooming in the immaculate beds edged with blue and white mosaic stones formed a delightful juxtaposition of natural beauty and formal gardening.

"What a lovely garden," I said, as Father Thomas sat down beside me with Marcy on the other side.

"Yes, Mrs. Pease keeps it flourishing very nicely." He leaned back on the bench to let the sun fall on his face. "What can I help you with?"

"We're interested in the fire at the manse ten years ago, and then the theft of the icons that followed. What can you tell us about your experience?"

He sat up and gave me a sharp look. "So much interest in those events these days! What do you want to know?"

Well, now I wanted to know who else was interested, but I decided to save that question for later. "Tell us about the fire. Did you see who started it?"

He shook his head. "I woke up in the middle of the night to find my house filling with smoke. It was all I could do to gather my pets and run out the door." He shook his head sadly. "They say you grab what's most important to you when faced with just minutes to escape with your life. I chose my dog, Grace, and my three rabbits. My Bible that was passed down to me from my grandfather went up in flames. The rabbits are all gone now, and Grace is getting on in years, but I've never regretted that choice. They were living beings in my care—a sacred responsibility." He turned to me with a smile. "I bought another Bible from your uncle's bookshop the following week."

"I'm sure you made the right choice, Father," I said. "I hope Uncle Vance gave you a discount on the Bible."

He laughed. "The entire community was very supportive. When we discovered that the icons were missing, all the spiritual leaders in town gathered together for a prayer service. We were not successful in praying the icons back home, however. Now, I hear that they might be about to resurface on the art market. I'm not sure how someone could buy them knowing they were sacred stolen objects, but I'm often confounded by the ways of the world."

I took a deep breath before asking the most important question, "Have you ever been able to figure out who set the fire and stole the icons?"

He stroked his long salt and pepper beard, his eyes focused on the past. "What woke me up that night was the sound of shattering glass. Someone had thrown a rock through my window. I looked out the window to see two figures outside, running away. Only then did I notice the smoke and realize that my life might be in danger." He brought his gaze back to the present. "I believe that evil exists in the world, my dears, but I also believe that the power of God is stronger in all cases. Despite their evil actions, one of those miscreants took care to alert me to my plight. He may have burned down my home and stolen my church's holy icons, but he also saved my life."

Marcy and I drank in this story in awe. "Wow," she breathed. "And you have no idea who the two people were? Male, female, old, young?"

He shrugged. "I would say they were both men, not kids. I did hear a name, or at least I thought I did."

Marcy and I exchanged a startled glance. "What was the name?" I said.

"Well, I can't say exactly. One man called to the other in such a way that I took it to be the man's name. It was a short name that started with an S—that's the only thing I can say. I didn't put that in the police report, because it was so imprecise." He shrugged. "Beyond that, I have no idea. No one showed up to confession." His eyes twinkled at us. "So, what is your interest? Surely, neither one of you is here to confess."

I smiled. "No, not me. I feel like the story of the icons has something to do with the fire that broke out on the *Northern Dream* this week, as well as the fire at the Grizzly Bar yesterday. As you say, there is evil in the world." I took a deep breath. "You said there's been a lot of interest in this story lately? Can I ask who is interested?"

"Rachelle Simonson, of course. I think she's planning a special edition of the *Ptarmigan Times*. I got a call from the *New York Times*, of all things. Let's see, a newcomer to town stopped by yesterday evening, asking about the icons in particular. He had a picture of both of the missing ones and wanted to see the remaining archangel."

"Was his name Seth?" I whispered.

He shot me a startled glance. "You know him? He struck me as having an unhealthy interest in our icons. I didn't feel right about showing him the third one."

"Did he explain why he was so interested?"

Father Thomas merely shook his head and started to get up. "I suppose you also want to see the Archangel Gabriel?"

Marcy caught her breath.

I glanced over at her before responding, "I would love to, but only if it's convenient, and appropriate for us to see it. Mostly, I just want to make sure that it's still here."

That stopped him in his tracks. "You think it might have been stolen too? Come with me."

He hustled into the church, closing the door behind us. "Wait here," he said, and disappeared behind the iconostasis while the two of us stood in the open area.

"That icon hasn't been seen during services for many years," Marcy whispered to me. "Father Thomas must be very impressed with you."

"Only because you're here with me," I whispered back. "Have you seen the icon since the other two were stolen?"

She shook her head. "I don't think so." She heaved a sigh. "I hope it's still there, right where Father Thomas put it ten years ago."

Within minutes, Father Thomas reappeared. He held a small, wooden painting in his hands. I was amazed at the opulence of the icon. A large gold halo surrounded the head of the Archangel Gabriel, and the detailed feathers on his wings made me think that he could take flight to the heavens at any moment. "Safe and sound," Father Thomas said in relief.

"Thank goodness," Marcy breathed.

I glanced over my shoulder to make sure Seth wasn't lurking in an alcove of the church. "Keep it hidden for now, Father Thomas. You could even ask for help from the troopers to protect it, and you. I'm worried about what might happen next."

He patted my hand. "I keep it in a safe place, while I await the day that it can be reunited with the missing icons to make a whole once more."

"Thank you so much for your time, Father Thomas." As Marcy and I walked out of the church, he disappeared behind the iconostasis once more. I hoped that he and his icon would be safe.

Marcy fairly skipped down the winding path. "That was an extremely satisfying sleuthing session. 'A short name that started with S.' One of the two thieves must have been Seth."

"Well done, Agent George. Then Angus and I are almost positive that we saw Chuck in a newspaper photo of the crowd watching the church fire. I think we've identified our icon thieves."

• • •

We walked past the Grizzly Bar on our way back to the café and bookshop. The 'Open' sign was on the door, and classic rock music emanated from within. It was still early in bar hours, time enough to have a quick word with Kirk before it got too busy.

I laid a hand on Marcy's arm. "I'm going to stop in to say hi to Kirk. Want to come with me?"

She shot me a sly glance. "I need to get back to the café before Ricky takes off for the day." She waved airily. "Enjoy!"

I laughed and turned to go in, when Seth Corliss pushed his way out through the swinging saloon doors.

He stopped abruptly. "Junetta Beale. Now it's definitely you who are following me."

I could feel a blush rising on my cheeks as I thought about my snooping on his boat last night. I hoped he wasn't a mind reader. I fell back on my tired refrain. "How's my brother, Seth?"

He rolled his eyes. "If you want to know, you'd better go ask him yourself. Ask him to Sunday dinner or something." He nodded pointedly at the sidewalk behind me.

I moved aside to let him pass. I hated to do it, but I let him have the last word. I turned my back on him and walked into the bar.

There were a couple of people sitting at a booth in the corner, ignoring everything around them. That suited me just fine.

Kirk watched me come in. A huge smile broke out on his face. "Great to see you, babe." He poured me a beer before I had even approached the bar.

I sat down on a barstool and took a cool sip. "Looks like you've gotten things put back together again, Kirk." I took a long look around, to see if anything had been destroyed. The familiar array of expired fishing and hunting licenses adorned the rough board walls, the fishing nets and buoys hung down from the ceiling, and the huge stuffed brown bear still stood by the door in its glass case, like a fierce bouncer. "I'm actually here on a mission. Angus wants to know if Riley survived the fire."

Kirk cast a fond glance at the huge bear. "You can tell him Riley's fine—not even any smoke damage."

"Wait a minute! How did you know I was talking about the bear? I thought Angus just made up his name."

He laughed in delight. "He did, first day he came to town. He told me that everything needs a name, so I let him choose. Riley works for me."

I regarded the ferocious bear. "Okay, Riley it is. I'll tell Angus that it's all good."

He picked up a bar rag to wipe down the spotless counter. "It was nice of him to ask. The fire mostly stayed in the storeroom. We lost a bit of whiskey, but nothing more than that. I'll bet my insurance company doesn't often pay out for whiskey. The muckety-mucks might think that somebody's pulling a fast one."

"Yeah, they probably think you just threw a humongous party. But, seriously, do you know who could have set the fire?"

He shook his head. "The fire investigators said somebody lighted a candle in the midst of the whiskey and left it there to do the dirty work. They said it likely burned for a couple hours before it set anything else on fire. Could have been anybody."

I was pretty sure I knew the answer, but I had to ask, "Was there any security camera footage or anything?"

"Babe, you sound just like Nels. I don't have any cameras, or any enemies. Occasionally, I have to stop serving someone when they've had enough, and I've had to call the troopers once or twice when all else fails, but I don't think anyone holds it against me."

I glanced over my shoulder. "I saw Seth Corliss leaving just now. What do you know about him?"

He grinned at me, a grin that said, "What don't I know about him?" Good old Kirk! "He's up from California on his boat. He says this is his first time in Alaska, and he really wants to find a gold nugget while he's here. He was asking about you, babe, as a matter of fact. Is he bothering you?"

I shook my head. "Not really. He just seems to pop up everywhere I go, like he's stalking me or something."

Kirk leaned his elbows on the bar, coming in close. His voice was as serious as I'd ever heard it. "Have you mentioned this to Nels? Stalking is no good, babe. Bad things can happen."

I shivered. Bad things had been happening. "I'll be sure to tell him. I wanted to ask you—do you believe Seth when he says he's never been here before? Do you remember him coming in the bar years ago? Maybe the same time as Teena and Chuck?"

He shook his head. "That was ten years ago. You know I was just twenty, so I wasn't even old enough to serve alcohol yet. Old Brinker was glad of a hand behind the bar, but he poured the drinks--mostly." He winked at me.

I laughed. I remembered Old Brinker. He had retired to Arizona six or seven years ago, leaving the bar in good hands with Kirk. I could see him cheerfully bending the rules without any qualms whatsoever. "Other duties as assigned—is that it, Kirk?"

He shrugged, a grin on his face.

"Did Seth ever come in during that time? Did he know Teena or Chuck?"

He shook his head slowly. "No, I'm sure I never saw him before he brought you all back from Price Island. Here's the thing about Seth, though—he strikes me as the kind of guy who might change his appearance—like a spy or something. Maybe he was here ten years ago, but as somebody else."

A chill ran down my back. There was definitely something funny about Seth. Could he be using an alias, and if so, why? Was it to hide the fact that he was a killer?

Kirk leaned in close again and dropped his voice to a whisper. "Don't look now, babe, he's back."

I whirled around, expecting to see Seth morphing into somebody else before my very eyes. What I saw was Liam, a pleased smile on his face, approaching me.

I spun back around to see Kirk shaking his head at me. "You don't get the 'don't look now' part, do you, babe?"

"I guess not," I said ruefully. "Hey, Liam, how's your day been?"

He gave me a hug and a kiss on the cheek and led me to an empty table out of earshot of the bar. "We took a flightseeing tour that landed on the glacier. Pretty amazing!" He pulled out his phone to show me the magnificent pictures he'd taken of the Tongass Glacier from the air and then from its surface. The photos showed an otherworldly landscape of blue and white spires of ice broken up by crevasses as far as the eye could see. "Nothing like this in Florida," Liam said.

I oohed and aahed over the pictures. "Did all three of you go?"

"Yeah, Lacey, and I, and Flint." He showed me a selfie of the three of them posing in such a way as to emphasize the height of the ice spires.

"Any word from Teena?"

He shook his head. "She took off. I'm not even thinking about her anymore." Before I could respond, he went on, "I'm not thinking about that horrible boat trip and that dead body anymore either. Lacey and I are reclaiming this trip for our wedding. We're leaving all the bad stuff behind." He gave me a sidelong glance. "We're leaving tomorrow on the ferry to catch a flight home from Juneau. The ferry leaves at 11:30—we'll be on it."

I frowned. "Have you checked with Nels? He might want you to stay in town until he solves the case."

He shook his head vigorously. "He can't hold us here, unless he arrests us. Since he doesn't have grounds to arrest us, he'll have to be okay with us leaving." He held up a finger to silence me. "That's the law."

"Okay. Still, I think it would be courteous to tell him that you're leaving." I didn't add, 'If you don't tell him, I will,' but I'm pretty sure Liam got the message.

He simply shrugged and changed the subject. "How about dinner with the three of us on our last evening in town?"

I smiled at him. "Sure, why not? I've got some things to wrap up at the bookshop first. Where should I meet you?"

"We did the Orca Inn last night, which was amazing, as you said. But it would be nice to try something more suitable for the masses. What do you suggest?"

I bit my lip at his characterization of most of my fellow townsfolk. "How about the Schooner? Best fish and chips in town. But I should warn you, everything's fried there. They're all about tasty over healthful, and nobody ever complains."

"All right, we can go for tasty, just this once."

"And no complaining." We agreed to meet at six thirty, and I headed back to the bookshop.

Chapter Twenty-three

Uncle Vance and Patrick were getting things ready to close up for the night. I stopped in the doorway to watch the two of them moving through the bookshelves, reshelving a book here, straightening a table display there. They kept the place running so efficiently that I didn't even need to be there at all. It was a great business model. I ran my finger along the spines of a shelf of fresh new paperbacks. I could spend exactly as much time as I wanted among my beloved books, with flexibility to take off and do other things. Too bad the other thing right now was trying to figure out a murder case.

I said goodbye to the two of them and locked up after them. I wanted a few minutes alone to sort through some things in my mind. I dragged one of my easy chairs up to the true crime section, hoping to soak up some crime solving energy through osmosis. I thought about lighting a candle, like Angus, to manifest the killer to expose themselves. But I didn't. I didn't want the killer to show up here when I was by myself, and I didn't want to risk burning down my beautiful bookshop. No more fires for me!

I closed my eyes to consider what I knew. I had four suspects from the *Northern Dream* trip, plus another in the form of Seth. There were three distinct fires. Two icons had been stolen. One man was dead.

I opened my eyes and shook myself. I wasn't writing a children's picture book—I needed to figure out who killed Chuck Woodhouse. I jumped up from my chair, beating back the image of Chuck's body lying in the underbrush. I hustled into the back room and pulled out a few pieces of computer paper. Time to construct a timeline.

The first paper went like this:

<u>*Ten Years Ago:*</u>

-Two men set fire to manse and stole two icons from Orthodox church.

-Teena was in town—she met Chuck at Grizzly Bar.

-Chuck was in town—he was exhilarated about something. He was in newspaper picture.

-Flint was in town, working on fishing trawler.

-Seth was probably in town. Father Thomas heard arsonist call his name.

-Liam and Lacey were not in town.

On the second paper I listed recent events:

<u>*Tuesday:*</u>
-Northern Dream set on fire.
  (Liam, Lacey, Flint, Teena)

<u>*Wednesday:*</u>
-Chuck's body found.
  (Liam, Lacey, Flint, Teena, Seth)

<u>*Thursday:*</u>
-Teena is gone.
-Grizzly Bar set on fire—Liam, Lacey, Flint with me at glacier.
  (Seth, Teena)

But a long-burning candle set the fire—it could have been any one of them.

I puzzled over these pages for a very long time. I couldn't finger one person who could have been present for all the events, other than Teena. But if Chuck and Seth were the two icon thieves and the icons were at the center of the mystery, where did Teena come in? Maybe she was an accomplice? She met Chuck at the bar—he was exhilarated by something—probably the successful theft of the icons. Maybe that's when she got involved. They arranged a rendezvous on Price Island to reunite the two stolen icons after ten years. Teena set fire to the *Northern Dream* so we would all be shipwrecked there, while Seth moored the *Sea After Sea* on the other side of the island. During the handoff Chuck was killed, most likely by Seth, and then Teena took off with the icons. Could that be the answer?

I could feel a weight of stress sliding off my shoulders. The killer wasn't a member of Liam's bridal party after all. Teena was an accomplice, but she wasn't a murderer. Seth, on the other hand, played the part of killer very convincingly. I picked up my phone to call Nels.

He answered on the first ring. "Junetta. I've only got two minutes."

"Seth's your killer." I hung up.

He called me right back. "I've still got a minute and fifty-nine seconds. What makes you say that?"

"It's all about the stolen icons. I can place both Seth and Chuck at the arson scene. Chuck was in the newspaper photo, and Father Thomas heard one of the arsonists call Seth's name."

I could almost see him shaking his head on the other end of the phone. "Sounds like the flimsiest of circumstantial evidence. I happen to know that Uncle Vance was at the arson scene, because he told me about it at the time in great detail. That doesn't make him a suspect."

I chose to ignore his reasonable logic. "I've worked out that Chuck and Seth must have stolen the icons, then Teena was brought in as an accomplice, and then they all met up on Price Island to transfer the icons which were about to come on the market. In the process, one of them killed Chuck. I'm sure it wasn't Teena, which leaves Seth as the killer."

"Why not Teena?"

At least he was listening to me. "I talked to Teena before she took off. She was sad that Chuck was dead. She legitimately cared about him. I know she didn't kill him."

"So, you interviewed Father Thomas, and he told you that he heard the name 'Seth' in the midst of a conflagration ten years ago?"

"Well, he didn't actually say, 'Seth.' He remembers a short name that starts with 'S.' It had to be Seth."

Nels blew out a gusty breath. "That's all your evidence against Seth, that Father Thomas heard a short name that starts with 'S?' That could have been anything. Two minutes are up."

"Wait! I found out something when I checked out Seth's boat yesterday."

"Wait, what?"

"Okay, I might have had a look around Seth's boat when he wasn't onboard."

He didn't explode. All he said was, "I don't want to hear about it."

"There's one thing I found interesting."

"Stop. Don't tell me anything you found from your trespassing on Seth's boat." He cleared his throat. "We troopers have to get a warrant to search someone's private property. It has to do with something called law and order."

"Okay, get a warrant and search his sleeping cabin, where you might find a book on Russian America that tells all about the icons in Southeast Alaska. I've got a copy of it in the bookshop, as a matter of fact. Seth was using a business card as a bookmark—a business card from Norm Oliver."

"Yeah, I told you that Norman Oliver owns the *Sea After Sea*."

Things started to click into place. I knew it was all about the icons. "What you didn't tell me is that he also owns an art and antiques business and is right now on his way to New York City where the art auctions take place. He's after those stolen icons."

"How do you know this?"

"Aside from a bit of snooping around, which you don't want to know about, I got my information from my source in New York City—Angus Montgomery."

He gave an exasperated laugh. "You and Angus! Last time you teamed up, I had to rescue you from a killer."

"Revisionist history!" I cried. "If you remember; that killer was tied up when you arrived in the clearing. No rescue necessary."

"Okay, you're right. Good job. Please don't go after this killer, Junetta. There's a devious plot going on here, and bad things seem to happen to whoever gets in the way. I will check out Seth Corliss, I promise you."

"Great! I'll leave Seth to you. He won't give me the time of day, anyway."

He chuckled. "Otherwise, you would have finished with him long ago. One more thing before I go. The lab results came back on your water bottle. The residue at the bottom was from sleeping pills. Someone was trying to keep you from poking your nose into their business during the night, like you do."

I refrained from taking the bait. "That suggests that killing Chuck was premeditated."

"Possibly—or to disguise a different crime."

I heard muffled voices on the other end of the line, and then Nels said, "Listen, I gotta go. Stay out of trouble, Junetta."

"No worries. I'm just off to have dinner with three former murder suspects. If any of them moves back into the active category, I'll call you."

We hung up.

Chapter Twenty-four

I met the group at the Schooner, as arranged. Lacey looked askance at the plain board walls darkened by grease, and the vinyl covered booths, but she must have been tutored by Liam, because she didn't complain. My friend, Sammie, dropped off a pile of dingy menus with a cheery hello. "I heard you've been through fire and water to come here, Junetta," she said. "Appetizers are on the house."

I thanked her and leaned in to the group. "They've got the finest fried green beans in the country. I definitely recommend them."

Liam shuddered but refrained from comment. I ordered the beans for the table, and fish and chips all around. "My treat."

Liam and Flint both laid their phones on the table next to them, face down. Must be a power thing that attorneys do. Lacey had hers in full play, taking photos of the food when it arrived.

I prevailed on them to each try at least one fried green bean. Liam and Lacey stopped at a nibble, but Flint went back for seconds. "This takes me back," he said to me. "Sometimes we'd stop here after school, and my buddies always went for the fried green beans."

Liam's phone rang. He turned it over to see who was calling. "Excuse me, I need to take this." He got up from the table and held the phone to his ear as he made his way out the door.

Lacey and Flint took the interruption in stride. Lacey turned to me with a sweet smile, "Junetta, could you please ask the waitress to close those blinds? The sun is getting in my eyes."

"Spoken like a true Southeast Alaskan," I said, getting up from the table to seek out Sammie. It felt a bit like Lacey was trying to get me out of the way for a private word with Flint. If that was her goal, I certainly wasn't going to stand in her way.

I chatted with Sammie for a few minutes before making my request. "Sammie, could you please close the blinds across the way, so the sun doesn't get in Lacey's eyes?" I waved a hand at Lacey, who had her head bent close to Flint's. As I watched, she reached out to take his hand, talking earnestly all the while.

It was a public place—I was allowed to watch.

Sammie adjusted the blinds, and I ambled back to our table just as Liam came through the front door. Lacey's private moment with Flint was over.

Liam laid his phone back on the table and sat down, exuding energy and purpose. "That was Callum Oliver," he said to Flint, apparently not noticing Flint's flushed face. "He says his dad is coming to Florida after a trip to New York, and he wants to arrange a meeting with the firm."

My ears perked up. "Callum Oliver? Did I meet him when I was in Florida last year?"

Liam shrugged. "You might have. Callum's a fraternity brother of mine from undergrad at Florida State. Now, he works with his family's antiques agency, and he retains us for his legal work." He gave me an exaggerated wink. "It's not what you know, it's who you know, right?"

I smiled at him, my thoughts whirling in other directions. "You'd fit right in as a resident of Ptarmigan Port."

Liam laughed. "Sure, you know everyone in town, Junie. But they probably don't give you as much value-add as my contacts with the Oliver family give me."

"Hmm," I mumbled, declining to rise to his bait. My family and friends in Ptarmigan Port were the salt of the earth, who loved me and would always have my back. There was nothing more valuable than that. I didn't feel like telling Liam how offensive his comment really was. My thoughts were occupied with the Oliver family, headed up by Norman Oliver, no doubt. Liam's law firm, where he worked alongside Flint, represented Norman Oliver in his business dealings. Liam undoubtedly knew about

Oliver's interest in the missing Ptarmigan Port icons which were supposedly about to resurface. Had he conspired with Oliver to recover an icon from Chuck on Price Island? Suddenly, Seth had strong competition as the front-runner in the role of icon thief / murderer. I hadn't been able to identify a motive for Liam before now, but an old friendship, especially with a fraternity brother, could be a powerful force in some shady business dealings that may or may not have included murder.

I picked at the rest of my dinner as the conversation flowed around me. I had been so sure that Seth was the killer. Now, I just didn't know. I could be having dinner with a murderer after all.

Liam and Lacey talked animatedly of their upcoming flight back to Florida and how soon they planned to hit the beach when they arrived. I pictured Lacey on the beach wearing a floppy sunhat and fashionable sunglasses, drinking cocktails with her man by her side. I wasn't a hundred per cent sure which man would have that honor, although, if I had to guess, I would say that Lacey had just told Flint that she was committing to Liam at long last.

When dinner was over, we walked down the sidewalk to the Grizzly Bar for a nightcap. Kirk greeted me enthusiastically as we walked in, "Junetta, great to see you, babe, and all your Florida friends too. Beers all around?"

"Thanks, Kirk, that would be great."

We settled in a booth by the pool table. Kirk arrived with the beers before we had even had time to take off our jackets. He distributed the bottles, leaving one still on his tray. "You're a woman down this evening. Is Teena coming around?"

Incredibly, Kirk was behind the times. True, he had been cleaning up after a fire, so I could cut him some slack, just this once.

"Teena has left town," I said, with a side glance at my companions. Nobody else chimed in.

Kirk looked surprised. "You mean, when she walked out of the bar the other night, she went clean out of town? Wow, I wouldn't have predicted that. I would have thought she would savor every moment of her time here." He gave me his goofy grin. "I guess you never know how people are going to react." He sauntered back to the bar, holding the beer he'd brought out for Teena in one hand.

Uncle Vance and his buddy Davey sat together at a booth in the corner, drinking beer. Surprisingly, Seth sat with them, as relaxed as could be. Nels hadn't arrested him, then. Was that because he had worked out that Liam was the guilty party? Maybe I should bow out now and leave the case to Nels.

Come on, who was I kidding?

From across the bar, Davey waved me over. "Have you seen Nels around lately? It's only, I had something I wanted to tell him."

I walked over and sat down beside him. Lowering my voice so the whole bar wouldn't hear Davey's message to Trooper Nels, I said, "What is it?"

"Well, there's something funny going on up at the old Warner place. When I was out walking my dog on Wednesday night, I saw a vehicle drive up and somebody heaving things into the cabin. Kimmy was howling when we went by. She does that when there are bears around. I didn't stop in case there was a bear, and then I haven't been that way since. I just think Nels should check it out."

"What kind of car was it?" Seth's question startled me. He still leaned back in his chair in that relaxed pose, but his attention was sharply focused on Davey.

Davey shrugged. "I don't know—some kind of dark SUV."

"Well, the bears are certainly out," I said. "Patrick had one break into his car the other night…" I paused mid-sentence. A series of pictures flashed through my mind: Patrick showing me photos of his dark SUV that was broken into by a bear. That was Tuesday morning. Then, on Thursday morning, the day we discovered that Teena was missing, he said his car had been driven overnight. He insisted that this time it wasn't a bear.

"I'll be in touch with Nels," I told Davey. I hustled back to our table. "Sorry, guys, I need to get going. Enjoy your last night in Alaska!" I pulled out my phone to send a quick text to Nels, 'Meet me at the old Warner place.'

His response came back immediately, 'Got it.'

Before I could pocket the phone again, Liam snatched it out of my fingers. "Meet me at the old Warner place," he read aloud in a high-pitched voice. "Oooh. Who is this secret assignation with, Junetta?" He pointed at the bar. "Kirk is right here. Or maybe it's Beefsteak that you're meeting?"

I grabbed my phone back from him. "My texts are none of your business, Liam. See you later." I threw on my jacket and stalked out the door.

There was a flurry of movement behind me, as Liam, Flint, and Seth all got up to leave, with Lacey protesting at the general exodus. I guess we'd see who got to the old Warner place first. I hoped it would be Nels.

The other two men disappeared, but Liam ran after me. I jumped in my car and locked the doors. He pounded on my driver's side window. I cracked it down an inch.

"Come on, Junie, don't be mad. I'm just playing."

"I am not playing." I revved my engine. "I'll see you at the ferry terminal tomorrow, Liam, to send you off in style. Goodnight." He had to jump back as I peeled out of the parking spot. As I drove past him, he shouted, "Where's the old Warner place?"

Well, he was going to have to ask for directions, something he was not particularly skilled at. I waved a backward hand at him and took off down the road.

The old Warner place was on the edge of the graveyard on the east side of town, accessed by either of two long driveways on opposite sides of the building. It was originally the caretaker's cabin, dating back to the mid 1940s. By the seventies, the graveyard was officially full, and the caretaker was let go. The cabin was abandoned. It had stood empty ever since, but there was no desire in town to tear it down. It made the perfect haunted house for Halloween. Every October, the old Warner place was plastered with spooky decorations and frequented by ghouls of all descriptions. I remembered one year when I was in high school, the parents of school-aged children tried to reform the cabin's reputation by staging a Halloween candy hunt in the graveyard. It was a nice thought, but the mischief makers took it as a new opportunity to haunt not just the cabin but the graveyard as well. I was pretty sure Nels was one of the ringleaders that year, but I'd never gotten him to confess. The errant teens of those days had grown up to become our town's new leaders, who all had a soft spot in their hearts for the old Warner place and the happy memories of their escapades there. There was no risk of it getting torn down anytime soon.

I pulled up in the overgrown front driveway, hoping that Nels chose the same one. I sat for a moment, taking in the sinister look of the abandoned cabin. It was still summer, and twilight was just now falling. No spooky decorations had gone up yet, but the darkened windows and moss-covered roof breathed danger to me. Was Teena using it as a hideout, waiting for interest in the murder to die down before finding a quiet way to leave town? Was she waiting for Seth to join her right this minute?

I stayed in my car until Nels pulled up beside me.

He jumped out of his vehicle. "What's up, Junetta?"

"Davey said you should check this place out. He said he saw a dark SUV drive up Wednesday night and somebody hauling stuff into the cabin. He thought there might be a bear around, so he didn't go inside to check on things."

"Okay…?"

"So, that was the night that Teena went missing, and Patrick said his car had been taken that night." I gazed at the windows. "Maybe she's inside. And you should know that Seth is on his way here, too, and Liam and Flint."

He placed both hands on his hips and glared at me. "So, instead of telling me to check out a potential crime scene, you arrange to meet me there so you can play at solving a mystery? You can't help yourself, can you?"

"Nels, this isn't about me. This is about stolen icons and a dead man, and a missing woman who could be lying in wait to hit us over the head."

As if on cue, a figure leaped out from behind Nels's car and whacked him on the head, dropping him like a stone.

It wasn't Teena, or even Seth. It was Flint.

I screamed and dodged away from his upraised arm, putting my car in between us. "What the heck, Flint!" I shouted.

He bent and fumbled at Nels's belt, coming up with his service revolver. Nels didn't move.

Flint pointed the gun at me. "Shut up!" He walked up to me, covering me with the revolver. "You wanted to go to the old Warner place? All right, in you go."

He marched me to the door, the revolver barrel pressed into my back. With one eye on me, he pushed the door open. He shoved me inside and slammed the door behind me.

In the semidarkness, I wasn't sure at first if he was inside the cabin with me or if he'd merely shut me in. Then I heard his heavy breathing. He struck a match, which lit his face in a parody of the Halloween goblins. "This old cabin is full of dry, rotting wood, even in a rainforest. Such a shame for it to go up in flames, don't you think?"

I backed away from him, my eye on the barrel of Nels's gun. I bumped into something hard, from which came a muffled yelp. Tearing my gaze away from Flint, I looked behind me with eyes that were adjusting to the low light. Teena lay on a cot, struggling against the ropes that held her tied up, a foul gag in her mouth. She wasn't an accomplice, but a victim!

Time enough to help her later. I needed to neutralize Flint, or I would become his next victim.

"Flint, how can you do this?" I said, silently cursing my wavery voice. "You stood shoulder to shoulder with me and stared down a charging bear. We were on the same team."

He snorted. "I was never on your team. I do what I have to do to survive. In that moment, my needs aligned with yours, but that doesn't mean I owe you anything." He turned away from me to shift a stone on the hearth. "You shouldn't have gotten in my way."

I gauged the distance between us, wondering if I could rush him and grab the gun before he had time to shoot me. "Nels will get you. You can't keep him down long."

He looked over his shoulder. "Your brother is probably dead right now. But if not, he will be soon. I hit him as hard as I hit Chuck, and look what happened to him."

A chill ran through me. Nels couldn't be dead! What would I do without him? I closed my eyes, just for an instant, and breathed a desperate prayer for his survival. But I needed to look out for my own survival, unaided.

I realized that Flint had just confessed to Chuck's murder. Too bad I wasn't wearing a wire to capture his words.

Flint didn't seem worried about giving himself away. He pulled out the loose stone, to reveal an alcove hidden within. He reached in and drew out a small packet. It was about the size of a hardback book, or a compact wooden icon gifted to Ptarmigan Port by the Russian tsar.

While his back was turned, I grabbed the first thing that came to hand—a coil of rope lying on the floor by the cot. I hid it behind my back.

Flint slid the icon into his coat pocket and turned back around to face me. He picked up a pitcher that was sitting on the table. "Goodbye, Junetta. I can't say it's been real, but that's not your fault." He sloshed the liquid in the pitcher across the floor and lit another match. The room leapt into flames.

Flint threw open the door, but he didn't get far. I flung one end of the rope around his shins and caught it on the other side. I pulled both ends tight, sweeping Flint's feet out from under him. He fell forward, crashing into Seth, who stood in the doorway, his own gun drawn. Both men sprawled outside. Flint lost his grip on Nels's gun, which skittered harmlessly off in the twilight. Seth's gun rebounded into the cabin, and I snatched it up before the two men untangled themselves. I dropped it into my pocket.

I dodged around the fire to get to Teena on the cot. She was tied to the metal frame in several places, too tightly for me to untie her. But the cot itself wasn't tied down. I shoved it as hard as I could, pushing it past the growing flames toward the two men on the threshold. They had both regained their footing and were shouting at each other over the noise of the fire. I gave a mighty heave and bowled the two of them over with Teena on her cot. I slammed the cabin door shut behind me to contain the fire inside.

I pulled out my phone and dialed 911 even as I continued to push the cot away from the cabin. When Stella answered, I shouted into the phone, "Send help to the old Warner place. Fire, killer, Nels is knocked out." I dropped the phone into my pocket without disconnecting and pulled out Seth's gun with one smooth motion. Nels would have been proud, if he wasn't unconscious and possibly dead. I pointed the gun at the two men. "Freeze!"

They actually froze. For one brief, shining moment, I was in complete control. Then, Flint shoved Seth in the chest and turned to run away.

"Stop!" I shouted. He must have known that I wouldn't shoot him. But he didn't reckon on Seth.

Flint got maybe five yards, not enough for a first down, when Seth dropped him with a flying tackle worthy of the finest football player. He whipped out his wallet and shoved it in Flint's face while straddling him to the ground. "FBI," he shouted.

Chapter Twenty-five

I couldn't believe my ears.

Smoke poured out the broken windows of the haunted cabin. I slid Seth's gun back into my pocket, just in case FBI was a bogus alias of his, and then bent down to check on Nels. He still lay unmoving, but he was clearly breathing and therefore not dead. I dropped my head on his chest, just for a moment, as relief overwhelmed me. I should have filled him in on the situation before calling him here to sort out this mess.

I lifted my head to see Seth advancing on me. He held a utility knife in one hand. I jumped to my feet and pulled his gun out of my pocket and pointed it straight at him. "Drop the knife."

He lifted both hands in the air, still clutching the knife. "I'm an FBI agent, working undercover. The knife is to cut the ropes." He waved a hand at Teena, still bound on the cot. "Give me my gun, and I'll set her free."

Both hands were shaking as I lowered the gun. "I'll keep it until the troopers arrive." I slid it back into my pocket. "Give me the knife and I'll cut the ropes."

He shrugged and handed over the knife. "I've got Flint secured for the troopers. I can see you don't trust me, so I won't try to help you." He sat down on a log.

I took a deep, deep breath, trying to steady my shaking hands before taking a knife to Teena's bonds. I started with the gag.

Her eyes bugged out as I brought the knife close to her face. In the growing darkness, she probably couldn't tell friend from foe.

"It's okay, Teena, it's Junetta. I'm going to set you free. It's over."

I sliced the fabric and pulled the gag away from her face.

She worked her jaw a minute and then spat out, "I'm going to kill that Flint!"

I worked on the ropes tying her to the cot. "I think he was going to kill you, so the feeling is mutual. But be careful what you say—Seth is an FBI agent in real life. He might think you're a danger to his prisoner."

Her eyes darted to where Seth sat on the log. He gave a friendly wave.

This evening was starting to feel surreal.

I sawed through the last rope and helped Teena off the cot. Sirens wailed in the distance, becoming louder and louder as they approached. I'd always felt startled and anxious by the sound of sirens, taking them as an indication that something bad was happening. Now, they sounded like the trumpets of the cavalry coming over the hill to the rescue. I couldn't imagine a more welcome sound.

The surreal feeling intensified as the parking area was overrun by troopers, firefighters, and an ambulance. They loaded Nels up on a stretcher and assisted Teena into the ambulance as well. A volunteer firefighter dropped a blanket around my shoulders where I sat on Teena's cot, before joining his team to put out the fire. A trooper teamed up with Seth to escort Flint to a squad car. They sped off.

Trooper Mark came over to sit down next to me on the cot. "You okay?"

I nodded, trying to brush off the tears that flowed down my cheeks. I clutched the blanket around me with shaking hands. Before I could say anything else, he said, "I'll take you home. You can pick up your car tomorrow." He loaded me into his vehicle without further ado, and we drove away.

• • •

I prevailed on Trooper Mark to swing past the Front Street Clinic, the closest thing we had to an ER, to check on Nels. After an interminable wait, they allowed us in to see him. We found him awake and fretting at his forced inaction.

"We got our man," Mark said. "Not the guy we went there for, as it happens."

Nels nodded, wincing at what must have been a humongous headache. "Are you okay?" he said to me.

"I'll leave you two alone for a short minute, then I'm running Junetta home." Mark tactfully withdrew.

"I'm fine." My lips trembled. "I'm sorry I dragged you out to an ambush without telling you what was going on. Thank goodness you're going to be okay."

He shook his head gently, wincing again. "You can't help yourself, can you? I assume you had old Flint trussed up by the time my troopers arrived?"

"Well, old Seth surprised me by pulling out an FBI badge, but only after I'd knocked him down twice and commandeered his gun." I grinned at my brother. "Never underestimate the power of movable furniture."

He held up his arms, and I leaned down to wrap him in a hug. "No more murder inquiries, okay?" he said. "They're bad for my health."

I patted his shoulder and stood up. "Shall we call Mom?"

I placed the call on Nels's phone. When Mom answered, I said, "Just a quick hello, since we talked about my adventures last night. It's Nels's turn, today. Love you, bye." I handed the phone to Nels and waved on my way out the door. I was pretty sure he wouldn't have called Mom without my big sisterly influence. I smiled to myself all the way home in Trooper Mark's car.

Thank goodness, it was over!

Chapter Twenty-six

I woke up the next morning to sunshine streaming in through a crack in my blackout curtains and a ding on my phone. The text from Nels said, 'Meet me at the station.' I chuckled and typed back, 'Got it.' He must be feeling better.

When I got to the Public Safety Building, I saw that I wasn't the only one to receive a text from Nels. A couple of card tables were set up in front of the cells. Around the tables sat Liam, Lacey, and Teena, sitting silently and eyeing one another warily. Seth Corliss sat next to Jeff Stevens, the only practicing lawyer in Ptarmigan Port. An earnest man nearing retirement age who enjoyed sport fishing above all else, Jeff usually concerned himself with wills and estates. A murder inquiry was a stretch for him. I imagined that Nels invited him here just to check all the boxes. Next to Jeff was an older man with a long beard who I didn't recognize. He was dressed in a blue two-piece jogging suit with a stocking cap covering his salt and pepper hair. I looked again—it was Father Thomas. Devoid of his ecclesiastical trappings, he looked like any other middle-aged man out for a bit of morning exercise. Nels leaned on the edge of a desk, commanding the room. Even Flint was there, behind bars. I sat down in the empty chair next to Father Thomas without a word.

"Now that we're all here, I want to go over this case from beginning to end, to make sure that justice prevails." With this pompous speech, Nels opened the proceedings.

"Father Thomas, ten years ago, you were the victim of an arson fire at the manse, which was a diversion to cover the theft of two icons from the Orthodox Church," he went on. "Flint Sands and Chuck Woodhouse were the two men who perpetrated those crimes, who you saw through the flames that night. Each man took one of the stolen icons." He looked over at Flint, "Do you have anything to add at this point?"

Flint crossed his arms over his chest and said nothing.

'Flint Sands'—a short name that started with an S. On the night of the fire at the manse, Chuck must have called out to Flint, using his last name. I guess Nels was right, I didn't have much to go on there.

Nels went on, "Teena Styles, you met Chuck in Ptarmigan Port shortly after the theft of the icons. What did you know at that time?"

Everyone shifted their gaze to Teena. She looked pale and wan today, and her multiple yarn bracelets couldn't cover the dark bruises on her wrists. She wore her silver Celtic knot necklace— Nels must have returned it to her. She said softly, "He told me he had come into possession of something that would secure his future. He didn't say what, and I didn't care. I was only interested in the present at that point." She looked down at her hands. "It secured his future, all right. Poor Chuck."

Stella plunked a paper cup of police coffee down in front of me. She leaned down and whispered, "Poor lamb, she was tied up for days while everyone thought she was a killer."

"I know," I whispered back, catching a frown from Nels. I took a sip of the sludgy coffee.

Nels cleared his throat. "Fast forward ten years. Flint arranged to meet Chuck on Price Island to recover Chuck's icon and take both of them to a buyer. He staged the fire on the *Northern Dream* and drugged Captain Evan to ensure that the entire party would end up on the island."

Liam burst out, "Why did you have to involve the rest of us in your scheme, Flint? We could have drowned. Why not just charter a boat, sail out to the island, grab the icon, and head back to town? You ruined our pre-wedding trip to Alaska for no reason. Make no mistake, you're no longer best man at my wedding!"

I bit the inside of my cheek to keep from laughing. It truly wasn't funny, except it kinda was.

Flint sat stolidly on the bench behind bars, still saying nothing.

Nels eyed Flint as if offering him the chance to set the record straight. "As far as I can make out, Flint wanted backup in case he couldn't handle Chuck. His communications with Chuck led him to believe that Chuck had become unstable over the years. The reports from the rest of the party bear this out. Chuck's behavior on the island was paranoid and threatening. During the night when the handoff took place, Flint hit Chuck over the head and killed him. It remains to be seen if it was in self-defense." Again, he looked inquiringly at Flint, who stayed silent. "You can work that out with your attorney."

"Chuck wasn't a threat," Teena blurted out. "He was putting on an act, for some unknown reason. When I talked to him in the night, it was just like old times. There was nothing unstable about him."

"Interesting," Nels said. He resumed his presentation, "As often happens to killers, the fear of discovery led to more and more desperate actions. When Kirk Dunbar mentioned that he remembered Teena and Chuck together ten years ago, Flint realized two things: one, Kirk had a phenomenal memory and needed to be silenced, and two, Teena might know of the original icon theft and connect the dots, so she needed to be neutralized. He set a fire at the Grizzly Bar and kidnapped Teena."

"He kept me tied up so everyone would think I had skipped town because I had killed Chuck." Teena glared at Flint. "You were going to kill me in the end, weren't you, in some devious way that would hide your own involvement. You just couldn't think of something cunning enough."

Flint shifted on the bench and looked away from her.

I couldn't help chiming in, "You stole Patrick's car in the night to kidnap Teena. You caused that sweet young guy a lot of unnecessary anxiety, on top of everything else."

Nels shot me a quelling glance. "Then, layered on top of this unfolding plot, was the presence of Seth Corliss, who kept us all guessing as to his true motives and involvement. Maybe you could fill us in, Seth."

Seth laid his badge on the table for us all to see. "I'm an FBI agent."

This simple statement caused quite the sensation. Liam jumped up from the table, and Lacey cried out in surprise. Father Thomas began to chuckle. "You sure fooled me."

Nels said, "I checked his credentials—he's the real deal." He motioned to Seth. "Go on."

"The bureau got involved when Chuck alerted us to the upcoming icon transfer. Evidently, he didn't trust his partner, who he did not name. He negotiated a reduced sentence if he delivered both icons as well as his partner to us.

"So, the bureau started rumors about the icons coming onto the market. I went undercover and approached Norman Oliver, an art dealer who was known to skirt on the edges of the law. He jumped at the chance to acquire the stolen icons. He set me up on the *Sea After Sea*, and I conveyed Chuck to the rendezvous."

"Sounds like entrapment to me," Flint growled, speaking for the first time.

Seth just shrugged. "We'll let the lawyers sort that one out. At any rate, Chuck insisted that I allow him to go to the meeting alone. If I hadn't listened to him, if I had gone with him, he might be alive right now, and the only crime Flint would be facing would be arson and theft from ten years ago. That's something I have to live with."

We sat in silence for a minute, then Seth went on, "By the time the fog lifted the next morning and I could motor around the island, Chuck was dead and his body was concealed, and a whole group of shipwrecked passengers were acting very suspiciously. So, I remained undercover and tried to sort things out. If I could have had half an hour alone with the two men on the island before the troopers showed up, I imagine I could have figured it all out."

"Is that why you insisted on leaving them behind, even when there was obviously room for all of us onboard? 'My boat, my rules.' That was pretty rude, if you ask me." Lacey tossed her head and wrapped Liam's hand in her own.

Seth gave a sheepish smile. "I couldn't very well say that I needed to get the two men alone to interrogate them as to which one was Chuck's partner in an icon heist. I had to resort to being a jerk. Sorry. I know you all took me for a murderer, while I was suspecting each of you in turn."

"We were all running around suspecting each other," I said. I looked at Liam, Lacey, and Teena. "It was awful."

Nels shot me a glance of compassion, of all things. "Well, we got the right guy in the end."

Flint stood up. "Actually, you don't have anything on me. When I get back where I belong, you'll be hearing from my real lawyer." He sneered at Jeff Stevens.

Nels reached behind him and picked up a small, wrapped object from the desk. He pulled back the wrapping to reveal a glorious, gold-highlighted icon of a winged figure with a glowing halo around his head—the Archangel Michael. "This icon, stolen from St. Michael's Russian Orthodox Church in 2005, was recovered from your jacket pocket last night. I imagine the lab will find both Chuck's and your fingerprints on it." He laid the icon on the table and said to Father Thomas, "We need to process it before returning it to the church, but it won't find its way to any shady art dealer. I promise you that."

Father Thomas placed his palms together and bowed his head to Nels in thanks. "And the Madonna and child?"

"We'll get it back," Nels said. "I'm sure our friend Flint, here, will help with that, in exchange for some kind of plea deal."

"This is a load of circumstantial evidence," Flint snapped. "Improper policing methods. Illegal search and seizure. You've got nothing but conjecture to go on."

Nels held up a finger. "If nothing else, we have a witness who saw you strike an Alaska State Trooper over the head, knocking him out."

"And I know who kidnapped me," Teena cried.

Flint scowled around the group, and then his gaze fell on me. He pointed a finger through the bars at me. "I would have gotten away with everything if it wasn't for you. You kept poking your nose into every little thing and running to your trooper brother with your wild speculations." He sneered at Seth. "For all your undercover FBI nonsense, you were outdone by a shopkeeper who specializes in children's books. That's something else you have to live with." He sat back down on his bench, folded his arms on his chest, and turned his face away from us.

Seth exchanged a glance and a shrug with Nels. "The FBI is always happy to receive tips from the public."

Nels stood up from his perch on the desk. He came over to me and shook my hand heartily. "Your wild speculations won out in the end, Sis. Try not to let it go to your head."

Before I could respond, Father Thomas spoke up. "I wouldn't be in possession of this holy icon without you, my dear," he said. "There is a reward for the icons' return, you know. I couldn't think of a better person to claim it."

I smiled at him, a tad embarrassed by all the attention. At the end of the day, I had picked the wrong person as the killer, sullying my sleuth reputation. That was something I would have to live with.

Liam broke the mood. "This is all very well, but we're going to miss the ferry if we don't get going." He looked over at Flint. "I guess you're going to miss it, regardless." He stood up and took Lacey's hand. "Ready to go, sweetheart?"

Lacey wiped a tear from her cheek. She allowed Liam to pull her to her feet. She turned to Flint, just for a moment. "I've always thought of you as a friend, Flint. A close friend. You used me on this trip, and you ruined our time here. I'll never forget that." She kept steady eyes on Flint, who clenched his fists but didn't say a word. Lacey twined her arm with Liam's and leaned against his shoulder, placing a gentle hand on her fiancé's cheek in an intimate caress. With her eyes locked on Liam's, she said, "Goodbye, Flint."

Chapter Twenty-seven

In the end, I took the three of them to the ferry. We only had time for a fleeting goodbye before they needed to be on board. I gave Teena a warm hug. "Come back to Ptarmigan Port any time, Teena. I'll take you out to the garnet cliffs or build a city of fairy houses with you. I knew you couldn't be a killer."

She hugged me back. "Thanks for having faith in me, and for persisting in your wild speculations."

Lacey was next. I hugged her as well, although it may have been more reserved on both of our parts. "I'm sorry your bridal trip turned out so disastrously, Lacey. I hope you'll keep some fond memories of your time here, though."

She slipped out of my embrace and took Liam's hand. "They say adversity can bring two people closer together." She looked deep into his eyes. "I'm counting on that to be true."

Liam squeezed her hand and then dropped it to give me a full body hug. "You're the best, Junie," he whispered in my ear. "I've always said that." He raised his voice, "Thanks for keeping us all alive, and for figuring out who was innocent and who was guilty in the end. I, for one, will remember the good parts of our visit here. Maybe next time we'll come up on a cruise ship."

Lacey smiled and mumbled, "I would like that."

The three of them walked down the ramp to board the ferry. Teena turned to wave, and Liam and Lacey walked straight ahead, hand in hand.

• • •

I found a bench on the dock to watch the ferry finish boarding passengers and cast off for departure. The run to Juneau should be lovely, with the sunshine and calm seas. Maybe they would see some whales. I spied their group along the rail and waved. All three waved back at me as the ferry got underway.

As the ferry steamed away from the dock, another boat came into view, anchored in the harbor. It was the *Northern Dream*. She bobbed on the slight wake from the ferry, as if to reassure me that she was still alive. I longed to dive into the sea and swim to her side, hop on board, and assess the damage from the fire. But I knew the water was icy cold. For the moment, I had to content myself with a visual inspection across the waves. All the port windows were broken, and the surrounding wood was blackened by the flames. A portion of the port rail sagged over the side and trailed in the water like a twisted strand of seaweed. I didn't see any holes in the hull that would put her at risk of sinking. She had a bedraggled air, but her spirit wasn't broken.

I heard a thumping sound on the boards of the dock behind me. I turned to see Uncle Vance coming toward me, leaning on his walking stick with Cosmo in tow. The little dog gave a joyful yip and ran to the end of his leash to swarm into my lap and cover me with doggy kisses.

"Hi, Uncle Vance," I said, ruffling Cosmo's fur as he wriggled in my lap.

Uncle Vance nodded in response. "Last I saw you, you were charging out of the Grizzly Bar to trap a killer. Nels should make you a deputy if you're going to keep up this foolishness."

I flashed him a big smile. "You're allowed to say you're proud of me, you know."

He grunted. "I'm just glad you're okay." He waved a hand at the *Northern Dream*. "I gave her a once over while you all were busy catching the criminal who did this to her." He sat down on the bench beside me. "The engine room is a mess, but the fire was mostly confined there. Shutting the door was the best thing you could have done. It'll take some hard work, but her sailing days aren't over yet."

I reached out to take his hand, touched by the fierce love in Uncle Vance's voice for the ancient boat that had been in our family for generations. "What about the books?"

He shook his head. "The books didn't get burned up, but I'd say they're ruined. The whole boat smells like a campfire laid with wet logs." He stood up, bowing to Cosmo's eager desire to explore every inch of the dock without delay. "You can buy other books."

I waved a cheery goodbye and watched him walk down the dock with Cosmo poking his nose into every enticing thing along the way. I breathed in the fresh salty air in relief and contentment. The *Northern Dream* was salvageable. I could buy new books. Maybe I would be able to claim that five-thousand-dollar reward for the return of the icons—although I was sure it would give me more joy to buy Father Thomas some new bunnies and a state-of-the-art rabbit hutch for them to live in. I chuckled at the thought. With time and hard work, everything would get back to the way it should be.

I pulled out my phone and dialed Angus.

He picked up on the first ring. "Junetta. Marcy told me you took off last night to confront a killer. How did it go down?"

"Wait, Marcy told you? How did she know? I haven't even talked to her since it happened."

He chuckled. "I guess you live in a small town or something. Evidently, Kirk told Marcy, and she texted me this morning to see what I knew and to fill me in on developments. It's good to have sources. Tell me everything."

So, I told him.

When the whole convoluted story was told, he gave a low whistle. "Thank goodness you're safe! It sounds like Flint didn't care who he hurt to get his way. My friend at Columbia will be ecstatic to learn that the icons will be restored to the church after all this time. I wouldn't be surprised if he made a pilgrimage to Ptarmigan Port to see them." His voice took on a shy note, "Speaking of pilgrimages to Ptarmigan Port…"

My heartbeat quickened.

"I'm finding that I can't conduct the historical research for my dissertation without being on site in Alaska. I didn't want to tell you about it until everything was settled. I've applied for and received a study grant to fund a year's stay in Ptarmigan Port."

I gasped out loud.

"The grant will pay for housing, and I have an application in for a part time position at the Ptarmigan Port Historical Society. I'll be right down the street from you, rather than thousands of miles and four time zones away. What would you think about that?"

I could hear the catch in my voice as I said, "I'll pick you up at the ferry with bells on to welcome you to paradise!"

• • •

Finally, I made my way to the Last Chance Café for a proper cup of coffee. The lunch rush had ebbed, and Marcy sat at a table near the counter, digging into a bowl of soup. When she saw me come in, she got up to give me a hug. "What news on the case, Agent Beale?" She fixed me coffee and soup and sat down with me.

I took a deep, grateful swallow. "You know all about it. You tell me, Agent George."

She laughed. "I do have my ear to the ground. I heard that Seth wasn't a killer so much as an FBI agent, and Flint was caught red-handed. It sounded like Trooper Nels went to make the arrest but got whacked on the head, leaving his sister to do all the dirty work." She gave me an affectionate smile. "And I know something you don't know."

"If it has to do with Angus, I just spoke to him. Evidently, you and he are conspiring to keep each other informed."

She grinned. "It's all part of Operation Boyfriend Befuddlement. I don't know if you remember the Attraction Axiom—if you actually like the guy, the tactics have to change accordingly."

I laughed so hard my coffee went up my nose. "How can I remember something you just made up on the spot? Did Angus tell you he's moving to Ptarmigan Port?"

She exclaimed over this news, which was evidently new to her. When she had fully expressed her delight for me, she said, "That's not actually what I wanted to tell you, though." She pointed to a secluded table in the far corner of the café. "Look who's back."

I turned around to look, then jumped up to join the elderly man at the quiet table. "Captain Evan, I'm so glad you're back, safe and sound!"

About the Author

Photo by Mike Barnhill

Greta McKennan is a wife, mother, and author, living her dream in the boreal rainforest of Juneau, Alaska. In addition to her *Southeast Alaska Mysteries,* she is the author of the *Stitch in Time* Mystery series. She enjoys a long walk in the woods on that rare sunny day and reading cozy mysteries when it rains. Her growing collection of Agatha Christie novels threatens to take over her bookshelves. Her author heroines include Louisa May Alcott, Mary Stewart, and M.M. Kaye, among many, many others. You can find her online at www.gretamckennan.com.